THE LAST CRUZ

A Novel by

CAITLIN AVERY

The Last Cruz, Published November, 2015

Editorial and Proofreading Services: Kellyann Zuzulo, Stephanie Peters, Karen Grennan

Interior Layout and Cover Design: Howard Johnson, Howard Communigrafix, Inc:

Photo Credits: Cover, Motorcross Poster, © sengerg, Shutterstock 13765300 Author photo by Just So Designs—Susan Ogar Photography

Title Page: Skull Day of the Dead, ©Jiewsurreal, iStock by Getty Images 56745040

Chapter Opener: Cross (Tattoo Flash Illustration Set), © m.j.h 1nkle, Depositphotos 60295953

Endpapers: Map of Mexico, © Olinchuk, Shutterstock 192502859

 **SDP Publishing**

Published by SDP Publishing, an imprint of SDP Publishing Solutions, LLC.

SDP Publishing
Permissions Department
PO Box 26, East Bridgewater, MA 02333
or email your request to info@SDPPublishing.com.

ISBN-13 (print): 978-0-9968426-5-5

ISBN-13 (ebook): 978-0-9968426-6-2

Library of Congress Control Number: 2015956880

Printed in the United States of America

*This story, and every tidbit
I wrote before it,*

*is dedicated to my mother,
Bette Lynn Sidlo.*

1945–2015

"Your ABC's became my poetry …"

———∞∞∞———

1

LOS ANGELES

Catrina squeezed into her racer-back swimsuit, pulled on her Juicy Couture sweats, and flipped through the tops in her closet before she found a loose-fitting, long-sleeved tee. Traveling incognito meant steering clear of the apparel her agent insisted she normally wear around town. Next, she packed her wetsuit, standard attire for Pacific surfing in October. Grabbing her Aveda 80 sunscreen, she smeared it above her brow, down her nose, and across her cheeks before tossing it in her beach bag and snagging a beach towel from the dresser.

"Your water's boiling!" Chris hollered from his sinkhole on the couch.

Cat knew better than to ask him to turn it off, so she took one good look at herself in the full-length mirror and sighed. She tilted her chin first left and then right, but her neck still looked camel-like. She slipped a hand down her pasty thigh that was heavier these days than it should be. With a look of disgust, she grabbed a rubber band from the crystal dish on her vanity, wound her long blonde hair into a low bun, and headed downstairs in her beach-bum attire.

As she maneuvered the tight turns of Mulholland Drive in her Mercedes SUV, Cat carefully sipped peppermint tea and made a mental list of everything she had to do today. Laundry would be done and ready to pack by two, and she would stop at the dry cleaners on the way home. She needed to remember to pack a sweater in case the weather got cool in Baja. October was typically sunny in Mexico, but Cat was prone to chills whenever the temp dropped below sixty.

The traffic coming off Interstate 405 onto Sepulveda looked like the parking lot of a car dealership. Cat rolled her eyes. Surf spots usually got crowded by 9:00 a.m. Luckily, the northbound side of Pacific Coast Highway was open. Cat banged a U-turn before Malibu Cove and claimed the perfect ocean-side parking spot on the shoulder.

The clear autumn air was a fresh welcome when she stepped from the car. Squinting into the wind, she scanned the waves for the best place to paddle out, when a flurry of photographers caught her eye.

"*Shoot*," she murmured, ducking to hide her famous face, while second-guessing her decision to surf at this popular spot. Relief replaced disbelief as she realized the photogs were rushing in the opposite direction. Straightening, she held her palm above her eyes and tried to identify the man with the black lab who seemed to have captured their collective attention.

"It's Mel Gibson," a man's voice behind her said. She turned and recognized a nameless, shaggy-haired acquaintance who commonly surfed at the same spots she did.

Thank God, she thought, pulling her visor over her eyes. Mad Max's presence was guaranteed to keep the paparazzi off her scent. She grabbed her board and headed toward the shore, safely anonymous to the scavengers of Tinseltown.

The choppy water made her gasp, inspiring Cat to paddle out quickly. Four-foot-high breakers caught the sunlight, casting palpable beams around Cat like the rays from the crystal prism that hung in her kitchen—a gift from her mom after she landed the lead in *Darkstar*. As the sun rose over Santa Monica Bay, Cat felt at home, a rarity in the life of a rising star.

⚶

Back in Beverly Hills by noon, Cat edged her way, arms overflowing with wet gear, through the back door of the garage onto the porch. Midday sun fed the bougainvillea vines that hung over the rear entrance. They needed to be cut back, but she was hesitant to tell the gardeners to trim them while they were in bloom; the fuchsia petals were too pretty to sacrifice. At six-foot-one, Cat routinely snagged herself on the thorns. Inside the kitchen, she dumped her bag on a high-backed leather dining chair and opened the fridge to find something healthy to eat. She never had much of an appetite. After two hours of surfing, she felt weak in the knees and sort of shaky, but hunger remained elusive.

Out of habit, she tossed a frozen salmon patty on the counter to thaw and grabbed some preshredded slaw, hoping this staple meal would seem appealing after a hot shower. Gathering her stuff, she rounded the corner and almost ran down the housekeeper.

"Oh," Elva yelped in surprise. "Ms. Lang, how are you?"

"Sorry," Cat said, "I forgot you were here. No car today?"

"My husband has it. I came on the bus."

"That's quite a hike at the end of the day," Cat remarked. Her home in the Hollywood Hills was a mile up Laurel Canyon, but the bus stop was at the top, about a mile higher.

"Let me know when you're done, and I'll give you a ride." She looked sympathetically at Elva, a heavyset Hispanic woman whose stronger days were behind her. "Is Chris here?"

"No, ma'am, Señior Marrrc left as soon as I got here." Elva had worked for Chris for ten years and still couldn't pronounce the name Marx correctly. It pleased Cat to hear his name altered by Spanglish. Nepotism ranked high, in order of Hollywood advantage, and scripts written by a grandnephew of the Marx brothers had given Chris an eternal edge. They often teased one another about their birthrights; she called him Marrrrrc, and he called her Stretch.

"Just don't call me Stretch Marx," she said when he proposed upon learning that she was pregnant.

Elva was steering the Dyson out of the linen closet, so Cat headed upstairs to escape the noise of the vacuum.

"Your laundry is on the bed. I'll be done vacuuming soon!" Elva called out.

"Thanks!" yelled Cat.

Her clothes were folded neatly on the bed. It amused her that Elva folded her underwear. She would put most of the clothes away, although she needed as many undies as she could stuff in her saddlebag for her impending vacation. She had no problem wearing the same tees over and over again, and her riding pants might not get washed until she returned home, but clean panties were a creature comfort she could not live without. As she walked to and from her walk-in closet, her cell phone rang. Tapping her Bluetooth, she sang, "Hello?"

"How's it hanging?" asked Sis with her unmistakable twang.

"High and tight," joked Cat, an homage to their father. "How's the ride?"

"Boor-ring. I hate the highway—got to find me some dirt!" Sissy paused to take a noisy slurp of soda and went on. "You got a big old tub of hot water waiting for me, right?"

"It's ready. What time you think you'll be here?"

"About six. We're a hundred miles outta Tucson now, just stopped for some Mickey D's."

Cat snickered at her larger-than-life sister chowing down a Big Mac and asked, "Did you say 'we'?"

"Yes-sir-ee! I'm bringing an assistant." Cat swallowed and tried to speak, but the audacity stunned her into silence. Her cheeks heated as anger swelled in her throat. Never short on words or courage, Sissy hammered Cat's reserve.

"Her name's Rey. She's my teammate, a real expert ... you'll see."

"How old is she?" asked Cat.

"Eighteen," said Sis. Cat was twenty-five, and the five-year age difference between her and Sis was enough of a gap. Another young sidekick would make Cat feel like an old puss.

"I thought it was just going to be the two of us," Cat said with a huff, gripping the phone tighter in her fist.

Avoiding an apology, Sis produced an excuse. "It was an impulsive invite, over drinks Friday night. She rides to Mexico all the time. I thought she'd be a good tour guide."

Cat paused, waiting for some semblance of concession from Sis. It didn't happen. 'Anger is ugly,' as their Mom would say, so Cat dutifully acquiesced. "I'll have Elva dress both guestrooms."

"You only have *one* maid for two guestrooms? How will she find time to fold your underwear?" Humor was Sis's way. Her Texas twang made sarcasm sound sweet.

Cat turned a cheek and chuckled at her sister's pluck. "I need all the help I can get to protect this house from my dirtball sister. You don't mind sleeping on rubber sheets, do you?"

"Don't get your pressed panties in a knot. I'll sleep in the barnyard."

"You can take the girl outta the country ..." Cat rolled her eyes. "Okay, see you when you get here."

⚜

By 5:00 p.m., Cat's to-do list was done. Pack (check). Bank (check). Order sushi (check). She was cooling her heels when the front door swung open, and Chris rushed in with a to-go bag from Mr. Chou.

"Want some Chinese?"

Cat shook her head and grimaced.

"Don't want to mess with that bikini bod?" provoked Chris.

Cat frowned at his obtuse suggestion. She hated Chinese—it had nothing to do with her agent's insistence that she get her prepregnancy body back.

Noting her sourpuss face, Chris inquired, "What's a matter? Did I offend?"

"Sis is bringing a *friend*," Cat explained.

"What friend?"

"A teammate," Cat spit, increasingly pissed about Sis's inclusion of a friend. "I can't believe the nerve of her."

"Two-for-one instruction," Chris quipped.

The king of narcissism, Chris's lack of sympathy was typical. As usual, he squashed her statement like a steamroller. "Keep your eyes on the prize. We got to get you ready for the role of a lifetime. I pitched to Sony today ... they *love* the story. It looks like our million-dollar baby is back!"

Cat was stunned by his insensitivity. "I can't believe you just said that."

Chris countered with concision. "You can always get pregnant again, but an idea like this is hard to come by." His levity pierced her grief.

Unlike Cat, Chris was relieved when they lost the baby. He recently admitted he didn't really want to be a dad. Now Cat was beginning to think she didn't really want to be his wife. This getaway had taken on new meaning.

Cat was arranging the sushi selection when the sound of dual engines announced her sister's arrival. Cat threw open the front door, rushed down the driveway, and watched as the leather-clad women parked their behemoth machines. The private road was a steep one, so it took a little maneuvering to prop the high clearance bikes uphill against the curb.

Sissy cut the engine first, threw her leg over the saddle, and popped her helmet off to reveal spiky blonde hair with streaks of red—the same poppy hue as her Honda. Rey stood a good bit shorter than Sissy and looked like a child, if not for the bright orange KTM she commanded. The massive dirt bike balanced precariously underneath her left thigh as she tipped it onto the kickstand but slid off the uphill side to set her right foot on higher ground. The women unzipped their jackets and walked toward Cat with their helmets in hand.

"Howdy," boomed Sis. A boisterous embrace between sisters was followed by a quick introduction, before all three of them crowded into the entryway.

"I'll take your jackets—just toss your helmets anywhere." Cat leaned toward the stairs and called, "Chris, they're here!"

"Where's that little corncake? Burrowing in his mouse house?" Sissy loved to harp on the height difference between Cat and her little man.

"I heard that," Chris said as he tramped down the stairs, walking tall.

They embraced, and Sissy asked, "How's it hanging?"

"Like a turkey wattle. Who's this pretty young thing?" Chris asked. Cat read that his atypical height advantage over her was the turn-on.

"This is Rey," said Sis, presenting her ostensibly reserved friend. Rey smiled and shook his hand shyly.

"Nice to meet you," Chris said. Rey's gaze remained down; she seemed flustered.

Cat eyed the new girl with jealousy, not for Chris's attraction to her, but Sis's. Honoring the ideals of pageant etiquette, Cat showered her rival with civility.

"Welcome to our humble abode. Come on in the kitchen. I bought a boatload of sushi." They filed around the bend to find a culinary showstopper, complete with salmon, tuna, and eel sashimi, and a platter full of Caterpillar, Rainbow, and "real crab" California rolls.

"Holy sea cow," said Sis, "that's a lot of raw fish!"

"Worth every penny." Cat grinned as she grabbed porcelain plates from the cupboard. "Dig in!"

Chris stepped back. "I'm all set. I'll be upstairs if you need me. Enjoy the feast." With that, he slipped around the corner and went into hiding.

Cat excused his quick departure. "When he's working on a script, nothing can stop him." She gazed at Rey, who stood motionless by the butcher block. "Do you want chopsticks, Rey?"

"I've never had raw fish before."

"Try it—for the halibut!" joked Sis, who was willing to try anything once. Cat grabbed the take-out menu and read aloud the components of each piece, then showed Rey how to mix the wasabi into the soy sauce for added heat. After a few hesitant bites, Rey became a convert. They consumed the entire order in less than an hour, and Cat's unusual hunger attack was sated. As she began to clean up the kitchen, the girls gave a rundown on their two-day adventure from Texas. They laughed as they recounted their overnight stay in Tucson, where they swindled a bunch of guys out of three hundred dollars at the pool table. Apparently, Rey was quite the pool shark.

"Speaking of sharks, do you scuba dive, Rey?" Cat asked.

Rey cracked a half smile. "Not since our family sold the yacht."

"She's a little out of touch with reality," Sissy scoffed to Rey.

"Well, I'm sure you two will find plenty of *other* things to do in Cabo," Cat suggested coolly, already sensing she was bound to be an outcast in this trio. Frustrated about Rey's inclusion on this trip, she brushed past Sis and said, "I'm going to check on the hot tub, if you guys want to put your suits on."

Stepping onto the porch, Cat inhaled the early evening air. "Anger is ugly," she reminded herself, fighting to keep her mouth from scowling.

Heading over to the wine fridge, Cat grabbed a bottle of Dom Pérignon and hung three flutes upside down in her fingers so she could transport the party to the hot tub area. An ice bucket had been placed within reach of the tub as part of Cat's meticulous planning throughout the day. She set the glasses down carefully on the ground and popped open the bottle. When Sis and Rey exited from the kitchen onto the deck, Cat handed each of them a crystal glass, with

THE LAST CRUZ   15

a crystal grin fixed firmly on her hostess with the most-ess face. She was banking on the fact that her lifestyle could be the golden spoke in her role as third wheel ... it certainly appealed to Sissy.

"This is living," Sis exclaimed, taking a chug of champagne. "Thank you, *Darkstar.*"

"*Darkstar?*" asked Rey.

"The movie," said Sis, staring at Rey like she was an alien.

Rey shook her head. Sis looked pleased by Rey's dis of Cat's claim to fame, but questioned Rey's poker face. "You seriously don't know it?"

"I'm kidding. Of course I do. It was awesome!" Rey's praise took Cat by surprise. "When's your next one coming out?"

"That's what this trip is about," explained Cat.

"She wants to play me on the big screen," injected Sis.

Cat ignored her sister and turned to her new fan instead. "Chris is working on a script about the first female rider to make it to the top in Motocross. He wants me to learn how to ride off-road again so I can play the lead."

"Which gives us two whole weeks to pull a rabbit out of a hat," Sis said, looking steamed. Sending a wave of hot water toward Cat, Sis attacked: "Why don't you just teach me how to act? There's not a lot of trick to mastering that."

Cat was taken aback by Sissy's insult. "You need to 'act' like a human being."

"Spare me."

"Should I spare you more charity?" Cat asked. Her voice was flat, but tinted by tension. Sis's mouth tightened to a thin red line, and she looked ready for a challenge.

"Hey," said Rey, smartly interrupting. "This is a win-win situation. Cat gets trained by two amazing racers, and we get a two-week vacation—pretty sweet, if you ask me."

Steam rose from Sissy's torso as she scraped her fingers through her sweaty do, then splashed water on her head to cool off. Climbing out of the tub, she reached behind her ear and removed a tiny gadget. Submerging herself once again, she dipped down, popped to the surface, and made a fluttery finger gesture to Cat, who gestured back. Rey looked confused. The sisters signaled back and forth again, before Cat laughed, and Sissy dunked under. Breaking the surface once more, Sissy turned to Rey and spit a stream of water toward her.

Rey called Sissy *la perra*, in Spanish, a word Cat had never heard.

"I can't hear you!" Sis hollered.

"You can read lips," reminded Cat, urging Sis to mind her manners. Rey's expression showed she was in the dark about Sissy's hearing.

"I'm deaf," confessed Sis.

"What?" asked Rey.

"That's my line," shouted Sis.

"Why don't you talk funny?" asked Rey.

"Most folks think I doooo."

"Doctors think it's because she practiced reading aloud as a kid," answered Cat, who was used to explaining Sis's secret to people after they became aware that Sis was deaf. Sis was famous for hiding weakness, and her implants made her disability almost invisible, if not for the tiny gadget that hid behind her ear.

Rey squared off to face Sissy. "So that's why your coach uses so many hand signals with you? I thought you guys had some special language you use to keep his advice private."

"It's sign language," said Sis. "Comes in handy on the bike. But this is called *flipping*." As an example, she sent a message to Cat that said, *I can flip faster than you can.*

Sis took a dip again and left Cat to explain. "We both know how to sign, but flipping is a mix, like Spanglish." Cat flushed at her cultural faux pas, but Rey didn't seem slighted. Feeling a familiar tightening in her left hip, Cat moved closer to one of the jets to help release it. She'd had recurring problems ever since she'd broken that leg riding off-road as a kid. That break had made her left tibia a full inch shorter than her right, and while Cat had learned to hide the limp, the imbalance in her hips often made her back ache.

Sissy lifted her butt onto the edge of the tub, leaned over, grabbed her sound processor, then tucked it behind her ear again. "I can hear everything with the implants, so we don't flip much anymore. But it's great when we need to speak secretly." With that, Sis flipped, *Sorry I was rude.* To which Cat replied, *You're a dirt bag.*

⚡

"Hey!" said Sis, talking out loud again. "We still haven't seen your bike."

"Oh yeah!" Cat said, trying to match Sis's interest. "I can't wait to get on the thing!"

"What do you mean? You haven't ridden it?" Sis didn't sound surprised.

"It was delivered last week, and I don't have anyone to ride with."

"So your agent still thinks you're going on a *spa* vacation?"

Cat nodded.

"Why lie?" asked Rey.

"I'm not allowed to risk life or limb," Cat explained, "so my agent thinks we're going on more of a Club Med kind of vacation."

Sis shook her head. Cat could tell by the way Sis raised her brows that she thought Cat was a pansy-ass when it came to handling her handlers.

"Let's go check out the death trap," snickered Sis, laughing at Cat, not with her.

They toweled off and then shuffled across the porch to the garage and spent a few minutes analyzing Cat's sparkling clean machine. "An 800," said Rey, "that's a big thumper." Cat smiled, feeling pleased with her purchase.

"How many miles you got on her?"

"Sixteen," Cat confessed, waiting for a snide remark from Sis.

"New is not the coolest adjective," said Sis. "This thing could use a scratch or two."

"Nothing wrong with being the first one to break the bitch in," said Rey with a wink. "This shit is clean, though—I ain't never seen such a sparkling white bike."

Cat felt hot under the collar as they started to rib her. She was already a little tense around Rey and nervous about getting back in the saddle. She figured a good night's rest was the best way to deal with her stress. "Well, I'm sure she'll get dirty tomorrow," conceded Cat. "Speaking of tomorrow, I'm ready for bed. You're welcome to stay up if you like, but I need my sleep."

"You got any more of that tasty champagne?" asked Sis.

"There's wine in the cooler." Cat pointed to the wine fridge on the deck, and Sis grimaced. "There's beer in the kitchen," Cat added, and Sis grinned. "Help yourself to whatever you'd like inside," Cat said. "I'll be up at seven to cook breakfast."

Sis followed Cat toward the door, before turning to ask if Rey was ready to double fist it: "Dos mas?"

"Yeah," Rey said, ready to catch a buzz now that Cat was not there to witness it. As she waited for Sis to return, Rey's mind filled with concern.

After worrying all day about how her plan would pan out with a stranger in tow, Rey was beginning to realize that Cat was gullible and eager to please, a great combination when it came to choosing a wingman. The only problem was Cat's inexperience on the bike.

An extreme rider since the age of sixteen, Rey couldn't help but sense Cat's reticence. If it was any indication of her attitude in general, this trip would be an impossible undertaking. Per Sissy's insistence, Rey planned to take these girls deep into the Mexican desert, where mule paths reigned. It was the kind of terrain that if you got scared, you got stuck, and if stuck, you were screwed. Good thing Rey knew so many locals. Her Mexican connections, however shady, would come in handy if the shit hit the fan.

Rey was tempted to ask Sis if she had any idea what she was getting Cat into, but didn't want to deter her. Rey had good reason to want to ride side by side with Cat … she was the perfect diversion. A celebrity gringo was exactly what Rey needed to survive this mission without a hitch. Ever since the close call at her last border crossing, Rey had been praying for a lucky star, and Cat was just that. She might be slow, but she had a famous face and plenty of pesos, and no matter what language you spoke, money talked in Mexico. Rey knew firsthand that there were only two outcomes when it came to trouble in Mexico. Most of the time, you could buy yourself out of the situation. The alternative was death.

CHAPTER 2

LOS ANGELES TO CORONADO

"I 'll be back with the forecast, right after this commercial break...." The DJ's voice pierced Cat's skull. Blood thumped through her head as she rolled onto her back and pulled up the covers. *Ugh!* Champagne and hot tubs were a reckless combination. She shifted to a seated position and moaned, then grabbed water from her nightstand. Daylight filtered dimly through a crack in the blackout curtains. It bounced off the clear plastic face mask that was propped on the edge of Chris's bedside table.

As Cat's consciousness grew, she noticed a pelting against the windowpane that was barely audible above the buzz of the breathing machine that Chris used to combat his sleep apnea. The fact that it was still running meant Chris had come to bed last night, but had left in a rush to get an idea down again. Rising carefully to her feet, Cat padded toward the pitter-patter and peeled back the blinds to find water streaming down the glass due to overflow from the blossom-stuffed rain gutters. It was pouring.

Cat rushed to the radio to crank up the volume. The weather report was grim. "Unusually low temps for this time of year, we'll see a high of sixty today, with off-and-on showers. Expect to see clear skies again by late afternoon, and we'll be back to sunny and seventy-five tomorrow. Remember to take special precaution on the roads today, folks. There's a lot of oil on the road; it's been a while since our last deluge here...."

The clock read 7:45. Cat had slept longer than she intended. Guess it didn't matter now. Shoot! This was a major wrench in the plan. She hurried to greet any early risers. Clomping downstairs, Cat saw Chris on the couch in the living room, his laptop leaning back at the same lazy angle as his trunk. He looked exhausted, but his fingers were awake, beating the keys before pausing to depress the "Backspace" and erase. He let out a sigh that inspired Cat to act cheerful despite her anxiety about the weather.

"Hey, hon," she said, pausing on her way to the kitchen. In his classic request for silence in the a.m., Chris leaned back and pulled his palms down his face, seemingly irritated by Cat's friendly greeting. "Have the girls been down yet?" she asked, ignoring his "poor me" attitude.

"I haven't seen them." His superlow monotone spoke volumes; dawn was not a good time to engage him.

"Sorry you didn't sleep. I hope the girls didn't disturb you." Squinting against the light, Cat uttered, "My head hurts" as she moved into the kitchen to grab a bottle of ibuprofen from the cupboard above the fridge. "Can you believe this weather? Nice timing, huh?"

Chris sat silently. Cat opened the fridge to grab the eggs and found the bag of French roast beans sitting where the creamer should be. Opening the coffee cabinet, she found the creamer and made the switch.

"Do you want more coffee?" Cat inquired.

"No thanks, I'm going upstairs to lie down. Come say goodbye before you leave, okay?" Tying his fuzzy brown robe, he slumped as he stood, looking like a hobbit as he shuffled away.

Cat had just adjusted to the light of day when Sissy and Rey trooped down the stairs. "Rain in LA!" Sis exclaimed, grabbing the top of Cat's back in a pinch, like a massage gone wrong. Cat turned to escape the vice grip, forcing Sis to put her hands on her own hips for sassy emphasis: "I guess your cherry's getting popped twice today—first ride on the highway, first ride in the rain."

"Oy vey," Cat muttered, using a favorite term of Chris's grandmother. She had watched the forecast every day this week. The weather channel was even tagged as her favorite. Problem was, she'd only been checking on Mexico. "It never rains here, I swear. I can't believe we have to postpone our trip," she said half-heartedly, unable to keep the wistful hope from her voice. Sissy glared at her.

"We don't cancel a trip because of weather. This is how you learn, sister."

"Can we wait for it to clear?" Cat sounded scared.

"We didn't come all this way to sit on our butts," Sis said.

"Actually, we did," injected Rey, "but only while speeding."

Sissy cracked her knuckles like she might sucker punch Cat if she played the coward card before the ride even began.

"Let's have breakfast, and see what the weather looks like in an hour or two," Cat said, looking eagerly from Rey to Sissy. They agreed to delay their departure only after Sis admitted that water, coffee, and "greasy meat" were three things she needed to cure her hangover. "How about some homemade hash browns?" Cat asked, blurting out the most time-consuming recipe she could think of.

"Latkes for all of us," announced Sis, in reference to Chris's heritage. Cat smiled at her sister's ribbing and pulled out a frying pan.

By 11:00 a.m., the rain had stopped. The clouds, heavy and dark, remained threatening, but Sis pointed out that it was a two-and-a-half-hour ride to the hotel in San Diego, and traffic would be thinnest at midday. Cat felt her chest tighten, the way it had when she performed her tap-dancing talent trick for the Miss Teen Texas pageant. She had run out of bargaining chips—the start of the trip was upon her.

Sissy and Rey were securing their saddlebags to their bikes on the street when Cat entered the garage to greet her machine. Her bags had been secured yesterday, so her only prep for the impending ride was to figure out how to get the bike out of its space in the back corner. "Hey, Sis, would you mind backing it out for me?" Cat tilted her head toward the BMW bike.

Sissy shook her head "no" from her spot on the street, then she made her way back up the driveway to offer her first dose of coaching. "I ain't your personal assistant, girl. Pull up your big girl panties and just do it."

Cat reluctantly threw her leg over the saddle and settled in. Taking a moment to squeeze the clutch a couple of times, she ran through all five gears with her right toe: one down, five up ... piece of cake. Then she tested her turn signals, honked the horn once to make sure it was working, and completed her prep work by pulling an extension cord out of her jacket pocket. She leaned over to plug it into the underside of the bike, next to the gas tank.

"What's that?" asked Sis. "Your umbilical cord?"

"When Pop taught you to become one with the bike, he didn't mean *literally*," Sis ribbed.

"Very funny," Cat lied. "It's the plug for my electric vest," she mumbled sheepishly.

Cat turned the setting on "high" to prepare for the cooler than average air and eased back into her seat. Sis returned to her parking spot on the street, ignoring Cat's rudimentary first challenge. Sis climbed on her bike and turned the key, joining Rey in revving her engine.

Ready as she would ever be, Cat turned the key and started her machine. Fuel injection meant no need for revving. The putter of the engine was smooth, nothing like the rising scream the motocross bikes produced as Sis and Rey had to twist their throttles to reduce the sputtering coming from their non-fuel injected engines. Putting a choke hold on her clutch, Cat brought the gas up, pressed down on the foot lever, then released the brake and the clutch to get the bike moving. It edged forward, glided through the door of the garage, and tipped down the decline. She clutched the handles in a death grip as she coasted down the driveway. Nerves and excitement spread a wide smile on her face. She stopped on a dime at the bottom of the driveway.

Sis was unimpressed. "Great, you can coast. Now show us something you can boast about." With that, Sis popped a wheelie and jolted off down the street. Rey followed in quick pursuit.

"You can do this," whispered Cat, her breath hot with anticipation. She pulled the clutch, released the hand brake, and began rolling down the street. Then she tentatively pushed the gear lever up with her big toe to find second, gaining momentum. Feigning control, she managed a meek honk as her final goodbye to Chris, sound asleep and oblivious inside his palace.

Sis and Rey idled at the bottom of the street, waiting for traffic to thin enough for Cat to make a quick left turn onto the main road. They knew better than to rattle her nerves at this stage in the game. It would only slow them down further. Not surprisingly, Cat negotiated the S-curves and the potholes of Laurel Canyon with caution, and the speed demons up ahead drove slowly so Cat could catch up to them. The late morning traffic was light, but the road was wet, with a small river gurgling along its edge. The streets of LA were banked to guide the water off the sides. But the walls of Laurel Canyon climbed abruptly uphill, and the runoff gully was small.

Cat felt squeezed by the narrowness of her lane, but she felt good in the saddle, and her heart eventually slowed to a regular beat. She convinced the girls to follow Cahuenga

Boulevard south to the 405. The minor detour through the city would cut out the worst of the Westside's six-lane freeway between the Valley and LAX. Traffic thinned past the airport, and Cat knew they'd be able to open it up at that point. She was concerned about freeway speed but was even more afraid of splitting lanes.

"It's like a video game," Sissy hollered at a stop light. "Imagine everyone's out to kill you. Just be on guard and you'll be fine." Cat found no solace in this suggestion.

Sis and Rey stayed in the lanes as long as traffic was moving and reserved splitting for the red lights, when they carefully edged their way up to the front of the line. Cat followed their lead and was happy to see folks actually move out of the way for her. Cruising more quickly than normal through town, Cat thought of how nice it would be to get around town on a bike during rush hour, and hoped she could convince her agent to let her ride around town after she made it home safely.

South of Fairfax Avenue, the scenery changed. Ladera Heights gave rise to a dirtier version of the city. South of the 90210 zip code, the potholes took hold of the road, and the sheen of the oil and water-filled puddles masked their depth. Cat was caught off guard by the first hole that jostled her bike. It sent a jolt of vibration through her forearms. She managed to avoid any slips as she slalomed around the dips in the road.

The grid system in LA meant that intersections were labeled impeccably, but as the women approached the airport, Cat's sense of direction became confused. With all the potholes in the worn-out road, Cat kept her head down to avoid the dips, all while navigating a crowded part of town she was not familiar with. Her trips to the airport typically included a driver in a town car, and Cat was really missing the AC and cool leather seats; sweat from humidity and stress ran down her neck. Sissy and Rey looked completely at ease in front of her as they followed the signs to LAX down La Tijera Boulevard. At one of the last lights en route to the freeway, Rey's engine quit. She reached down and flipped a switch as the engine sputtered and went silent, seamlessly starting it back up again. This cued Sis to veer into the gas station at the base of the on-ramp to the 405. She turned in first, followed by Rey, and a panicky Cat, who almost missed the turn.

As Sis and Rey filled their tanks and checked their tire pressure, Cat asked Rey why her bike had stalled.

"Out of gas, had to switch to the reserve," Rey explained.

"Can that happen while I'm driving?" Cat inquired, rolling through her rolodex of possible problems.

"Fancy bikes have a gas light," assured Rey, glancing at Cat's speedometer. "You even have an onboard computer on that thing." There was a hint of envy in her tone.

Sis tapped the gas nozzle and set it back in its holster on the pump, moving in for a look. "Oh, man, a GPS—that'll come in handy."

Cat beamed, suddenly more comfortable with her choice of such a high-end vehicle. "There's a trip counter, too. Should I reset it?" Cat asked.

Sis reset her odometer and did the same for Cat. "Let's top off your tank," she said, handing the nozzle to Cat. "Next time the gas light comes on, make a note of the mileage.

That way, you'll know how many miles you get per tank. The gas light gives you a one-gallon warning, about fifty miles. In the back country, we may need more than that."

"Our reserve tanks give us about a hundred miles," added Rey.

"Look how much tread I've worn already," said Sis, looking at her tires. "Pavement sure does a number on the knobbies. I can't wait to hit the dirt again."

Cat tried to absorb what they were saying, but she was distracted by rising anxiety. The sound of the adjacent freeway was giving her palpitations. As Rey headed off to find the restroom, Sissy offered a quick pep talk to Cat.

"You can do this," Sis assured her. "It's like riding a bike. In this case, the speed keeps you upright." Distressed, Cat was not convinced, until Sis softened and offered a rare indication that she cared about Cat's security. "I'm not going to let anything happen to you, but why don't you give me your credit card, just in case ..." Sis's joke was accompanied by a look that said *lighten up*, and Cat laughed at her sister's self-serving suggestion.

When Rey returned, the three of them started up their engines and then zippered and snapped their jackets in preparation for the rainy-day wind of the freeway. Sis pantomimed to Rey that she should take up the rear to sandwich the newbie. Then they pulled into formation, and Cat staggered herself in the middle. Giving it some gas, Sissy flipped Cat some final words of encouragement. *You can do this—it's going to be fun!* Popping her signature wheelie, she headed up the on ramp.

CHAPTER 3

ORANGE COUNTY

They'd been riding for all of twenty minutes when the skies opened up, and it started to pour again. Traffic slowed to sixty, and Sissy downshifted with the pack of cars. Speed blew the rain off Cat's face mask, but her accelerated breathing kept steaming up the inside of her visor. Notches on the adjustment allowed her to crack it open at the bottom, but every few seconds the mask would blow closed again. It took all her courage to release her grip to produce an air slit. Her clutch hand was readily available, but the wind pushed her back every time she let go for an instant. Her right wrist felt weak from holding the throttle.

Cat recognized the tenderness as the same type of ache she felt after an hour of yoga. She worried the strain would limit her riding. If not her wrist, then her recurring problems with her left leg could be a problem. So many excuses not to continue, yet here she was, committed to at least two weeks of this. Cat had always been soft compared to Sissy. This was Cat's chance to prove she could develop bravado. *Get it together* was the mantra she repeated as the rain pelted her head and the road kept on coming.

As quickly as the showers had begun, they suddenly gave way to a crease in the clouds where the sun shone through. As they approached Irvine, Cat discovered that elevating her wrist to align it with her knuckles took the pain away. She also realized that when the rain stopped, she felt less inclined to hinge forward. Rising to an upright position took some of the weight off her hands and the strain off her hamstring. Easing up was the key to relaxing. An hour of riding had brought a valuable lesson. It would be amazing to see what a couple of weeks could do.

The sun bore down on them as the 405 freeway bore down on I-5. Orange County inspired many memories of Cat's early years of surfing. Modeling work had allowed Cat to surf in Hawaii, Costa Rica, and Australia, but she found her favorite breakers on her home turf, and had fallen in love with the sport on the beaches that stretched from Malibu to San Diego. Newport, Huntington, Laguna, Oceanside, Del Mar, and La Jolla were as accessible as they were incomparable.

Surfing was her favorite way to escape the grind of her Hollywood lifestyle, but it hadn't always been that way. Like the early days of being afraid of the fiercest waves, she was ready to face her fear of riding. It was time to quit being typecast as a brittle bombshell. This motorcycle was going to empower her as she entered a new frontier. Not so much literally, but mindfully. She had a strong premonition that life would never be the same after all she was about to see and do in Mexico. Cat was in need of a new attitude, and this trip was her ticket to freedom and courage.

As Cat's vacation motivations kicked into gear, she committed to try every new opportunity that arose. Renewed energy made her hungry, and her stomach growled when the iconic zigzag of In-and-Out Burger's yellow arrow appeared on the horizon. Billed as the best burgers this side of the Mississippi, the beach bums Cat knew couldn't get enough of the place. But Cat's eternally restricted diet dictated that she never indulge in such artery-clogging atrocities. She decided it was time to satisfy the devil inside her. A double-double with hand-cut fries would be the perfect treat. She had no doubt that greasy meat would appeal to her comrades. Surging forward, she passed Sissy on the left and flipped, *Time to eat!* Then she tagged her right-turn signal and exited the off-ramp.

Squeezing into a triangular spot at the front of the lot, the ladies quickly unmasked themselves.

"Yow-zer ma-chow-zers, I'm hungry!" declared Sis.

Cat's enthusiasm waned as she noticed a group of young boys sitting at an outdoor table, pointing at them. Cat was always unnerved by this kind of attention. In an attempt to stifle their stares, Sis hollered at the gawkers, "Take a picture, it lasts longer!"

Taking her literally, the boys whipped out their phones and began snapping shots. "Next time, pick a better one-liner," snapped Rey as she moved in front of Cat and tried to block them. Cat mumbled, "Sorry," then lowered her head, just like a celebrity trying to dodge fans. Unfortunately, the skintight superhero suit her character had worn in *Darkstar* closely resembled Cat's dirt bike attire. She was hard-pressed to pose as a civilian.

"It's no use," muttered Cat.

"What did you expect?" asked Sis. "You get paid for this. If Angelina passed a bunch of teens wearing leathers, she'd be hassled too," she added brusquely. Since Cat's film debut in 2010, fan warfare had been a recurring theme in the Lang sisters' reunions, and the success of *Darkstar* had created a whole new level of FANaticism, a term coined by Sis. Neither of them could stand it, but Cat claimed there was no turning back now that she was a bona fide movie star.

During her last visit to Texas a year ago, Cat had created a similar stir when she showed up to watch Sis's race. The constant attention Cat received on what was supposed to be Sis's big day had driven a wedge between a formerly supportive Sis and her famous sibling. So it was again, at this not-so-fast food chain, where Cat was forced to chat with her fans. While Sissy and Rey stood in line with the mere mortals, Cat signed a baseball cap, four napkins, a notebook, and one grease-stained hamburger wrap. Finally sitting down to eat, she heard the manager say that he'd like to dip her in a vat of hot oil and take a bite. Cat picked up a fry and nibbled meekly, having promptly lost her appetite.

"What's a-matter, Cat, fame got your tongue?" antagonized Sis.

"Just tell them to leave you alone," said Rey.

Cat sighed. "It's impossible to keep them at bay."

In an attempt to relieve the situation, Sissy ate like an

animal. A teardrop of ketchup clung to the corner of her mouth as she spoke. "If a bench racer did that to me, I'd dis 'em, or run 'em over." Sis snorted as she smeared ketchup from her face to her sleeve.

Cat knew Sis's dream of becoming a household name meant race fans would begin to follow Sis in similar fashion. "Being a bitch is bad for business," Cat reminded her.

Lunch ended when a man with a strong stench asked Cat for her hand in marriage.

"Hey!" shouted Sis, as they slunk through the exit. "Catrina has left the building!"

"Thanks," whispered Cat, her head bowed by the weight of the movie world.

"That's *annoying*," noted Rey as they marched across the lot toward their bikes.

"Welcome to my life," interjected Cat with a wilted grin.

They mounted their bikes. "That was fun," announced Sis sourly. She slipped her helmet on and slapped her face mask down.

As the trio continued toward San Diego, chaparral-spotted dunes lined the freeway. They passed the exit for SeaWorld around quarter past two, three hours post-departure. Sissy flipped Cat a sign, asking, *How much longer? I have to piss.*

Cat responded *Ten minutes or less*, then accelerated to take the lead and guide them into Coronado. As downtown loomed behind them, the four-lane freeway dissolved into two, and the median filled with sand and succulents, a preview of their sea view. The beach vibes swelled as the salt wind blew around them. Spotting the red-tiled roof of their hotel destination in the distance, Cat pointed to it and downshifted onto the bridge to Coronado. The first leg of the trip was done.

Cruising around the half-moon driveway of the Hotel Coronado, they pulled up to the front and cut their engines. The valets did a double take when the women pulled off their helmets and shook out their hair. The men did a triple take when they recognized Cat. Falling over themselves to assist this A-list guest, they directed Cat and her companions to the VIP parking adjacent to the grand entrance. Then the bellhop approached and helped load their saddlebags onto his golden cart. Having hung behind her more experienced sister for the ride, Cat reversed her role and led the younger women into the lobby. She showed the confidence of someone who had seen her fair share of five-star accommodations.

Rey was clearly awed by the place. "This is the nicest hotel I've ever seen," she whispered to Sis. A three-tiered chandelier cast rainbows around the room as the sun caught the crystals through skylights in the vaulted ceiling. As Cat approached the desk, Rey's eyes bulged. "Have I died and gone to heaven?'

"Nice place," replied Sis nonchalantly.

Cat waved them over to ask if three beds were necessary. "I reserved a suite with two king-size beds, but they offered us an upgrade if we need it," Cat said.

Rey snickered at the audacity of the situation. "Most trips to Mexico have me sleeping in the sand and pissing behind cacti," Rey muttered quietly to Sis. "I'll sleep on the floor," said Rey, without shame.

"Madam," the hotelier interjected, "we will not have anyone sleeping on the floor here. Let me call the head hostess upstairs and inquire about the grand suite. I believe it's ready for occupancy." Moments later, the women were guided to the antique birdcage elevator for liftoff to the penthouse.

The bellhop was waiting there for them. He opened the door to reveal a Victorian masterpiece. Antiques lined the walls. Plush chairs draped with woven throws set a warm tone to the place, and a couch fit for a queen faced the balcony. The bellhop drew the sheer curtains back to let the sunshine in. Chocolate-covered cherries sheened as the light brightened the room. Jumbo shrimp nestled in a bowl of crushed ice. A bottle of Pierre Jouet leaned inside a sterling silver wine bucket. Sissy tossed her boots off as Cat slipped a tip to the bellhop and bid him farewell.

"Holy shit, look at the bathroom!" belted Sissy, inviting Rey to take a peek. They gazed into the tiled expanse, complete with claw-foot tub and a vanity bigger than Sis's bedroom back in Texas. "I guess some things are *not* bigger in Texas!" Sis boomed.

"We're going to rough it for the rest of our ride, so I wanted to do something special tonight," explained Cat. Twelve hundred dollars was a small price to pay for the response she was getting from her allies.

"Let's get out of this gear and hit the deck!" announced Sis.

Cat slipped onto the private balcony for a glance at the sea. "It looks a little choppy for surfing," she said, thinking out loud. She was about to re-enter the suite to change into her suit when Sissy glided out of the bathroom wrapped in a fluffy white robe, her toes poking out of a pair of memory foam slippers. "I'm ready for my close-up," she purred à la Marilyn Monroe. Then she dropped the act and shed her cover-up to reveal a cherry-red, Brazilian-cut bikini.

Sissy was extremely fit. Hitting the jumps and the bumpity-bumps all day was like doing thousands of squats in a row. She was as lean as she was mean, and her physique resembled that of an Olympian, but she had the bones of a Viking and a punked-out ruby red 'do. Her teeny-weeny bikini didn't seem so audacious in the darkness of Cat's deck last night, but against the backdrop of this nineteenth-century palace, it edged close to inappropriate.

Making excuses to mask her concern about exposing the other upper class guests to her scantily clad sister, Cat declared, "The waves look lame and the sand is wet. Let's lay out up here for a bit." Cat felt like a snob as she recognized her discomfort at the idea of parading around the place with her loud-mouthed sister and her Mexican friend, but she figured it was better to keep them confined to the privacy of the penthouse suite and let the Rockefellers float around the kidney-shaped pools below.

Lying out on the bountiful balcony was good enough for Sis and Rey, who wanted to be close to the sun, and so they smothered themselves in tanning oil. Cat, who was used to the strictures of makeup artists, donned a large-brimmed hat and SPF 50. The younger girls guzzled champagne and devoured the chocolate treats, while Cat munched on shrimp cocktail. As the sun began to sink, they discussed their game plan for the next day. When Cat rose to run inside and grab the maps she had, Rey insisted she sit. "I know the border towns like the back of my hand," Rey reminded them.

"Where to tomorrow?" asked Sis.

"Just west of Tijuana," Rey explained. "There's a fifty-mile stretch of road that's roughly maintained. It's a perfect place for Cat to start training."

Cat's chest constricted as the reality of the next leg of the adventure sank in.

"The ride on the freeway today was easy compared to tomorrow. The soft sand will take a little more getting used to," warned Sis. Tension in Cat's left leg crept up as a reminder of the serious injury she'd sustained as a kid.

"Let's hope the dirt offers a softer landing this time," added Cat nervously.

"There are two kinds of riders—those who have crashed and those who will. Then there are the repeat offenders." Sis shoved Cat's bad leg with the back of her hand, nudging as if Cat was part of some badass club now.

"Have you crashed in the past?" asked Rey.

"She *wiped*. And never rode again," explained Sis.

"I crashed when I was ten," added Cat. "I had a compound fracture in my left leg, and my mom wouldn't let me ride after that—she thought it would ruin my chance at Miss Texas."

"You competed in Miss Texas?" asked Rey with a glint in her eye that said that was impressive.

Cat paused, then said, "I was crowned Miss Teen, right before I left for Paris."

Sis rolled her eyes. Rey raised her brows. Cat glanced at the girls and noticed that Rey's necklace had left an army-green mark at the nape of her neck. "Your necklace got tarnished in the hot tub—is it sterling?"

"Yeah," said Rey, instinctively reaching up to clasp her dual crosses. She futilely rubbed them with the corner of her towel.

"There's a jewelry store downstairs. I can ask the bellhop to have them cleaned for you," offered Cat.

"I never take them off. I have a cloth I use to shine them," said Rey.

"Are they handmade?" asked Sis.

"My father made them for my mother and me," said Rey with no further explanation.

"For a special occasion?" asked Cat.

"He made them when I was born. My mom died when I was little, so now I wear both of them."

The sisters waited, but Rey remained elusive. "I'm sorry for your loss. It's a really beautiful necklace," said Cat. A glance passed between Sis and Cat. Their family had secrets they knew Rey could relate to, but talking about their dead baby brother was not a subject Cat felt like sharing.

A short time later, Cat declared she'd had enough sun exposure. She excused herself and stepped into the shelter of the suite, closing the sliding glass door behind her.

⚜

Rey watched as Sis smirked at Cat's backside. "No tan lines for Miss Perfect," Sis scoffed.

"She seems pretty cool to me," said Rey, whose misgivings about meeting Sissy's Beverly Hills sister were overshadowed by Cat's generosity, a trait that Rey was rarely a recipient of.

"Yeah, well, I've listened to her complain about her royal life since the day she left Texas. She complains about fame, but that's the bed she's made."

"I'd be totally pissed if people stared at *me* all the time," declared Rey.

"I just wish she'd embrace her star-kissed life, or leave it. I could use her help at home."

"Everyone has their row to hoe," Rey said. Her history was as painful as they come.

"Yo, don't call me 'ho,'" joked Sis. Rey laughed at her crazy friend and kicked back to soak up the sun again.

CHAPTER 4

TIJUANA TO LAGUNA SALADA

C at pumped the gas and zigzagged behind her comrades as they wedged their way through traffic. Honking motorists sanctioned them for cutting the line. She chose a lane and prayed that Sis would follow suit as Rey continued her beeline toward Mexico. At six foot one, Cat had a solid view of Rey until her facemask fogged with humidity. In the five miles from the Hotel Coronado to the border, the scene had changed as dramatically as the weather.

"I swear, it never rains here," Cat had said apologetically when the women stepped out of the hotel into sopping wet San Diego. Still wet after yet another early morning downpour, the colors of Coronado were vivid: purple and red bougainvillea blooms dripped along the chalk-white walls. Manicured lawns hemmed by the waxy green leaves of palm trees that dotted the yards and boulevards.

Despite the cooling effect of the recent precipitation, the atmosphere at the border reflected a much more realistic sense of the desert—cacti, sand, and heat-reflective stucco. As the women approached the entrance to Tijuana, rust-colored mud covered everything. On the opposite side of the highway, a beat-up truck hauled an old-school silver bullet camper spattered with mud. It reminded Cat of a burrito with mole.

She flipped her visor up as it fogged again and motioned to Sis that her clutch hand was tired.

"No sense shifting in this shit," Sis yelled above the noise. "We may as well walk the rest of it." She cut her engine, took off her helmet, and clipped it around her handlebars. Her short white hair remained spiked in spite of the sweat that ran down her brow.

"I hope we don't lose Rey," Cat said, acknowledging her sister's sacrifice in hanging back with her.

"Won't be the first time I adjust my pace for the newbie." This ribbing was classic Sis.

The road wore a layer of tan sand that hid the lines between lanes. As the sisters straddled their bikes and walked them side by side, Cat caught a glimpse of Rey at the security check. She admired Rey's daredevil flair as she hopped down to touch the ground at the stop sign. At five foot three, her legs weren't long enough to reach the ground simultaneously, so at each stop she had to drop off to the left, keeping her right knee draped across the saddle. Baby-faced Rey could've passed for a kid if not for the bright orange KTM dirt bike she commanded.

Following Rey's brief interaction with a guard, Cat lost

sight of her as she slipped under a sign that read "Bienvenido a México."

Even with the engine off, the heat of the surrounding cars and lack of riding wind brought beads of sweat to Cat's neck that pooled around her collarbones and ran down her back. Her armored jacket felt like a sauna in the relatively mild eighty degrees, and she wondered how it would feel when it got really hot. Like stomping her toe to forget a headache, Cat focused on a more manageable source of discomfort. "My wrist is starting to bug me," she admitted to Sis.

Sissy had broken her right wrist in September during a big competition. She showed little empathy, but offered a few good suggestions. "Try stretching your forearm, that's where the finger muscles are." Sis pressed her hand back while balancing her bike on her tippy toes. "Neutral is easiest on the wrist," Sis explained, holding her hand straight out from her arm. "Collapsing your wrist puts pressure on it." She rolled her knuckles over as an example. "It can cause carpal tunnel or tendonitis. Try to keep it aligned, and we'll get you some anti-inflammatories."

"I brought Advil," said Cat, who hadn't had a period since her miscarriage two months ago and was expecting it any minute.

After a quick interaction with the border-crossing guard, during which Cat signed an obligatory autograph for the man's teenage son, the sisters pulled into the lot behind the border patrol office to reunite with Rey, who was polishing off a bottle of water.

"Been here a while?" asked Sis.

"Twenty minutes," she claimed. "I've never seen a line going *this* way."

"How'd you get across so fast?" asked Cat.

"They welcomed me back," said Rey with a smile.

Cat grabbed ibuprofen from her saddlebag and opened a bottle of water, but before she could take a sip, Sis took the bottle without asking and dumped half of it on her head. "See why I didn't take a shower?"

"Can you at least save me a sip?" asked Cat.

Sis handed the bottle back while spiking her wet hair with her spare hand. "Don't worry, Clean Freak," Sis teased, "I don't have cooties."

Cat thought about wiping the mouth of the bottle on her clean tee, but she wanted to get one full day of fresh out of it. Lord knew it would probably be the last day of cleanliness for a while. She held the bottle without touching her lips to it and then wiped her hands on her water-resistant pants.

The threesome made their way through the clog of cars trying to enter the highway toward downtown Tijuana. Rey took the lead to guide the sisters toward the tourism office where Cat insisted they purchase liability insurance. "There's no point reporting a crash down here," Rey argued. Cat, whose body was insured for a million bucks, opted to follow precaution and paid to cover all of them.

"We can get our visas at the port in Ensenada, when we buy our ferry tickets for the Day of the Dead," Rey explained as if it had been discussed.

"What ferry?" asked Cat.

"Rey told me about a place on the mainland where they

have amazing Day of the Dead celebrations...." Sis squinted and tried to recall the location.

"Lake Pátzcuaro," Rey said.

"I really want to check it out," prodded Sis. "How far is it from Baja?"

"It's eight hours from Mazatlán," said Rey, "and a straight shot north back to Texas." Sis and Rey's attempt to extend the itinerary seemed brazen to Cat, who was the benefactor of this vacation. Cabo was the end of the line in Cat's mind, but Day of the Dead sounded cool. Feeling steamrolled, Cat knew her "coaches" would deserve a bonus if things went well.

"If you make me look like a pro by the end of this, I'll gladly pay for the extra days."

The next stop was at a drug store with a hand-painted sign that read "La Farmacia."

"I hope they have batteries," Sis said as they entered.

"What kind do you need?" asked Rey.

"Small ones."

"For what?"

"The doohickey stuck to my brain," explained Sis, pointing to her processor behind her ear.

"I hope they have Evian," added Cat.

"Don't waste your money on fancy brands," Rey warned. "We'll dump half of it on our heads anyway."

"No Montezuma's Revenge for me," Cat declared, carrying three large bottles of the most expensive Mexican brand up to the counter. "Is this water good?" she asked the clerk, who had just handed Sis a battery pack from behind the counter. The clerk smiled, ignoring Cat's question.

Sis grabbed Rey's cache of sunflower seeds and generic water to set them next to the register as Cat pulled a hidden neck wallet from under her shirt. Rey retrieved a bunch of crumpled bills from her own woven wallet, but Sis motioned for her to forget it.

"Better get used to Miss Priss paying our way. She's a real philanthropist."

"I think you mean charitable person," Cat corrected. "And I'm happy to pay for provisions—that's the deal."

"Cool," said Sis, adding a pack of gum and two bags of cashews to their collection. "You can never have enough nuts." She winked.

"The salt will help us retain water," Rey explained. "And they're full of calories, if we get lost or stuck."

"I thought you knew where we were going," Cat said apprehensively.

"I cross these paths all the time," said Rey, "but the rain may have changed the terrain."

"And what happens if we get lost?" Cat demanded.

"I told Sis to bring sleeping bags," Rey said.

"Better add that to the list," said Sis.

"Dos ponchos, por favor," said Rey. The clerk stepped out from behind the counter and pulled down two colorful cotton ponchos from a clothesline outside the door. "You won't find camping gear around here," Rey said as an afterthought.

"I'd really like to sleep in a bed tonight," Cat said.

"When you head off-road, you got to be prepared to sleep in the sand," said Rey.

"I brought bug spray with DEET," said Cat enthusiastically.

"Scorpions love a warm place to sleep," Rey teased. "Just make sure to spray your feet."

Cat shot a look at Sis that said, *How could you forget to tell me about sleeping bags?* Then she handed the woman behind the counter a hundred-dollar traveler's check.

The clerk took one look at it and raised her brows before muttering something in Spanish. Rey translated: "Do you have anything smaller?"

Cat nodded. "You better get pesos," Rey recommended. "Small-town folk won't know what to do with those."

Cat's cheeks burned. "I'll cash some of them at the hotel tonight."

Luckily, she was able to cash one of them at the very next stop, when they paused just before Highway 2 to top off their tanks and grab lunch on the run.

"So where are we headed next?" asked Sis, pumping just a gallon in, prepping her tank for desolation.

"There's a dried-up lake bed about two hundred kilometers east called Laguna Salada—it makes a great race track, like the salt flats in Cali."

"Sounds good to me," said Sis, not even glancing at Cat for her opinion.

"I made reservations at a bed-and-breakfast in Ensenada," Cat exclaimed.

"We'll be there by dinner, and the long way will be worth the delay," Rey promised.

Cat paid pesos for her petrol before following Sis and Rey toward a taco cart parked alongside the gas station.

Lime juice ran down Sis's arm toward her elbow as she offered Cat a few pointers between bites. "It's been a little while since you rode."

"I know," said Cat, feeling nervous.

"Stand up to maintain traction on the dirt." Sis spoke with her mouth full. Cat bit her tongue to prevent commenting on her sister's sloppy eating.

"It'll keep your ass from getting rattled, too," piped Rey.

Sis continued her tutorial. "Don't grab the saddle with your knees or try to steer with your hips. Just focus on where you want to go and ignore the obstacles." She paused to lick her fingers. "We'll practice controlled slides once we've been riding for a while. Until then, try to avoid them."

"I don't need to practice wipeouts," Cat insisted.

"It was a high side you broke your leg on," said Sis, "just don't do that again."

"Stick to low sides," Rey suggested. "Better to slip than to flip."

"I'll just go slow," Cat assured them.

That's what I'm afraid of, flipped Sis.

CHAPTER 5

EL CHOLLA

Just outside of Tijuana, the ladies pulled off Highway 2 and headed into the wide-open desert. Civilization faded behind them. The dirt road was smooth as a baby's butt—a big fat baby with dimpled cheeks. Cat felt an impulse to cry as they said goodbye to the pavement, but the landscape quickly carried her back to Texas, where she remembered playing in the dirt with Sis.

The yard that surrounded their childhood home in El Paso had been filled with all kinds of stuff that gave Cat the heebie-jeebies: Angry looking cacti were the least of her worries since it was the fire ants and spiders seeking respite from the sun that most often spoiled her fun. The creepies, as Cat called them, restricted her use of the swing set and the toy water jets her father installed in the summertime.

Fortunately, Cat had been able to convince little Sis to

do the things she was afraid to do. As soon as Sis was old enough to sign, Cat learned to exploit her sister's pride by flipping *Don't be a priss.* Then Cat would test Sissy's courage by telling her to deal with the scary bugs. If Sis resisted, Cat would look at her with disgust and flip, *That's why they call you Sissy.*

Cat laughed in the privacy of her helmet at the irony of that mockery. With the body of an Olympian and the will of a warrior, Sissy had grown up to be a full-fledged champion; there was not a stitch of Sis that said wimpy. The sisters looked related, but that was it when it came to similarity. Cat was as scrawny as she was tall, with long blonde locks and super long legs that were supple and sexy. For all the years teenage Sis spent pumping up her quads on bumpity-bumps, Cat had spent balanced on a runway and posing for couture. Cat really hoped this trip would help her grow a pair of cojones. Her most recent flick, *Darkstar*, had turned her into a household name, but fame didn't change the way she felt about her empty existence. Cat didn't know why she felt so dissatisfied with life. Maybe it was her questionable engagement or recent miscarriage. Perhaps it was all the fanfare from strangers that was getting on her nerves, or her agent's constant harping: "Stay skinny, smile pretty, make more money." According to tabloids, she was living like a queen, but Cat was about to hang up her crown if something didn't change soon. It was time to decide what she wanted out of life, and Sis was the perfect muse in this ruse.

Sissy knew exactly what she wanted and how to get it. At the tender age of twenty, she was poised to become the only female in history to win the Triple Crown next year.

Her success in the male-dominated sport of motocross had inspired Cat and her fiancé to produce a movie about Sis's story. Cat was the obvious choice to portray the lead, but she had a long way to go when it came to portraying a badass. This trip had given Cat an exciting mission: She needed to learn how to imitate a master and to reconnect with her increasingly distant sister. Gazing at the fireball in front of her, Cat decided it was high time she quit letting Sis kick sand in her face, and try riding beside her for a while.

Cat trailed behind the racer girls for miles, eyes watering from all the dust being kicked up by their bikes. Sis gave her a nod as Cat rode up, standing on the pegs like a pro. The road was wide, but the side-by-side arrangement meant Cat had to choose a line and not meander into the soft sand to her left. The hard-packed path made Cat think that this road was well traveled, but there was not a soul in sight as the girls made their way across the scorched land toward the mountain range in the distance.

As their proximity to the peaks increased, a crosswind kicked in, forcing Cat to lean in and grip her handlebars more tightly. Soon the bumps in the road had evolved into lines like a washboard. Cat's forearms were practically numb by the time the path got flat again. Just when Cat was about to request a rest stop, the land leveled out and the packed sand of Laguna Salada came into view. She sighed with relief.

While Cat idled at the edge of the lake bed, Sis and Rey broke out of their steady motocross pace and cranked the throttle. In an instant, Sis and Rey were racing. Hitting ninety, they circled the oval "track" five times in as many minutes. Cat steered her bike cautiously around the ellipse, keeping her eyes down on the fast-passing ground as her comrades lapped her. She got faster with each loop, finally finding the courage to gaze up and wave across the way to the racers as they pulled over to take a break on the far side of the "track."

Cat came around the last bend and pulled up to Sis as Rey announced her need to piss. "It's pretty cool out here—" Cat began, but she was immediately interrupted by a commotion behind the cactus.

"*¡Carajo! ¡La puta!*" Rey cried out in pain.

Sis was off her bike first, followed by Cat who took a second to figure out where to set her kickstand in the soft sand. Hurrying awkwardly in her heavy boots, Cat found Sis hovering above Rey, who was on her hands and knees next to a twelve-foot cactus. A fist-sized spikey pom-pom dangled from her upper thigh.

"Aaaahhh!" Rey screamed angrily.

"Oh, no! What do we do?" Cat said. She knew better than to get close to the offending cacti. "It's a jumping cholla," she whispered, recognizing the dangerous cactus from her childhood. Sis nodded knowingly. The sisters analyzed the situation and found another bulb attached to Rey's hand and an egg-sized sticker in her chin.

"Don't move!" warned Cat. "They appear to be multiplying."

"Owwww! Get them off me!" Rey shrieked. The sisters looked at each other in dismay. Neither of them wanted to risk a similar fate by touching the barbed balls embedded in

Rey's skin. "Grab a stick, a rock, anything," Rey pleaded. "Uhhh, it hurts! Jesucristo! *Help me!*"

Sis and Cat scanned the ground, scrambling to find a tool that was long and strong enough to pull out the embedded thorns. Cat was the first one to score.

"I found a stick. It's not very thick, but ..." She rushed to Rey's aid. The dry and flimsy twig broke on the first attempt—the thorns pulled on Rey's skin but refused to relinquish their grip. Sissy immediately tried to scrape at them with a jagged rock she'd found. Again, the thorns stretched Rey's skin from her hand, but would not let go. Sissy tried again. This time the upper ring of thorns gave in, but the stubborn cactus pulled away from Rey's wrist and reattached itself closer to her knuckles.

"Ow wow wow wow! Stop, it stings!" howled Rey.

Sissy looked at Cat and flipped, *What do we do?* Cat hurried to her bike, unstrapped her poncho, and rushed over to pad the ground beneath Rey's knees. The cushion allowed her to rotate her weight without skinning her shins, so she reached up and picked a stronger stick that Sissy found. Fury burning in her eyes, Rey wedged the stick between the belly of the cactus and her skin, and pulled until the ball of thorns broke way. The baseball-size bulb landed softly at her feet. With all the strength she could muster, Rey stood up and kicked it as hard as she could. Simultaneously swearing at the earth, the sky, and the cacti, Rey screamed *fuck* in Spanish. "*¡Carajoooo!*"

"You want me to try the one stuck to your butt?" asked Sis, stifling her temptation to laugh.

Rey hobbled, hunched over and humiliated, toward

her bike. Her motorcycle pants were still bunched below her knees. Resting elbows on the seat for support in her bent-over position, Rey exposed her bare rear-end to her friend, then brought her knuckles to her mouth and bit down on them.

"Okay ... go," Rey coached. Cat placed her hand on Rey's back for moral support while Sissy dug the stick between the clinging cactus and Rey's derriere. It took about thirty seconds to get it. Three times, the damn thing released at the top, only to roll down and reinsert lower in Rey's leg. Finally, it gave as Rey caved into the pain and yelled, "Just get it, already!"

Moaning, Rey pulled up her cotton underwear and then slumped to the ground to rest on the poncho that Cat had repositioned. "Ow!" she cried again when she bumped the bud on her chin. A few quick tugs on the bulb from Sissy's grip that was shielded by a thick corner of the blanket, and the deed was done. Rey hung her head between her knees, careful not to touch the raised welt that was spotted with blood. She looked toasted.

"Have some water," said Cat, running through their supplies in her head, trying to think of something that might soothe Rey's pain. "I have ibuprofen!" She yanked her toiletry sack from the waterproof insert in her saddlebag and fished around for the bottle of pills. Retrieving the Advil, Cat bent down and gingerly shook two pills into her palm. Before she could offer them, Rey grabbed the entire bottle, tipped it back, and swallowed an undisclosed amount of medication. Then she twisted the cap off the water bottle with her teeth and guzzled the entire thing. Then Rey lay flat on her back in a heap. Sissy and Rey backed off to analyze the situation. Hoping to prevent any further distress for their collapsed friend, they privately discussed their next move via flipping.

$$\text{ꟺ}$$

The sun had sunk in the thirty-five minutes it took to free Rey from her prickly hijackers. The clock on Cat's bike read 5:15. Dinner in Ensenada seemed like a crap shoot now. Rey had said Ensenada was about two hours away if they rode "the way of the crow," but only if they hurried. This would be especially hard in the dark for the newbie, so the fast route seemed too sketchy. In addition to Cat's limitations, Rey was in no condition to stand, let alone sit on her injured ass, with an injured hand in charge of the gas. The alternate route along the highway would require backtracking all the way to Tijuana before heading south, and that would take close to four hours. It appeared they were destined to camp out, on this, their first night in Mexico.

Rey slept on as the sisters set out to gather firewood. Dry and brittle as it was, these sticks would serve as wonderful kindling. The trick was to find wood that could burn for the long run. Sissy was craving food when the cactus catastrophe began. Now that life was simple again, her awareness returned to her hunger. *I'm starving*, Sis signed. They had two big bags of sunflower seeds, but nothing else to eat.

CHAPTER 6

CABALLERO

As dusk settled over the dusty desert floor, the evening breeze picked up, and the flame of their measly campfire fought to maintain its fervor. Rey lay sprawled on the poncho next to the fire. Having passed out for an hour, she stirred as the cool night air tickled her senses. Suddenly, a horse appeared on the horizon. Cat dismissed it initially, assuming this passenger in the far-off distance was not set on a trajectory to interact with the three of them, but soon enough his path changed, and he steered his way toward them. As the rider neared, Cat could see he was a kid.

Rey opened her eyes as the approaching horse snorted. The boy on board was small and disheveled, although his horse looked healthy and well kept. The kid pulled on the reins about ten feet from the fire. He gazed down in silence, then slid off his saddle and landed with a *poof* in the loose

56

dust. Rey spoke groggily to him in Spanish, then introduced him as Carlos.

"Bracero?" Sissy asked, flexing her fluency.

"Caballero," he announced, with a hint of disdain. He was the real deal, a Mexican cowboy. Rey asked him a few more questions before informing a clearly curious Cat that he was riding back from a cattle drive.

"How old is he?" Cat whispered. His stature said twelve, his demeanor said thirty.

"*¿Cuántos años tienes?*" Sissy asked.

"*Dieciséis.*" Cat could count to twenty in Spanish and was shocked when he said sixteen. He was only two years younger than Rey. She raised her water bottle up as an offering. The boy shook his head. He spoke to Rey in such a way that indicated he was giving her a rundown on his travels while inquiring about their reason for being here. It irked Cat that she couldn't understand a word of it. When the conversation was done, he offered to gather them hardier wood for their fire. He appeared to be in no rush to leave, so they agreed. As he rode away, Rey began to move around the site with a vigor that said things were looking up for her.

"How you feeling?" asked Sis.

"Pretty sore," admitted Rey, "but I'll be fine tomorrow."

"Do you think we can trust that kid?" asked Cat. "He seems a little rough around the edges."

"He's a farm kid—tough stuff—it's not an easy way to make a living," Rey explained.

"He's a half pint," Sis said with contempt aimed at Cat. "He looks harmless to me."

Fifteen minutes later, the boy returned with a machete tucked under one leg. A loosely bound bushel of chopped logs balanced precariously behind his saddle. He asked what they had to eat.

"Nada," said Sis, scowling.

Carlos walked around the far side of his horse and untied the carcass of an armadillo that had previously gone unnoticed. "*¡Vamos a comer!*" he announced. Then without missing a beat, he tossed the thing on the ground in front of the horse, gave the stallion a slap on the rump, and backed away. The horse reared up on his hind legs, offered a quick whinny, and brought its front legs barreling down on top of the armadillo, smashing its shell like a lobster claw in a nutcracker. Cat's jaw dropped, and Sissy said, "*Ho*-ly shit!"

The horse reared up again and *whack*, came down hard, cutting the iron-clad critter in two. Cat gagged at the brutal sight of the prehistoric creature splayed and filleted on the ground. *I am* not *eating that*, Cat signed to Sis.

"You're going to cook it, right?" asked Sis.

Rey stood with both hands on her hips and snapped, "He's a cowboy, not a caveman!" Then she hauled herself up and moved to the far side of the fire to help pull the meat from the obliterated shell. Cat gagged and covered her mouth to hide her grimace. She wondered how she would survive the ride tomorrow without a hint of dinner. She had a small appetite, but twenty-four hours without food would make her weak and maybe weepy. She asked Rey if there were any other options of the vegetarian variety.

"We have a cactus garden in El Paso," Rey said. Cat shot her a look that questioned her cactus expertise. "Prickly pear should be an easy meal to score around here," Rey continued.

Fully aware of edible prickly pear, Sis raised her shoulders to say *What else can we do?* Then she took the lead, told Cat to follow her, and the sisters set out to find some edible vegetation under the light of the rising moon.

As soon as they were out of Rey's earshot, Cat aired her concerns to Sis. "I have a lot of money back there." She glanced over her shoulder. "I'm a little worried about the kid, he looks ... desperate."

"Give me a break," said Sis, "he's not after your money."

"And what's up with Rey suddenly acting like an expert on cacti?" Cat asked.

"Those 'sketchy' Mexicans are trying to help you right now, so don't be a bitch."

"I wouldn't need help if your friend had any sense. Why the hell did you bring her?"

"Because I didn't think I could stand two weeks alone with you!" Stunned and surprised by Sis's tongue-lashing, Cat had no comeback, but she suddenly wondered why Sis wanted to come here in the first place.

⚜

By the time they had carefully gathered enough cactus paddles, using yet another stick to pry them free and the outstretched bottom of their shirts as baskets, the moon had found its place high in the sky, illuminating the landscape in an eerie blue glow. As they approached the campfire, Cat saw Rey frowning, her raised arms gesturing frustration as if she was mid-argument with Carlos. Cat wondered what he had said that irked her; maybe he was complaining about the armadillo-fearing gringos, in the same way Cat suspected his foreignness.

Before Cat had a chance to ask Sis if she could understand what they were saying, a flash of light in the distance caught her eye. It was hard to tell how far off it was. She squinted, but the flashes had stopped. Cat was about to ask Sis if she'd seen it when Rey looked up guiltily and abruptly stopped talking to Carlos, a behavior that seemed only slightly strange compared to the rapid succession of flashes she had just seen. Cat looked in the direction of the lights again to try to figure out what it was, but it was gone. She hustled up alongside Sis, struggling to suppress her anxiety about what other alien being might be lurking out of eyesight.

Rey worked to rotate the armadillo meat on the crooked stick spit while Carlos instructed Sis to grab a paddle and rub the spines off on a rock. Sis translated his directions for Cat, and the two of them doubled up the corners of the poncho to use as mitts to protect their hands. Squatting side by side, they took turns rubbing the paddles on the rocks around the fire pit.

Carlos, who was tending to the roasted armadillo, stood as the sisters finished. He walked over, grabbed a well-worn cactus paddle in his bare hand, and held it in the hot flame until the skin began to shrivel and burn. Then he gripped the edge of it with his teeth and peeled the entire slab of skin off with one long pull. Without even flinching, he held it in the flame for a few minutes, then flipped it in his naked hand and scorched the other side. He offered the first one to Cat, giving her the international command to eat by touching his filthy fingers to his lips. Then he grabbed another paddle and repeated the process. The meat was mild and sweet, but more fibrous and less firm than an actual pear. She eventually consumed three more, while the others chewed on what Sis described as the "smoky and tough" meat of the armadillo.

When dinner was done, the girls did their best to wash up, using a trickle of water from the second to last of their bottles. Sis offered Carlos a taste of their water, but he refused. As he climbed back on his horse, the women thanked him for all his help, bilingually. Cat thought she caught Carlos giving Rey a look that said *be careful*, and was surprised that Rey nodded in response. Cat looked at Sis, but her sister seemed at ease with their eerie exchange.

Tension crept across Cat's back as she tried to guess what kind of threat would inspire such a serious-sounding warning from Carlos. Images of the hockey-masked Jason from *Halloween* stole the scene in her overactive brain. Cat chose to focus on the present tense, taking in the burly beauty of the silhouetted kid as he gracefully commanded his stallion to gallop. "He was harmless," Cat reminded herself. She only hoped the strange lights she had seen were a large pack of fireflies or some friendly passersby.

Opting to behave bravely, Cat settled in the dirt next to Sis, who was warming her hands by the fire. The way Rey was walking without a limp now showed she had recovered from her altercation with the cactus, a sign that they'd be back in the saddle come daylight. An odd vigor seemed to infuse Rey since Carlos had departed, despite the fact that her face remained swollen and red from the cholla barbs. The fire crackled and hissed as Cat kicked back on her hands, raising her eyes to stare out into the shadowy night. The full moon added depth to the sky and limned the mountain range in blue light.

"What does *Sangre de Cristo* mean?" asked Cat, jutting her chin at the mountains.

"Blood of Christ," said Rey. "They're named for their color at sunrise."

Cat was excited to see their claim to fame in the a.m. She was beginning to feel a real sense of peace when a coyote cried in the distance, and Cat recalled the reality of the situation ... and the threat of scorpions. She hugged her knees to her chest and shivered.

"Are there any animals out here we should be concerned about?" asked Cat.

"The coyotes are harmless, since we have no food with us," Rey claimed. "It's the random guys you can't always trust."

Cat smiled nervously at the irony of that statement.

Sissy asked Rey if she'd ever run into trouble traveling. After pausing for a few seconds, she shook her head.

"What brings you down here so much?" asked Cat.

"My father's a jeweler. He buys his silver from the mines. It's cheaper."

"Why doesn't he come?" asked Sissy.

"He used to, but he broke his back in a car wreck a few years ago. He's in a wheelchair now."

Cat pondered Rey's plight and thought of how difficult it must be to have your only parent handicapped. She felt sorry for Rey. Her sister knew all too well about living with a disability.

"Wow," Sis said, "is that why I've never seen him at the

races?" Rey nodded. "So how old were you when your mom died?" Sis asked softly.

"Three," answered Rey.

"How'd she die?" asked Sis.

As if Sis had uncorked a bottled volcano, Rey launched into the sordid story of her mother's journey to Mexico to visit family. She never returned. Rey's father thought she had abandoned them. The family in Mexico claimed Rey's mom had vanished and were distraught over her disappearance.

"My father didn't believe them—he thought they were helping her hide. But it turns out she had died."

"What happened?" asked Sis.

"She was one of the first *feminicidios*."

"What's that?" asked Cat.

Rey looked ready to slap the stupid off Cat's face. "You never heard of *las muertas de Juarez*?" Cat shook her head.

"It happened right across the border from El Paso."

"What was it?" asked Sis.

"Four hundred women, murdered in Juarez," said Rey. "All of them were tortured and violated."

Cat drew her palms across her face. "I can't believe we never heard of that," she said.

"It still happens to this day ... to girls as young as twelve." Rey's eyes turned toward the ground. "Mi madre was twenty," she said.

Rey's anger began to make sense to Cat, and she wondered if booze had anything to do with the accident that paralyzed Rey's father. The Lang clan was used to alcohol abuse in response to loss. Her own mother had faced an intolerable death, too, and had sought consolation in a bottle. It suddenly struck Cat how much she and Rey might actually have in common.

After a very long silence, Sis spoke. "Sorry about your mom."

"That's okay," said Rey, "it was a long time ago."

When it was time to stomp out the fire and get to sleep, the sisters lay one of the ponchos on the sand and used the other one to cover them. Cat created a small pillow out of her electric vest, while Sissy built a soft mound of sand under the blanket beneath her head. The ponchos offered incomplete protection for both sisters, since six-foot Sis was almost as tall as Catrina, but with windproof riding gear covering them from neck to toe, ample warmth was not an issue. They were fast asleep within minutes.

⚜

As soon as Rey was sure both sisters were oblivious, she snuck out of her sleeping bag and slipped into the shadows, settling into a protected pocket behind two rocks. She opened the plastic baggie and heaved a sigh of relief. One quick sniff would calm her nerves fast and help her forget about the past.

⚜

"Ahh!" Cat bellowed as she massaged her fiercely contracted hamstring.

Sis scrambled up to her feet in a flash and ran her hands through her hair as if a scary bug was about to crawl in her ear.

"Ugh," Cat moaned as she wrestled with her leg.

"What's a matter?" asked Sis.

"Leg cramp," moaned Cat.

"Hey," she whispered to Sis, "did you know about Rey's Mom?"

I knew her dad's a jeweler, signed Sis, *but she never told me about the other stuff.*

How long have you known her? Cat flipped.

About a year, responded Sis.

"Are you friends?" asked Cat out loud.

"We're teammates," Sis hissed. "How well do you know your costars, like the dude you screwed in *Darkstar*?"

"I didn't really have sex with him," Cat whispered.

"Well, damn, that was good acting."

Cat ignored Sis's cheap shot. "Do you know anything about this girl?"

"I haven't read her diary, but she seems like a decent human being."

"Aren't we all?" asked Cat sarcastically.

"Live and let live," said Sis, quoting their mother's favorite passage from the Bible, a staple retort she would give if anyone criticized her drinking. "Or should I say: Sleep and let sleep?" Sis seemed even more annoyed with Cat's inquiries about Rey than she had been last night, and Cat wondered again why she had agreed to come on this trip.

"Forgive me for crying, Your Highness."

"I'm *not* high," slurred Rey, apparently sleep talking. Cat furrowed her brows in confusion about the random interjection.

"No one's accusing you, Rey," said Sis, glaring at Cat as if to say *can it!*

At daybreak, Cat woke to the sound of retching and rubbed the sleep from her eyes to see Rey doubled over in the distance. "You all right?" called Cat as she rubbed her eyes again. "Hey, Rey—you okay?"

Sissy rolled over in the dirt and brushed a dusty hand through her filthy hair. "Your friend's getting sick over there," Cat mumbled to Sis.

"Maybe it was the armadillo meat," Sis whispered with a grimace.

Rey tilted her face to look at them, brushing spaghetti strands of dark brown hair from her face. "I'm fine," she said, before she violently hinged and puked again. When she recovered control, she stood up and arched her spine to relieve the strain in her back. "I was just lying there and felt sick." She wiped her mouth and accepted a bottle of water from Cat, who flashed back to all the times she had tried to sober up her drunken mother on the way to a pageant.

"Are you hot?" asked Cat. "Your cheeks are red. Or maybe it's a reflection from the sunrise." She looked beyond Rey at the ruby-red ridge in the distance. The mountain peaks increased in brilliance with the sunrise.

"I'm fine," Rey declared, excusing herself so she could rinse her mouth and wipe her face.

"You gonna be okay to ride?" called Sis from a distance.

"Yeah," said Rey with a shady squint. "No problemo."

7

LAGUNA SALADA TO ENSENADA

I'm so hungry I could eat a horse! flipped Sis as they passed a sign on the road that read "Ensenada 15 Km." The thought of watching Sissy eat armadillo was bad enough; the image of her dining on horse made Cat consider veganism. If only cactus paddles could satisfy her needs. After that wacky snack last night, Cat was too famished to resist carnivorous temptations, as long as they came in the form of steak and eggs. All she really needed was to get her grub on, after a suitable shower, of course.

She assumed Sis would insist on eating first, despite the fact that Rey still had vomit in her hair. Food trumped hygiene for Sis any day. Screw Rey, as Sis would say; for all her talent as a rider, she was a real klutz when it came to pissing. Being sloppy around notorious cacti seemed out of character for a person who portrayed herself as a desert expert. *Goes to show how little I know about her,* thought Cat, suddenly wary of the stranger in her midst.

When Ensenada came into view, the clock on Cat's bike read 10:00 a.m. There was still plenty of time to surf today, and after a hot meal, she'd have plenty of energy for it. The ride here had been easy, in spite of the fumes they were forced to inhale from all the diesel trucks along the way. In this part of Baja, eighteen-wheelers were a sign of abundance, and the women owed the smooth road to them. The Triple A guide said Ensenada was one of the most prosperous spots on Baja. The export of farm products and fish from the region funded the only paved road in the area.

Cat was salivating at the thought of fresh fish when she spotted her potential dinner. Slowing to a crawl in traffic on the six-lane highway, the women pulled alongside a man on foot carrying a lopsided prize. It was quite a sight. A forty-something Mexican, about five foot three, had an entire swordfish balanced precariously on his head. The sword hung down to his ankle and the tailfin draped to his knee, the fish bobbing in rhythm to the man's dogged march.

Cat flinched when a triple-axle truck narrowly missed the giant fish. Any taller and the man would have been struck by the side-view mirror. Cat was impressed with the fish and its captor, and hoped the guy survived long enough to cash in on his catch.

A few miles later, the trio arrived at the Casa de la Loma Dorada Inn, a day late for their reservation and five hours before check-in. Cat insisted that they freshen up before breakfast and pulled out all her star-studded stops to get in a room ASAP. Accustomed to the Los Angeles socialites who frequented the place, the staff was ready to accommodate their late arrival date. Cat asked for the same room she had booked yesterday because it was the only one in this four-room inn with two beds, and then she requested an additional trundle bed for Rey.

"Time for breakfast," insisted Sis.

"We can't go in the restaurant like this," argued Cat.

"Why not?" asked Rey, who looked peaked. Cat assumed that pale and sickly Rey needed food to settle her stomach, and caved in.

"I guess we can dine before a shower, but if anyone tries to take my picture, I'm gonna freak."

"You look pretty bleak—it shouldn't be a problem," quipped Sis.

The aroma of fresh tortillas trumped Cat's preference for sanitation over satiation. She forgot about her own stench as soon as they entered the dining room. Cat felt ravenous for the first time in her life. She scarfed down a plate of huevos rancheros and still had room for more. When they finished eating, Sis and Rey headed to the room while Cat stopped at the front desk to reserve a short board at the closest surf shop. Surfing always called to her, and this was the first step to getting her feet wet in Mexico.

Back in the room, Rey fretted over the info Carlos had shared with her. Sis asked if she could use the bathroom first, so Rey decided it was the perfect time for a quick run to the nearest *pharmacia*.

"I need to buy a phone card, so I can call mi papa."

"Cat will let you use her cell," offered Sis.

"I don't want to take advantage of your sister."

"She loves to throw her riches around."

"I'd rather fend for myself," said Rey. She hoped her insistence didn't sound desperate, even though that's the way she felt.

"Suit yourself," said Sis.

Rey slipped out of the room, clutching the hotel key. Her palm was sweaty against the key card. She needed to find a bag of balloons and get the heroin into safekeeping, before her urges got the best of her. Ensenada was the first of the tourist traps she would have to endure. Carlos made it clear that the police presence had intensified dramatically over the last few months, to assure tourists that they would be safe in spite of the increasingly violent drug trade. Rey was thinking about where in the world she could bag her stash when she turned the corner of the hallway and nearly ran down Cat.

"Sorry," said Rey, as she fought to mask her distraction. "I need to run to the store—want anything?"

"No, thanks," said Cat.

"Sis should be done in the shower, if you want to grab the next one," Rey called over her shoulder, rushing toward the exit. "I'll be back." She hurried onto the street.

Cat was bothered by Rey's intensity, especially in the wake of her illness at daybreak. She had a bad feeling and thought now would be the best time to discuss her distress with Sissy.

Sis was kicked back on her bed when Cat entered the room. "What's Rey up to?" Cat asked.

Sis rolled over to grab a bottle of water from the nightstand. "She said she needed to buy a calling card. I told her you'd let her use your phone, but she wants to pay her own way."

"She seems a little off today. She was sweating like a stuck pig and almost ran me down in the hallway. Is there something you're not telling me?" Cat busied herself packing a surf bag as a means to throw the focus off her increasing unease about Rey. She was applying fifty-dollar sunscreen across her cheeks when Sis basically stated her allegiance to Rey.

"You're *such* a snob sometimes."

"I've been nothing but nice since you guys arrived. I want to know how much you know about your friend, is all. She seems a little … messed up, and I don't want any trouble down here. We're in a foreign country, you know. I'm cool *riding* in the backcountry, but I don't want to *sleep* there again. *All right?*" Cat used her older-sister tone that said *Don't mess with my seniority.*

"O-*kay*," said Sis, turning to a teenybopper tone to lighten the tone of her aggression.

"Don't be a wiseass," cracked Cat. "Just keep an eye on her."

Cat threw some things in her beach bag, grabbed her wetsuit from her saddlebag, bid goodbye to Sis, and headed out the door for her first round of surfing, feeling vindicated by her effort to put Sis in her place. This was a gift vacation for her, and Cat was not about to deal with too much trouble from Ms. Mooch or her "plus one." She walked tall down the hallway, hoping she could catch Rey engaged in some action that might explain her sickly behavior. Peeking into the hotel bar room, she saw an empty space, no sign of the Latina she had envisioned drinking tequila.

Moving on to the task at hand, Cat waited impatiently in the lobby for the taxi to arrive. Her whole body ached; the tension of the last few days and sleeping on the ground had twisted even the most limber of her muscles. Surfing was one of the best ways to loosen her up, and Cat hoped there were enough breakers to ease her mind and lift her spirits. Neither of her companions had any interest in water sports, so this would the first of many opportunities for alone time.

As the cab driver rolled his VW bug slowly down the boulevard, Cat absorbed the bright white heat bouncing off the stucco walls by poking her head out the window. The smell of carnitas, cooked onion, and fresh baked tortillas made her hungry, and she welcomed the improvement in her appetite with relief—her inability to eat since the miscarriage had started to alarm Chris, and he constantly ragged on her for "dieting." Cat was actually considering a second breakfast when the cabbie pulled up to the surf shack. Offering him a hefty tip, Cat requested a pick up at two so she could get back for a midday snack.

The fact that she was scheduling her day around a need for regular feedings made her smile. This newfound craving gave her a rush, so she paused on her way out of the shop to eat a bunch of dried mango she'd scored as a presurf snack. Gazing up at the street above, she felt lit up by the festive colors that dotted the storefronts along the avenue. Accenting the rust-red roofs and blue awnings, ornamental stencil work danced above each doorway and windowsill. The downtown felt like a present waiting to be unwrapped, and Cat looked forward to an afternoon of touring the town, even if it meant keeping her distance from Sis and her suspicious friend.

Stepping in the soft sand of the ocean with the short board held above her head, Cat was surprised to find the water of the Todos Santos Bay was so much warmer than in LA. Seals swarmed, looking for handouts from the fisherman who dotted the pier to the north of her. A cargo ship crept slowly along the horizon, hauling goods that kept local restaurants in rank with the world's finest. Scuba flags dotted the scene, and she imagined one of those divers might actually be in the process of spearfishing her lunch.

Cruising along the surface, bobbing up and over the breakers on her way out to catch her first curl, she suddenly had the urge to abandon her board and dive deep. She couldn't wait to get under the surface again. Her last scuba trip had been a few months before her pregnancy. With all the sorrow that ensued after the miscarriage, and the downtime she needed to recover from it, diving had fallen by the wayside. Exploring the ocean was one of her only passions. Now here she was again, enjoying the mad dash of white-capped breakers.

The water was a deep blue hue and about ten degrees warmer than the briny green sea that lunged along the coast of So Cal. Her heart rate rose each time her arm pulled through the water. As she slipped her board around to face the coast, Cat panted, excited to leap to her feet with the next big one. Inhaling as the sea rose up behind her, she paddled hard until she felt the board lift and her body tilt forward.

This is living! She heaved herself up with an exhale. It instantly made up for all the time she spent pretending.

A couple of hours later, Cat was kicked back on the beach, catching her breath and some illicit rays, when she heard a car horn playing the cliché mariachi song: *da-da-da-da-DA da-da-da-da-DA, da-da-da-da-da-da-da.* An energetic wave from her cabbie told her it was time to pack it up and find her comrades.

Inside the warmth of the cab, Cat was pleasantly surprised when she spotted her sister's head bobbing above the crowds that filled the busy boulevard. Lost in her post-surf euphoria, she was over their previous confrontation and was feeling generous again, hoping to make it up to Sis with an offer to buy them lunch. When the taxi caught up with Rey and Sissy, Cat suddenly sensed intoxication; Rey stumbled and Sis laughed uproariously.

Cat told the cabbie to pull farther up and let her off at the next side street, so she could cut them off at the pass. *They're going to get arrested for public drunkenness,* she thought angrily. Barely two o'clock in the afternoon and based on Sissy's wobbly walk and glassy eyes, she was three sheets to the wind, and counting.

"Hey," Cat said, controlling her temper as the duo approached. "What have you guys been drinking?"

Sissy flashed a crooked smile at Cat and offered a riddle as a retort: "Why'd the Mex-s-ican dude throw 'is wife off the roofff?" Sis slurred. Cat stood there stone-faced.

"Te-quila!" sang Sis.

Cat was unimpressed by her antics, but Sis refused to apologize. "What's up, Sista?" Sis slung her arm over Cat's shoulder. The stink of booze on Sissy's breath fermented the air. Cat's hair might have caught fire had a flame been near.

"You having fun?" she asked, a bite in her voice. She stepped back from them. She'd already seen Rey hurl once and didn't want to be within reach if it happened again.

"It's the Annual Festival of Tequila this week!" Rey said. An inflatable margarita glass spun in the wind across the street. It hung from a sign strung above a bar that confirmed this.

"How did you get them to serve you?" Cat asked.

"They don't card down here," said Sis, as if this was common knowledge.

"Lucky us," said Cat flatly.

"*We want tacoooooooos!*" boomed Sis as she linked her arms with Cat. Cat felt transported to all the times her mother took her on shopping sprees during moments of happy insanity that accompanied their mother's alcoholic highs.

Fake it 'til you make it, Cat thought as she repeatedly had said back then. So she caved to Sis's joviality and joined in a raucous skip up the sidewalk. Sissy raised her knees like a pie-in-the-sky Dorothy, Rey walked stiffly as the Tin Man, and Cat, as the Cowardly Lion, reluctantly joined them as a means to corral them.

After lunch, Cat decided to get a massage while the young ones opted to sleep. A peaceful trip to the hotel spa was a necessity, considering Cat's waning patience. She was pissed that she'd gotten drawn into their adolescent tomfoolery, but ninety minutes of pampering gave her enough time to convince herself that Rey and Sis were acting like a couple of college kids on spring break. Granted, it was mid-October, and none of them had ever pursued higher education. But what did Cat know about adolescents? She had gone from thirteen to thirty in the time it took her to win a modeling contract and escape to Milan. Maybe it would be good for her to act like a juvenile every once in a while. She had a job to do here in Mexico, but it meant she was going to break every rule her mother had ever set for her.

After two phone calls to Chris and to Rick, her agent, Cat was feeling jaded. Chris never once asked her about her trip and would not shut up about his struggles with writing. It made her crazy to listen to him whine about nothing that really mattered.

"The lead sounds too butch," he complained. "And the premise of the story doesn't feel pungent enough."

Cat rolled her eyes but still goaded him to keep going. It didn't matter how the first draft of his screenplay turned out, he had the reputation to sell it to the highest bidder. A no-name writer would punch up the script and ultimately be blessed by a million-dollar paycheck, despite Chris's blatant imperfections. Cat was tempted to tell him to hire a Mexican day laborer to help with the authenticity. *You'll get the most bang for your buck!*

Swallowing her disdain, she offered Chris empathy instead. By the time she dialed her talent agent, she was hell-bent on cutting that conversation short.

"No, I haven't been out in the sun," she lied. "Yes, I'm

having fun." When she was done acting like she appreciated his queries, she told Slick Rick she would call him at the end of the week. She asked him to leave any urgent messages for her at home because her cell wasn't getting good reception. It was actually his pythonesque personality that was getting bad reception. She couldn't stand feeling squeezed—so she signed off with a "kiss, kiss," and then flipped him the bird as she pressed "End."

⚶

The dinner etiquette of Rey and Sis set the record straight as far as Cat was concerned. The girls were perfectly well behaved, and it appeared their madness in the afternoon had cleared the way for a mellow evening. However, when Cat offered to treat them to some fine wine and dining, Sis had teased, "Should I iron my thong?"

"El Rey Sol," Cat told the cabbie as he pulled out of the driveway of the Casa de la Loma Dorada Inn. "Muy bueno," he said, rubbing his fingers and thumb to indicate *pricey*. Cat took out her trusty guide and read, "'This internationally award-winning restaurant specializes in French and Mexican cuisine.' You two survived the armadillo ... how 'bout some escargot?" Cat asked.

"*Yuck,*" said Sis. Rey shook her head.

Once they were good settled into their bottle of wine at the restaurant, Cat took the helm and ordered a selection of the most palatable sounding appetizers. She paired each one with a lesson in etiquette and by the end of second course, the hooligans were acting like ladies. As a last hoorah, Sis and Rey ordered aperitifs to accompany

Cat's café and the chocolate soufflé she requested. Waiting patiently for dessert to arrive, their conversation returned to riding.

"So why'd you buy a Beemer?" Sis asked Cat.

"I liked the color," Cat quipped.

"It's white," said Rey, missing the joke.

"Who told you to buy a thumper?" asked Sis.

"A lot of guys ride Beemers in the biggest off-road rally in the world each year."

"No shit," said Sis.

"*Etiquette,*" Cat hissed.

"I was just commending you on your wild guess," said Sis. "Thumpers are all they ride at Dakar; that's the race you were talking about, right?" Cat nodded, like a teenybopper who already knew that.

"*Thumper's* a term for a single cylinder," added Rey. "All the cool girls ride thumpers." She winked.

"A thumper has the power you need to jump and peel around a dirt track," Sis said. "It won't win in a straightaway, but it can outrun bigger bikes in the tight turns."

Sipping on that compliment and beginning to feel like she fit in, Cat was excited to ride again. "So what's our next plan of action? I say we sleep in late tomorrow." Both of her companions beamed.

"Sounds good to me," hummed Sis.

Cat paused as their dessert was delivered. "I'm ready to ride kind of hard now," she admitted after the waiter left. "But before we leave town, there's a tourist attraction I really want to see."

Sis raised her eyebrows, as if waiting for Cat to propose

an artsy-fartsy museum visit. "According to the Triple A guide, La Bufadora is a blow spout that erupts at high tide," Cat suggested.

"Sounds like a *blast*," said Rey facetiously.

"Ha!" said Sis, elbowing her friend. "You're a real *fountain* of information, Cat!"

With a mischievous look in her eye, Sis took two of the silver spoons and squeezed a squirt of molten chocolate from the top of the soufflé. Sis and Rey erupted in giggles. Feeling Cheshire-like, Cat just grinned. Two days down, and she was starting to gain some control, both on *and* off her motorcycle.

CHAPTER 8

ENSENADA TO EL ROSARIO

Sissy woke up looking sick this time. "Wine does it to me every time," she said as they made their way down to breakfast. Rey was fine, and Cat was pleased to see she was not a regular troublemaker. Cat had sensed that Rey was up to no good yesterday, but after last night's fancy affairs, she felt assured that Sis and Rey were equally worthy travel companions. It became more apparent when the trio found themselves stopped by the federales shortly after their departure.

The air was dry and hotter than yesterday, and the confined space inside Cat's helmet felt like a closed car in the middle of summer. Dust was caked all over the exterior, including her face mask—just one of the reminders of their first venture into the deep desert. Feeling nervy, Cat decided to ride with the face mask flipped up, one, so she could breathe, and two, so she could keep inhaling the smells of Mexico. Today's olfactory cornucopia included churros, a snack they passed numerous times on the side of the road leaving Ensenada. When the cops stopped them just across from yet another churro cart, Cat's first thought was Mexican cops eat Mexican donuts—ha! They didn't seem friendly enough to crack a joke with, so Cat let Rey do all the talking.

Rey had an edge in Mexico, and when the police pulled them over and demanded a tariff on top of identification, Rey took over. Presenting an innocent smile and friendly Texas drawl, Rey batted her eyes like a sorority girl at the uniformed men. In the end, an exorbitant tax was demanded for permission to cross "federal territory."

Expressing her disgust, Rey reverted back to an ornery urban dropout as soon as the cops left; spitting on the ground and calling out, "Pigs!"

"That shit about 'federal territory' is bullshit ... there's no such thing," Rey explained. "But the federales get whatever they ask for here."

"How do they get away with that?" asked Cat.

"It's safer to pay than to question them."

Cat had paid, and she hoped that La Bufadora would be worth its weight in pesos. As they rode on, the route wound around a rocky cove populated by the telltale flags of scuba divers, and Cat was pulled by her longing to dive again. She really wanted to join them, but she had committed to ride today. She would have to wait for an opportunity to go solo again.

The road to the waterspout carved through glorious

curves and varying grades as it worked its way to the summit of the peninsula. It was the most beautiful section they'd seen so far. Vistas overlooked the sea from every cliff top. The riding was slow, due to the buses stuffed with tourists that lined the narrow strip of freshly asphalted roadway. Vendors selling food and crafts congregated along the one-lane road.

As the women pulled around the last bend, they managed to squeeze past the line of cars by riding on the gutter side. They missed the fee stop by default, as they pressed past a Winnebago that was holding up traffic. Cat heard the driver explain that he only had traveler's checks. Rey had advised Cat to grab cash, so there was no excuse for them not to pay, even though they had gotten away with it. Sissy and Rey didn't think twice about stopping. Sissy even flipped the bird after they snuck past the pay station.

Feeling like crap, Cat flipped, *I'm going back.*

You just paid a hundred bucks to see this stupid thing, Sis replied in reference to the bribery they had endured. Cat killed her engine and parked her bike. *It's the price you pay for fun,* she flipped. Then she gallantly returned to the pay station on foot as her comrades continued to the parking lot beyond the art carts. When Cat caught up with them, the three of them eased between the parked cars and stopped twenty feet from the entrance. After they locked their helmets together with the spiral cable Sissy brought, they made their way up the stairs to the viewing area.

"'La Bufadora is a marine geyser that blasts nearly one hundred feet into the air as a result of sea water trapped in a cave, exploding upwards,'" Cat read aloud from her guide as the women meandered up the steep slope. "'Every minute or so, the blow hole erupts with a thunderous noise above the exhibit hall that is built into the rocks twenty-four meters above the ocean.'" She had barely finished that sentence when a loud bang knocked the rock walls above and a plume of cool mist rained down on them.

"I want to see it!" said Sis as she rushed like a kid up the last section of walkway. Seconds later, they wedged their way to the lower level of the paved overlook, through hundreds of other visitors, to get to the rock barrier that overlooked the sea. Cat was taken by a pair of musicians who were energetically playing a xylophone together. Their cheerful tune reverberated off the inlet's stone walls, loud and boisterous, as long as the geyser was quiet. When it erupted, the boom and accompanying "Ooohs" drowned out the melody for a moment. One explosion soaked a group of kids who were standing in the wet zone, and their merry screeches struck a chord with Cat. As an infant began to cry in response to the commotion, she was brought back to the baby she had briefly carried.

"Look at the water dripping from the palms," said Rey. She pointed at a cluster of tropical trees clinging to the cliff above the blowhole. Cat was impressed by their determination to thrive despite regular whippings from a fire-hose-strength spray all day. She was mesmerized by the power of this natural phenomenon, but after twenty minutes, Sissy had seen enough.

"You guys ready to go?" Sis asked. Busy Sissy had never been good at standing still as a kid. Cat remembered regular turmoil at naptime, as their inept mother had tried tirelessly to rock baby Sissy to sleep. Cat's nursery rhymes came in handy whenever their mother dipped Sissy's "paci" in brandy. Cat would pluck the tainted paci from her mother's grasp and offer to take over. No matter how sweet Cat's song, sleep rarely came for Sis, but her puckered infant smile and comforted coos entertained the young Catrina and kept their mother from drugging an eternally active Sis.

Cat tried to shake the bleak images of the past as they headed down the granite stairs. In an effort to focus, Cat paused to take pictures with her phone. True to form, Sis hurried ahead, as if they were running out of time.

☩

The women were back on the road by eleven-thirty. It was a little more than sixty miles to Colonet, where they wanted to stop for lunch. Finally, on this fourth day of riding, the racer girls stopped offering Cat special consideration as they worked their way through tourist traffic back to Highway 1. Cat wasn't sure which terrified her more—riding the double yellow line, or gutter riding on the right. Both techniques were technically illegal, but riding on the right-hand side of vehicles was actually considered more dangerous than riding on the cars' passenger sides, against oncoming traffic. Splitting lanes up the middle could lead to a head-on collision, but it was safer to get out where everyone could see you.

Cat's instructor at the motorcycle safety course had discouraged both these tricks, but riding conservatively wasn't an option. Sissy and Rey had made it abundantly clear that Cat should keep up or get left behind. The switchbacks ended when the mountain road ran into the highway, thirty minutes south of La Bufadora. At this point, the four-lane highway had no divider, which meant they could ride right up the middle between cars heading the same way. Even though they had to punch it to pass the neighboring traffic going sixty, it still felt safer to Cat. She held her breath each time she gunned it to get around an eighteen-wheeler.

As the commercial district became past tense, the highway dropped down to follow the lowland along the sea, where olive crops and chili pepper farms lined the coast. The chaparral that covered the slopes and ran up from the road was reminiscent of the central California coast.

It's like California's sister shore, Cat thought. She found herself smiling at the metaphor of a couple of rugged sisters who remained connected despite distance and remote resistance. She sighed as her gaze traveled down the jagged cliffs, across rolling hills of tall grass, and into the infinite ocean laced with lush clumps of kelp. The crash of the waves made Cat's heart ache, like a junky who covets white caps of cocaine that lay waiting on a silver mirror. The ocean was Cat's looking glass—it reflected who she really wanted to be.

As she soared along the interstate, dolphins kept appearing off the coast, reminding her of her favorite spots in Malibu. No matter how often she saw them, the majestic sea creatures never ceased to thrill her. When she spotted a big one breaching, she felt it was teasing her … she could practically taste the salt on her lips.

※

Soon enough, they were cruising past open countryside in the Santo Tomas Valley, where the grapes were harvested for the winery they had visited the previous night. The vineyard took over the valley, and curlicue vines exuded vibrant life in an otherwise arid region. Then as quickly as it arrived, the hue went from extreme green to flan-colored sand.

Rey was looking forward to the chance to chill out solo for a while. Her nausea had returned at La Bufadora and was getting old. It didn't make sense for her to feel so sick from such a minor indulgence last night. Maybe it was nerves, or her fervor for wanting a taste test again. Someday, she hoped to learn how to say no to the dope fiend inside her; these drugs were her Achilles heel.

The sickness in her stomach made her think she would be better off if she were cut off, but her ever-growing obsession with the high made it impossible to forget. Resisting temptation had never been her forte, and the only kind of problem solving she felt good at was the kind that came from the perfect dose, up her nose. "Taking a little off the top" was one of the best benefits to transporting heroin, otherwise this money-making venture was just another job.

After an hour of riding, Rey's brain was exhausted from the internal argument she kept having about what her next move should be. Carlos's warning played on repeat in her head: "Be careful: the federales are cracking down on even the most minor mules these days." Along one particularly long stretch of boring highway, Rey became resigned to denying her urges and bagging all of it up tonight.

A short time later, she came up with a great excuse to duck away from the Lang sisters for most of the evening, and her resolve dissolved into an internal negotiation. Tonight, they were planning on bunking down in a very small town surrounded by a vast and empty desert. Finding an isolated spot to get high would be easy. *A few small lines,* she thought innocently, making deals with her conscience. *Just one last time,* she promised.

⚜

After three hours of riding, the next major town bore down on them. They spilled one by one off the busy roadway onto the dirt-covered main street of Colonet. Unfortunately, their chosen lunch was as dry and uninspiring as the flat land that surrounded them. Cat was pleasantly surprised that Rey picked up the tab this time, choosing a hole-in-the-wall establishment that advertised "gorditas." The only table in the place was too big for the space and was literally placed to hide a large hole in the wall.

The "dining room" was actually the kitchen in a rundown family home on the outskirts of town, which caught Cat off guard and made her self-conscious about bearing witness to the family's obvious poverty.

"Should we take our shoes off?" whispered Cat when she noticed none of the kids were wearing any.

"No," said Rey. "This is not the first time dusty strangers have dined here."

"This is cool," said Sis, "we get to see how the other half lives." Cat glared at her for speaking openly about the rather depressing differences.

"It's pretty common for people to open their homes to travelers. In-home dining means no overhead and twenty-four-hour service."

"It's all about the profit margin," acknowledged Cat,

feeling instantly better about it. Ready to face this unusual situation with grace, Cat offered an awkward smile as a toddler, an infant, and a chicken got out of the way to make space for the Amazonian sisters. At five two, Rey was the tallest Latina in the bunch, and Cat guessed the eldest person in the room, a weathered-looking grandma, to be just shy of four foot nine. While they waited for their food to cook, the elderly woman sat silent in the corner and stared at the trio with a conflicted mix of interest and mistrust, as if she was worried that one misstep by a blonde behemoth might squash a grandkid or the huevo-laying chicken.

Rey seemed completely at ease, chatting up the mother/cook in Spanish, but Cat couldn't get past the idea that the woman believed her humble household was being seen through her Beverly Hills eyes, and was insulted as a result. She kept her eyes turned down most of the time, trying to act as humble as possible. She did catch a glimpse of rusty water coming out of the worn-out faucet and opted to deny her instinct to drink when the cook set down three glasses in front of them

"Gracias," said Cat, canceling her next question about where she could excuse herself to wash her hands. Dust wouldn't harm her as much as a parasite could. The grandmother eyed her again with suspicion—lowering her eyelids like slits. Cat thought she looked angry, because the dullness in her face was not a trait that folks in LA tended to carry. *Jaded* was a term that actors used all the time in California, usually in reference to being rejected at auditions. This thin and wrinkled Mexican woman looked like life had rejected her, and it was all she could do to keep breathing, day after arduous day.

Right before their meal was served, Rey excused herself to the bathroom. Sissy took over the role of making small talk with the cook, while Cat made eyes at the baby, who was too young to understand oppression. It was teeny-weeny, only a few months old, but there was a sparkle in her round onyx irises that made Cat want to weep.

Connecting with the baby, Cat felt an ache deep in her abdomen where the seed had embedded itself for a time. She used her eyes to tell this tiny child that everything was going to be okay. She fought the urge to leave a hundred-dollar tip on the table, knowing it would usurp Rey's generosity. Instead, she promised herself that she would make a donation to an organization that helped the children of Mexico as soon as she returned to the States.

When the painfully long lunch break was done, Cat had the sense that their hour-long visit was merely a hiccup in that clan's daily activities. They'd barely made it out the front door when the toddler began to help with the dishes, standing tiptoe on a stool, offering the mother a chance to haul the baby up to her breast for its lunch.

Cat and Sissy flipped quick signs as they straddled their bikes. They agreed that the bland sandwiches were the worst food they'd had thus far. The second of their signs said they were both still hungry.

I'm just happy to be back on the bike, signed Sis.

Cat flipped *Yep* before she threw her head back and took a bunch of big gulps from her water bottle.

Rey felt an urge to get moving again, too. The unspoken struggles that filled that little room had reminded her of her own home; she wanted to deny those childhood memories and focus on having fun. Having excused herself to the bathroom to puke, she felt normal again. Queen Reyna was ready to ride, full stride and irrefutably convinced that she deserved to get high after all the misery she had survived in life.

CHAPTER 9

EL ROSARIO

T he off-roading began before they even returned to the highway. Sissy couldn't wait another mile to attack the rough terrain, so the women rode perpendicular to the highway for a time, laying three deep divots in the sand. They crisscrossed the land, altering their trajectory to dodge rocks and burrows. As the dips and bumps increased, Sis and Rey became increasingly flamboyant. With each hard turn, they produced a spray of dirt that rivaled La Bufadora's passion.

By the next water break, they were panting with exuberance and dousing their heads to cool off. Cat asked them to teach her how to master a skid stop. Rey gladly hopped on her bike to offer examples, while Sissy showered Cat with facts. First, Sissy said, "Turn those superbrakes off." She was referring to the antilock braking system that came standard on Beemers. The default setting meant the ABS system was activated whenever Cat turned her engine on, so she needed to disable them every time she got on the bike.

Sissy reminded her of the importance of using the foot brake that controlled the rear tire. "If you hit the hand brake too hard, your front tire will stop, and you'll go over the top." Cat remembered this vaguely from the wipeout she'd had as a kid.

As Rey continued to show off and spin out in the background, Sissy built Cat's trust about shooting her rear wheel around in a shower of dust. Finally, it was showtime. Cat gunned her engine, kicked it into first gear, and burned rubber before she grabbed traction and shot across the loose dirt. At the end of the imaginary path, she let off the gas, pushed down on the foot brake, and sent the bike into a tailspin that went well beyond 180 degrees. The momentum of the spin messed with her handling, and she wound up in a low slide. Her bike lay down, and she skidded right behind it. Luckily, it was a soft landing, so nothing but her ego received any damage. Shaken by her failure, Cat's heart pounded, her hair stood on end, and she broke out in a sweat, but there was no time for pussy footing as Sissy yelled for her to get up and try it again. She had to restart her engine, which had died when the bike got away from her, and once again she forgot that the ABS re-engaged. This time the bike tripped when she hit the brakes, and sent her flying. It felt like the ground came up to spank her, knocking the wind out of her lungs and making her cough so hard that she couldn't get up.

Sissy knelt by her sister's side and helped shake the sand out of her boots as she regained her senses. "That was awesome," Sissy said, patting Cat on the back. "Don't think, just get back on the bike," ordered Sissy, who remembered Cat's last major crash as the end of her childhood riding.

Cat's third and final pass was filled on blind faith. "I am *not* going to crash," she repeated out loud, replacing fear with determination. So on her third and final try, Cat went for it, hitting the rear brake with enough gusto and leaning hard and away from her destination, Cat sent an awesome fan of grit toward Rey, who was waiting and watching with her arms up as a sign of empowerment. All three woman expressed the same level of elation, whooping and hollering for a bit before Sis uttered the first word.

"Hats off!" Sis yelled. Her voice was guttural and proud. It was all Cat needed to feel as though she was back on track, both with riding and with gaining some hard-earned respect from Sis. She no longer cared about the role she was researching, and she wasn't afraid to fail again. This was the attitude she had lost when she was ten. No more pretending. Catrina Lang was just a simple girl from Texas, who had loved ripped jeans, popping wheelies, and releasing a sequence of squeals when her bike hit the hills going fifty. It wasn't dresses and tresses that defined her. It was sisterhood ... with all the struggle and love that came with a life-long connection. Cat was ready to get to the bottom of all the drama that had forged a divide in the devoted, yet strained, relationship between her and Sis.

When they stopped to refuel at the only gas station in

San Quintin, Cat grabbed her wallet, preparing to pay for all three of them.

Rey scrunched her face when she saw the exorbitant prices. "That's like three fifty a gallon," she scoffed.

"That's highway robbery," added Sis. "I guess we're at the mercy of this monopoly."

"I just hope this means there's some sort of civilization around here. Are we going to find a place to stay out here?" Cat was worried.

"El Rosario is pretty close," said Rey. "They should have a few motels to choose from."

"I'm about ready to call it quits," added Cat, who was feeling tired from the stress of pushing herself, physically and emotionally, all day. Trying to bridle her fear so she could appear braver than she felt was exhausting. So when Sis excused herself to ask the attendant to turn the air on for a top-off on her tire pressure, Cat opened up her trusty travel guide to quickly peruse the page for El Rosario, hoping to find a nice little bed-and-breakfast instead of a motel. It was immediately apparent to Cat that they'd be lucky to find clean sheets in what the Triple A book described as the less-than-stellar accommodations available in El Rosario. The motel was listed as "the last outpost of civilization" they'd find along the Highway 1 before it jetted off into no man's land en route to the eastern coast of Baja. This town sounded a little sketchy to Cat, but she would prefer to stay at a two-star motel than sleeping in the sand again.

"Well, it looks like tonight will be a little less fancy," said Cat as Sis set down the hissing air hose and screwed the cap back on her tire.

"Fancy is as fancy does," said Sis. "Hey, Rey, I thinks it's about time we show this sister of mine what fancy pants means when you're wearing leathers."

"Time for a little hopscotch?" Rey asked.

Cat had no idea what they were talking about, but when Sis said "Yes-sir-ee" and hopped back in the saddle, Cat assumed they were still a ways from taking a break for the day. She just prayed the ride didn't get too crazy.

It turned out that Cat was about to get schooled on how high a motorcycle could fly with ample velocity and the right rider. And Rey's bright orange KTM had an obvious leg up on Sis's red Honda when it came to launching, twisting, and flipping. As the land rose up from the sea, toward the megamesa that looked down on El Rosario, the opportunities to launch their bikes were unlimited, and as far as Cat could tell, Rey was actually better than Sis at jumping. Rey could hit a jump and let go of the handlebars, holding the bike with her thighs and land perfectly every time.

"This is what she's known for," Sis hollered after she pulled up alongside Cat, who had stopped to wipe the sweat from her eyes and grab a sip of water. The sisters paused to watch as Rey circled around and prepared to hit a jump that she had just sailed over with ease. The second time was spectacular; Rey hit the hard-packed mound of dirt and pulled up hard on her handlebars, sending her bike into an upright position, which she held through the landing, hitting the ground in a well-balanced wheelie.

At the next opportunity to launch, Rey misjudged her take-off, hitting the angled tip of a rectangular rock that jetted toward the sky. It shot her straight up as she lost contact with the granite slab. Rey's KTM landed on its tail end again, but almost landed on her back as the bike tilted beyond upright. What could been a bad crash was avoided by Rey's boundless experience. She managed to wrestle the front end forward by laying her torso over the handlebars. As the front tire slapped the ground, she ricocheted into a partial handstand and timbered off her bike to one side. Because the landing faced downhill, Rey rolled after the smackdown.

"Thank God for all the armor, huh?" Sissy said to Cat as they watched the scene come to a chaotic end. Rey appeared to be unscathed, but she took an awful long time to inspect her shoulder pads, making a myriad of adjustments to them.

"You okay?" Sissy asked Rey.

"Yeah," Rey called out unconvincingly, scrambling to a seated position and wedging her hand into the pocket that held her shoulder pad in place.

"Is your *jacket* all right?" scoffed Sis. Racers had strange love affairs with their equipment, but Rey seemed awfully anxious about the state of her protective padding. As Sis rolled in for a closer look, Rey threw her jacket on in a rush, as if she'd gotten caught with her hand in a cookie jar. Rey's bike was no worse for the workout, and a minute later, she was zipping up the hill with gusto.

After Rey's inspirational flight, Cat began to push her own limits as she scaled the walls of the empty river bed. Zooming up and down the embankment, she found the rhythm similar to rocking side to side down a water slide. Suffice it to say,

Cat was falling in love with riding again, and for the very first time. As a kid, she was hyperaware of the conflict it generated at home, so she never really embraced the fun of it. When she hung up her helmet after the crash, she was so afraid of the marital tension it created that she was ready to say goodbye forever.

Back in the saddle again her bike felt like an old friend with whom she'd had a falling out, but had always admired nonetheless. It was funny to feel at home in such a foreign place. She felt a connection to the land beneath her wheels. She wanted to lie down in the desert sand and let the warmth toast her bones. Her favorite place in the world was the ocean, the cold water always helped to jolt her out of the deep sleep she often walked around in and made her feel alive again. The ride today was giving her a similar rush, despite the not-so-cool temperature. Hot, sultry, salty sweat ran down her entire body and made Cat feel like she was a source of electricity. The same kind of love she felt for the sea was radiating through her, but the source was solid ground for once. Good thing, since the next two days would find these riders landlocked.

When Sis and Rey finally admitted that they had their fill of fun for the day, Sissy and Cat headed on alone to El Rosario. It took the sisters by surprise when Rey told them that a cousin of her mother's lived in a small town northeast of there, and she wanted to surprise her with an unannounced visit. She explained that it had been a while since they had spoken, so it'd be best if she showed up alone. Rey said she would find them later. Cat's guidebook said there were only three options for accommodations, and

Rey would have an easy time narrowing the sisters' location down with their red, white, and dust-covered motorbikes marking their location for her. So as the clock struck three, the women headed in two different directions.

⚜

Rey was pressed for time. She needed to fill the balloons with the heroin outside in the breezy early evening air and leave time for her to get high. The empty desert was the best place to enjoy a buzz. Two years ago, after a solo trip to the silver mines, Rey had enjoyed a nugget of black tar heroin. Hiding in the desert until her high wore off and she was safe to head home again, she had watched a trio of vultures circle above a cow carcass in the distance. Coyotes trimmed the meat while the second-tier scavengers waited patiently. That's how Rey saw her family that day; poor Latinas living in America, circling outside the hub of prosperity.

As she sat there in the sand, with no one but the birds to observe her, pain drained out of Rey's veins like the blood that seeped into the ground from the half-ingested heifer. It was all she could do to peel herself off the ground at the end of that round and return to the sobering facts of her depressing little life as she knew them. A few months later, Rey became a drug mule.

Today her high was marred by sorrow, too. Rey knew that, come tomorrow, she would have to wrestle with willpower. Now sealed, the balloons would be difficult to breach and that was supposed to save her. The federales were a real threat. If she got caught, Rey would be on the boss's shit list, otherwise known as hit list. If anyone discovered the pancake-shaped packages of marijuana stashed above her shoulder pads, Rey would be charged with a misdemeanor. They were meant to be a decoy, making Rey look like a college girl gone astray. Heroin, on the other hand, would expose her as a soldier, and that kind of bust would make her a target for the cartel's death squad.

Until now, drug running had been easy. The only trouble she had seen happened three months back. One of the American guards got frisky during a pat down at the border, and she called him on it. Her reaction had been a gutsy one and led to the threat of a strip search, which she desperately needed to avoid. Carrying five ounces of marijuana was enough to land her in prison on the American side. So the barely legal Latina flirted with the guy instead and wound up screwing him, fully clothed, in one of the search rooms. That was the only close call she'd had, and she didn't want to experience another.

Now Reyna took a few long snorts from the same straw she had carefully used to transfer most of the remaining white dust from the original package into the fingers of the white medical gloves she had purchased at the pharmacy. When she was done with both deeds, she pulled out her pocketknife, unfolded the little scissors, and carefully cut each finger off. Pinching each of the rubber fingers off, she tapped one at a time to compact the heroin, before tying them off tight, rendering them impenetrable and safe to swallow. Finishing the job just as the high kicked in, she leaned back in the sand, placed both hands behind her head, and enjoyed an hour of peaceful bliss.

When she floated back down to earth, she felt like a jerk.

The sisters were essentially carrying her on this expedition, and here she was, lying to them while she got high. Rey sighed and rose up out of the dust to brush herself off. Tomorrow was a new day. She gazed at the heavens and promised to pray first thing in the morning and ask for forgiveness. Then she shuffled back to her bike.

Sliding back on her saddle, she released the hand brake and coasted down the rocky sand path about a hundred yards from the highway, until a swift sound made her flip her headlamp off. A manmade wind swept up as a motorcade of official vehicles zoomed past the instantly invisible Rey.

What the hell is this? As the last of four elongated cars passed by her lookout above the highway, Rey tried to calm herself with the knowledge that the drugs were completely sealed. According to Carlos, they would be virtually undetectable, as long as drug dogs were nowhere in sight. When the coast was clear, Rey cruised toward the main avenue. She'd gone about a half mile when she spotted Sissy's bike parked next to Cat's outside a mediocre motel. She raised her eyebrows at the thought of Cat settling for such a so-so abode. *If a rich princess like Cat could do that,* thought Rey, *I should be able to stay clean for a few weeks.* Rey was not entirely convinced, but she was hopeful.

⚜

When the Langs pulled up in front of La Buena Onda and killed their switches, Sis smiled. The name of this motel meant a "place of good vibes, good feelings, a good wave." Sissy assumed Cat would love the metaphor for all that she held dear. This was the third and final option they had for accommodations in El Rosario. The first two were closed "for renovations."

"Looks like they need to be demolished," Sis said as she spit and then flipped her visor back down.

And you could use a little polish, Cat thought to herself as she unlocked the door and entered this dive.

The stink of tobacco that greeted them when they entered had not been included in the Triple A description. Sissy took one look at Cat's scrunched-up face and listed the reasons it was still a step up from camping: indoor plumbing, pillows (albeit only two), and pay-per-view TV. These amenities set the bar higher than the desert floor could.

Cat heard the recognizable roar of Rey's bike when she arrived, about the same time Sis came across *Darkstar* on cable. "Oh, I love this movie," whined Sissy, tongue-in-cheek.

"You better, 'cause it's paying our way," said Cat and jumped on her sister to wrestle the remote control from her hand, hoping to change the channel and remove Sis's excuse for more mockery.

"I will never let you live this down!" declared Sis, evading Cat's grasp and laughing. A knock on the door meant Rey had returned, so Sis turned up the volume as soon as Cat unlatched the dead bolt to let Rey in.

"Hey, Rey," roared Sis, "check *this* out!" She pointed to the TV. "Kitty Cat's speaking Spanish!" Sis cranked the volume to expose the low-tech Spanish dubbing.

"It's like those old Godzilla movies!" boomed Sis. Then she began to strut mechanically like Godzilla, swaying her butt like a heavy tail. "Grrrrrrrrr," Sis roared. "I'm an amphibian sex symbol!"

"Shhhh," Rey hushed, "let me listen! Maybe this time I'll understand the story line."

Cat rolled her eyes at Rey's quotation of *Darkstar*'s many critiques. "An action film doesn't need a story—it's all about the fight scenes." With that, Cat launched a double attack on her sister with the pair of lumpy pillows. A one-two punch to Sis's head inspired Sis to rib her even louder.

"Look at me, look at me," Sis screamed, poking fun at the cinematic version of Cat. Rey laughed out loud at their lunacy.

"You want to know what it's like to get hammered by your critics?" Cat asked. Then without further warning, she swung a pillow around and whacked Rey in the face, instigating a full-on pillow fight among the trio. A few minutes later, they sat back to catch their breath, and Cat had to wipe joyful tears from her eyes. For the first time since this trip began, Cat felt like she was totally in tune with her companions, and it made it well worth all their teasing.

CHAPTER 10

RAIN

As soon as Rey opened her eyes the next day, she felt an unbearable ache for more heroin. She grimaced at he thought of it being locked away, curling herself up in a fetal position to relieve the cramps in her abdomen that seemed to be linked to her urges. She was privately cursing herself when Sis came out of the bathroom and threw the curtains open to see what the weather looked like.

The loud sounds coming from the air conditioner had masked the fact that Sis was gazing at a torrential downpour.

"Dammit!" said Sis, rousing Cat from her beauty sleep.

Rey sighed as she realized that today was going to be even harder without the ride to ease her pain. Sis and Rey were both stubborn when it came to riding in the rain, but even the most seasoned adventurer would not pretend to enjoy conditions like this. Mud puddles were one thing, but getting swept down river could really put a damper on a day of riding. So Rey tried to absorb the enormity of her task of staying clean while being confined to a dingy motel room with two people who were clueless about her plight.

Cat rolled out of bed wearing shiny silk pajamas and cracked the burnt umber curtain to peek at the street. The bikes sat like dripping dogs banished to the back yard. Sissy squeezed next to Cat to take a look and pouted.

Rey pouted, too, as the urge to get high came in waves. Her body ached for the powerful powder hidden in her saddlebag, despite the fact that it was supposed to be off limits. While the sisters quietly discussed their frustration with the weather, Rey fantasized about the ways she could reunite with the heroin. What if the sisters decided to join her? What an amazing way to occupy a wasted day. What if Cat fell in love with the stuff and offered cash for the whole stash? Then Rey could replace it with an official delivery for the States. What if the movie star loved it *so* much that she ordered a regular supply for the rest of her life and eternally funded Rey's mania?

Addicts for hire, Rey imagined caustically. Cat as a dope fiend would certainly sell magazines: Starlet vs. Stardust; another one bites the—

"Hey, Rey, did you say there were some kick-ass rocks on the other side of the valley here?" asked Sis.

⚜

On the television, the weatherman described Hurricane Collette as moving up the southern coast of Mexico, with strong winds and heavy precipitation for the next twenty-four hours.

"Forget about the ride," said Cat, exhibiting shades of rich girl claustrophobia. "What are we supposed to do here?" Cat wrinkled her brows, looking totally grossed out by the grunge of the room and no longer interested in biding time with another pillow fight.

When the weather report returned to regular programming, Cat pointed to the TV. "Are we supposed to spend the entire day watching Mexican soap operas?" Sis increased the volume of the show, drowning out Cat's melodrama with superloud Spanish and driving Rey to the brink of insanity.

I gotta get the hell out of here, she thought, feeling desperate to escape this scene through some kind of inebriation. Luckily, Cat grabbed the clicker and switched off the set with a huff, before she moved into the bathroom to brush out her wind-blown, knotted locks.

"Everything I read said that October weather in Baja almost never includes rain. What a pain," the prima donna whined as she brushed harder in vain. "Ow!" she cried when her brush got stuck.

Rey wanted to claw Cat across the face, to show her what pain really felt like. *If this bitch complains one more time today, I'm going to fill a pillowcase with bricks and knock the shit out of her.* She fought to maintain her cool as her stomach churned, her head spun, and the urge to use became intolerable. The only question that mattered to Rey if she couldn't get high was where to find a drink. No room service at La Buena Onda, and Rey suspected there would only be one restaurant to choose from in this sleepy town. Hopefully, it had options for cocktails at breakfast, lunch, and dinner. If she couldn't take a toot, at least she could inhale tequila. Wasn't that what most American kids her age did while visiting Mexico?

Rey was programmed to eat at 7:00 a.m. every day, when her little sister Carla cooked a full breakfast before their dad headed to the garage to begin welding. Having slept until 9:00, Rey had missed that hour by a landslide, and she was hungry. Eating seemed like a contraindication to her queasiness. Rey was as annoyed as she was confused by this on-again nausea. It made her uncomfortable in a couple of ways. To be off her game physically and to inspire empathy were two symptoms of vulnerability that left Rey feeling shaky. She swallowed hard to push the seeds of weakness deep.

Finally, the sisters agreed that breakfast was the next step in the yet-to-be-determined way to spend this rained-out day. Rey followed with a little less gusto as Sis and Cat sprinted across the street to a very conveniently located restaurant. It was one-stop dining that offered food and cocktails from 6:00 a.m. until midnight, with a waiter who doubled as the bartender. Already soaked from her head to her feet, Sis appeared ready to wet her whistle as well. "Make it a double," ordered Sis, choosing bourbon to accompany her chicken-fried steak and eggs. "Can you bring hot sauce?" she asked as the guy ducked into the kitchen. Nine thirty was too early for a margarita.

"You drink like this at home?" asked Cat.

"Only when I'm on va-cay...." sang Sis with a wink, then she looked to Rey for backup.

Rey took little convincing. A booze binge was the next best thing to galloping off on the white horse. "I'll have a shot of Cuervo with a Modelo on the side," Rey said when the waiter returned.

Without uttering another word of judgment, Cat ordered a tequila sunrise.

"If you can't beat 'em, join 'em," Cat said with a grin. From the look she shot at Sis, Rey assumed this was yet another cutesy saying from their childhood.

By noon, they were blitzed, and Cat was in rare form. "I tolllll you, it was Mattie...whas-her-face. What-ser-name again?" The sisters were immersed in the details of a hometown friendship that ended right before Cat left for Europe at age eighteen. She was recounting the sad tale of how a close friend, someone whose last name escaped her, had stolen a tiny diamond ring off her dresser during a sleepover. Cat was the eldest grandchild and had inherited the ring from her paternal grandmother after she passed. It wasn't worth much besides sentiment, but it was the first betrayal Cat experienced, and she would never forget it.

"I nevah heard thish story. Why didn't-cha kicker ass?" slurred Sis before she folded into a fit of laughter, while Rey looked neither amused nor impressed as she slid her stool back and walked away without uttering a word to the sisters. Cat felt bad for cutting Rey out of the conversation. She called out, "Hey!" hoping to end the illusion of exclusion, but Rey continued her path toward the bar, swinging around a wooden pillar on the way. After grabbing a double shot, she slid to the opposite side of the room to scrounge around for a pool stick with a decent tip.

Cat watched as Rey responded to a question from a hunchbacked man in the corner. He slid his sombrero far enough back on his head so Cat could see his dirty, black-and-tan face and yellowed teeth. Rey smiled slyly at the man and accepted his invitation to play a game.

"I bet you she loses the first few," said Sis, smiling wryly.

"That guy doesn't look like much of a challenge," said Cat, clearly not understanding where Sis's head was at.

"That's what makes him the perfect fool. She'll give him false security by losing, and when he's ready to up the ante and bet some money, she'll pull out all the stops and mop the floor with him."

Sis was right; a couple of games later, Rey returned to ask Sis if she wanted to join her for a doubles game, asking Cat if they could borrow some pesos to make things interesting. Sissy jumped at the chance to pull the wool over these unsuspecting Mexican men. Cat was well aware of her sister's billiards ability and was wary of this charade, but alcohol weakened her caution, and she wished the girls well with a nod as she settled onto her barstool.

By early afternoon, Sis and Rey had run eight out of ten games and continued to control the table. It appeared that word had spread that there was a rally at the biggest restaurant in town. Those without work, which appeared to be everyone, squeezed in to witness these sharks take a bite out of the local economy.

Cat had been surrounded by beautiful people in stunning locations for years, but she had never felt as alive as she did sipping Hornitos shots in this slimy saloon. She squealed with shock as a scorpion skirted across her foot, and then gasped as the burly barmaid squashed it with her open-toed sandal. The original waiter/bartender had called in recruits, for what may have been the biggest party to ever hit the Cachando Toad. Rey said the name of this place meant "horny toad," and Cat smiled as she scanned the patrons that packed this not-so-sexy place.

Taking in this gnarly scene, Cat pinned the picture to her brain, hoping to share this memory with Chris so he could add it to his script. She had just pulled out her iPhone to take a couple of notes when a handsome older man slipped into the bar from the kitchen. He was short in stature but stood tall in his posture and was dressed in a crisp, navy blue suit. There was nobility in the way he looked around the crowd as if he was many social classes above them. His clean-cut hairdo was slicked back with what looked like oil, and Cat thought he blended in with this crowd like oil in vinegar.

Smug-faced, silver-haired, and sharply dressed, this fox was the kind Cat would engage in a chase. She couldn't take her eyes off this smooth character as he glided directly toward her. Cat had a lot of practice playing demure around dazzling men, but none had ever commanded her attention like this guy. He was not as statuesque as her typical protagonist, but he waltzed around like he owned the place. Cat always put power before physique, and he was a lot better looking than Chris.

Feeling vulnerable in her drunken state, Cat glanced at the pool table to gauge what stage of the game Sis and Rey were at. Cat saw Sis hang up her stick and motion for Rey to walk away. Cat was happy to see her companions head her way as the man closed in on Cat's location.

"How'd it go?" asked Cat as Sis approached, delaying the man's interjection.

"We decided to let those guys bet against a couple of losers for a while."

"They were getting a little pissed about losing," added Rey.

Sis nodded and explained, "We left our winnings for them, since they were acting like poor losers." Cat looked over at the men who were now glaring in their direction. Sis wouldn't leave well enough alone.

"Keep the money," she taunted. "Buy yourselves a little pain medication." She raised her drink as a way to clarify what she meant. "Maybe it'll sharpen their aim," she said to Rey with a snicker. Cat couldn't help but notice that the men did not appreciate Sis's mockery.

"I think you need to back of a bit," she told Sis. Sis shifted her focus to the man who was staring at her sister, telling Rey exactly how she felt about him. "Looks like Cat's caught another louse in her lair," snapped Sis, insulting Cat's admirer and Chris simultaneously.

"Maybe he's seen her somewhere," said Rey, obviously referring to *Darkstar*. Rey took another look at the guy and squinted with a quizzical look that made Cat think Rey may have recognized him. She was just about to ask if Rey knew him from somewhere when the man of mystery approached the three of them.

"Hola, señoritas," the man said, pretending to address all three of them, even though his sultry gaze rested solely on Cat.

"No espeaka espanole," Cat murmured coquettishly.

Sis shouldered closer and introduced herself in Spanish, acting as Cat's interpreter. He smiled briefly at Sis but didn't acknowledge her presence beyond that, a shallow sign that this guy already knew who Cat was and was simply not interested in conversing with her companions. This was not the first time this had happened around Sis, but his manner was so overt that Cat suddenly understood why her fame irritated her sister so. Cat's suspicion was confirmed when the man jumped right into the next question without waiting for Cat to introduce herself.

"What does the name Catrina Lang mean?" the man asked in Spanish. Unable to understand what he was saying, Cat was nonetheless flattered that such a handsome and seemingly sophisticated stranger was aware of who she was. She smiled again and looked to Sis for assistance. Cat could tell that Sis was irritated by his unabashed interest, but curiosity spurred her to ask Sis, "What did he say?"

"He wants to know what your *name* means," said Sis, swinging her index finger around in cuckoo motion.

"Catrina means pure," Cat said coolly, as she shot Sis a look that said *he seems nice.* "And Lang means long," Cat went on, peeking modestly at her own lanky legs, a move that clearly drove Sis to the brink of madness. Rey, who looked equally interested in who this guy was, translated Cat's retort, usurping Sis's chance to say something rude to him.

The man introduced himself as Paolo Cruz, adding in English, "Paolo means small." A small smile indicated that he was clearly aware of the irony.

"Just like Tom Cruise," Sis said. "He's short and cuckoo, too!"

"Cruz," the man continued, ignoring Sissy's insult, "means cross, as in *la crucifixion*."

Cat flashed an awkward smile at his pious pretension. She was beginning to see the man from Sis's perspective and was ready to agree that he should receive a big thumbs down. Cat was already taken, after all, and had never been the type of girl to blow off her crew for a rooster. The guy was visually stunning, but time was running out on his attempt to engage her in this cheesy conversation. The booze in Cat's system was clearly to blame, but taking this flirtation any further was a waste of time, and a sure-fire way to spur Sis into saying something outrageous. Knowing it was time to call it quits with him, Cat offered him a peek at her three-carat commitment when she clasped her hand around her glass and took a sip. As she launched into a gabfest with Sis and Rey in English, Señor Cruz excused himself politely and slid back through the mob toward the kitchen.

Sissy watched him go and commented, "I can't stand when guys act like they *know you*."

Obviously embarrassed by her booze-induced slip toward infidelity, Cat murmured, "Got to get it together." She looked at Sis. "You guys ready to leave?"

Rey agreed it was time to go, but Sissy ignored them and ordered tortilla chips and a beer. It was as if she was trying to get even with Cat for wasting even a little bit of time on the cheesy guy, who had obviously annoyed Sis. Cat was trying to establish what she could say to get Sis on the same page with her and Rey when the guys from the pool game shuffled toward the bar and stood behind them.

"Can we buy you a round?" One of the men who had fallen victim to the women's pool shark maneuvers waved the abandoned winnings in Sis's face.

"We're all set," Rey said in a cold tone.

"You should've taken your winnings and run," a second guy suggested.

"We're leaving," Rey said, glancing at Sis.

Cat didn't understand the language, but she caught the gist of Rey's message and threw money on the bar to cover the order. "Forget the beer," Cat murmured to her sister. She popped off her stool and motioned for the girls to follow, offering a friendly "toodle-oo" to the losers.

The ladies stumbled through the swinging wooden door into the gray light of the stormy day. Rain pelted Cat's hand as she shielded her eyes from water that poured off the roof. Her jacket was waterproof, but everything above and below was getting soaked.

Squinting through the heavy rain, it took the women a few tries to find a path across the flooded street. They bounded across a wide section that required one big hop at the end, then huddled together as each one dug around for the door key. Reaching hurriedly into her vest pocket, Cat retrieved the missing key. She was the first to rush into the room, and the first to get knocked on the head.

CHAPTER **11**

RANSACKED

When Cat came to, she had no recollection of what occurred. Opening her eyes, she felt a pain in the back of her skull. Touching the tender spot, her fingers came away covered in blood. She snapped out of her daze. Despite the sense of urgency, standing was slow going. Her left leg had stiffened in the position she had been lying. It scared her to lose her motor skills for a moment, but she slumped back down to let the numbness dissipate.

She gazed around the room. All the furniture was overturned, and the contents of their saddlebags looked like they had exploded. A single pair of Cat's underwear had been flung into the air during what seemed like it had been a melee. It hung, totally exposed, from the lampshade that had bashed when it crashed to the floor. Cat sat up slowly, trying to get a grasp of what had happened. The details of the day were still clear in her memory, right up until the moment she opened the door to their room. Feeling increasingly distressed as the mess came into focus, Cat called out to Sissy.

A moaning sound issued from the other side of the room. "Aaaaah." Sis was hidden behind the overturned mattress. Cat scooted toward the desk to turn on the light, but the bulb had been smashed in the melee. She leaned to her left and reached for the doorknob, her left hamstring cramping as blood returned to the immobilized limb. The door opened inward blocking her view of the street, but gray light illuminated the room. "Oh my God," Cat cried in reaction to the total destruction.

"Ooooo, my wrist," whined Sissy, breathless. "I think it's broken again …" Cat could see that Sis was trying to move the mattress with her feet, apparently incapable of using her hands.

Cat began to rush to her sister's aide, but the pain in her head instantly increased with her speed, so she paused to let the pounding subside and asked Sis if she was bleeding anywhere. Like the Hulk busting out of an entrapment via rage, Sis kicked the mattress with all her might and shoved it just enough that Cat could see her face and upper body. Sis grimaced in pain as she hugged her right wrist to her chest. It was a look of weakness that Cat would never have associated with Sissy. Cat could see she had a gash on her forehead, but it looked like the bleeding had ended. Her shirt was drenched in blood. Moving in to try to get across the angled mattress, she stepped cautiously so as not to crush Sis's still hidden feet. As soon as she leaned on her left leg and lifted her right, Cat felt a searing pain shoot through her left hip.

"Where's Rey?" whispered Cat, breathing heavy to shake off the pain. It was pretty clear there was one missing person. Sis didn't answer as she rolled over and managed to edge herself out from under the mattress. Heaving a sigh of relief, she rolled onto her knees, carefully cradling her limp wrist.

Cat inched around the fallen furniture. "Hey, Rey!" she called. There was no response. Panic set in. "What the hell *happened*?" Cat's voice went shrill as she slumped to the floor again. The severity of her current hangover indicated it had been a while since their departure from the bar, but fading daylight assured her they had not been "out" for long.

Cat's head began to pound. "We have to get out of here!" Foggy with panic and pain, she couldn't establish the next move. Sissy finally got to her feet and stumbled into the bathroom.

"I look like a fucking freak," Sis said, peering at her head in the etched mirror. She rubbed her hair into a spiky mess. Turning on the faucet, Sis grabbed the yellowed towel and dabbed at the blood on her face. "Flesh wound," she confirmed. The jagged cut was about an inch long and centered in her forehead.

"Where's Rey?" Cat said. She felt like she was hyperventilating.

"Let me see your head," Sissy said calmly. Gingerly parting Cat's blood-caked hair, Sis murmured, "You got a nasty nick, too. But you'll be fine. I'm going to leave it, so it'll congeal."

Sissy had a lot of experience with varying degrees of injuries and knew when someone needed real medical attention. Squeezing out of the bathroom past Cat, Sissy said, "I have a wrist brace in my saddlebag." She rummaged around her pants pocket with her good hand and pulled out the key to her saddlebag.

When she retrieved a deflated air cast, she unrolled it, puffed it up, and gently set her wrist on it. "Ah-ah-ah-ah-ah," she panted. Cat heard something outside and put her index finger to her lips, suddenly aware that their attackers might still be within earshot. Then she initiated the switch to flipping. With a look in her eyes that said *please don't cry out again,* Cat fluttered her hands in rapid-fire silence, asking Sis if she thought she could ride. Cat wanted nothing more than to get back on the road as quickly as possible.

Sis nodded yes, although the care with which she had eased her wrist into the cast told Cat she might be bluffing. Sis was not one to admit to incompetence, so Cat let Sis get on with it, and the two of them threw their strewn stuff back in their saddlebags. When that task was finished, Sis took the lead and poked her head out the door. *The coast is clear,* she flipped with the only hand that could, and Cat followed right behind her as they crept out the door and into the darkening day.

"What time is it?" whispered Sis.

Cat glanced down and realized her watch was gone, then immediately extended her hand to confirm the whereabouts of her diamond. Its presence reassured her as she gently opened the door to look for her beloved timepiece. It lay on the dresser, mysteriously untouched.

"The thugs left my Rolex ... and my ring." She pushed through the menagerie of overturned furniture to snag the watch. The face read 5:26.

The disheveled sisters were frantically fastening their bags to their bikes when Cat heard a slow, muffled moan. "Do you hear that?" asked Cat. Rey moaned again. "She's out back!" Cat exclaimed. They bounded around the building.

Rey was soaked to the bone and shivering. Her face looked like a bunch of plums, and one eye was sealed shut. Cat was afraid to touch her, but Sis grabbed her under the arms.

"Are you okay?" Sis asked, hauling Rey to her feet.

"Soy fino. Sólo frío." Rey's teeth chattered.

"She's cold," stated Sis. "Can you go grab something?" Rey's jacket was gone, so Sis held her steady while Cat ran to the bikes to grab a cover-up. When Cat returned, the girls were huddled together, discussing what happened.

"It was guys ... from the bar," rasped Rey.

"We should call the cops," Sis suggested.

"We have to get outta here," Cat said.

"Where's my jacket?" asked Rey.

"We have to leave!" Cat pleaded, focused solely on escape. She was desperate to get to the next big city, but Rey was in no condition to ride. "I have a cashmere sweater you can wear," Cat offered. Sissy rolled her eyes.

Sis decided that Rey and Cat should swap bikes, so Rey could use Cat's plug-in vest and heated grips. Even with the warm tropical wind, Rey's soaked clothes would invite hypothermia once they got up to speed. Cat's bike was tall for her, but once she got rolling, Rey wouldn't need to put her feet down. A poncho on top of the electric vest would have to be warm enough for now. Rey said that if they followed Highway 1 they would hit Guerrero Negro by nine.

As the rigorous haul began, Cat couldn't shake the feeling that her life was permanently altered. She had never been exposed to such violence before, and she had no recollection of what happened after she opened the door to their motel room. *Sissy must have seen something,* she thought as she worked through the story in her head. *But she would've said something. Wouldn't she?* Sis and Rey were still standing in the rain when Cat got sacked, so what did they know that Cat didn't?

Fear eased into paranoia as Cat began to suspect the others were keeping secrets. She was the odd man out as she squeezed her fingers around the unfamiliar grips of Rey's bike. She wished she was safe and sound at home, preparing a character for a hefty drama instead of living it.

Rey gripped the handlebars intensely. The heat from the grips radiated through her palms but had virtually no effect on the outside of her fingers, and the freeze made her weak. She was glacial on the outside, but her heart was filled with heat ... anger that life was about to hit a wall once and for all. All she ever wanted was to feel secure and happy. As a teenager, Rey had steered clear of trouble, keeping her drinking under control and taking frustration out on the race track, but honest work felt like an uphill battle. Heroin had offered enormous rewards by comparison, and the drug money felt heroic as Rey made a more comfortable life for her family. They needed the extra money; it was more than any of them could earn legitimately in the "land of opportunity."

As time wore on, Rey realized she had joined the ranks of an army that required going AWOL if she ever decided to quit. A quote Rey had read in a high school English class reverberated in her mind. *Being human is hard, female is harder, and life as a Latina is occasionally downright grizzly.* Rey felt grizzly, like the bear—ready to tear her next threat to pieces.

She was full of rage, and her riding was reckless as desperate thoughts wracked her battered brain. They had been attacked because of the drugs in Rey's jacket—and now the healing power and the monetary value of the magic white powder were moot, because some dude found out about her loot and nabbed it. She had no idea who he was, and didn't need to. Her only concern was how she could replace what he had taken.

Cat didn't know what the hell to think as she struggled to keep up with the pace that Sis was setting. Everything about this was unsettling, but the strangest thing was how calm Rey seemed in the face of a brutal attack. *Why did they take Rey's jacket?* Cat wondered. She began to feel weak with worry, so in an attempt to focus on something calming, Cat started to sing a version of "Row, Row, Row Your Boat" that she had sung to Sis when they were kids.

Tick, tick, tickle your sister, 'til she has to pee,

Wearily, wearily, wearily, wearily,

Sissy never screams.

Cat overrode her worry with the image of Sissy's toddler giggle, and eventually that helped her switch from "woe is me" to "someday we'll have a good laugh about this."

As Cat remembered Sis's refusal to cave as a kid, she decided that since the two of them were related, Cat should be able to dig deep and find what she needed to keep going. Wind blasts and a record hangover would not stop her—if Sis could get through this, then so would she. Cat watched Sis duck as her wrist took the brunt of a bump on a sunken suspension bridge that spanned the flooded arroyo. The spray was huge as Sis zoomed across the flooded wooden planks of the overpass. Cat slowed way down as Sis hit the water, hoping to control the lighter weight KTM. The race bike handled as well as her BMW, and soon enough she was safely on the other side of the rushing river.

Cat needed to relieve herself, so she made a motion to pull over, and the women stopped in their tracks. Dusk hovered over them, creating a semidarkness that was coverage enough. They took turns squatting, and with the diuretic effects of the alcohol, went like racehorses after drinking from a water trough. The frenetic energy that had gotten them so far, so fast, was beginning to wane. Cat yawned, and soon Sis and Rey followed suit.

"How you feeling—are you warm enough?" Cat felt sorry for the rather pathetic Rey. She looked like a waterlogged ferret. Rey nodded half-heartedly as if so say *don't talk to me*. There was nothing left to do but push on.

For the next few hundred kilometers, the girls battled high winds and light rain while pushing into deep darkness—both in the sky above and their psyches. Cat knew she would make it to the next stop, but she was beginning to doubt her decision to continue with this trip. LA was a quick flight away. Her head hurt from the booze, the cut on her head, and the sneaking suspicion that the race girls were troublemakers. She figured she could hand the young ones the rest of her cash, sell her bike to the biggest local bidder, and go back to being a pampered actress.

As the threesome rounded the last of the switchbacks at the summit above the Laguna Chapala basin, they could see distant lights of civilization. Random glimpses of a small town peeked from among the low hills as they rode downward again. By the time they arrived, the rain was done, and they were able to grab a quick bite at a gas station in Guerrero Negro, where the girls got an unofficial weather report from a trucker ... Collette was headed out to sea.

This tidbit refueled each of them. Cat was amazed by what clear skies and a bag of chips could do for her attitude. After a double dose of ibuprofen and a couple of greasy taquitos, Sis no longer seemed crazed from pain and low blood sugar. Cat even slipped into the bathroom with Rey and a professional compact to camouflage Rey's bruises and render her somewhat presentable.

As they slipped back on the bikes for one last push toward accommodations, Cat was ready to accept any version of habitat they could find. *How bad could it be after that run?*

CHAPTER **12**

GUERRERO NEGRO TO LORETO

"'A huge steel monument of an eagle straddles the 28th parallel in the Vizcaino Desert.'" Cat buried her nose in the book and continued. "'Placed as a border between the Pacific and Mountain time zones'... Oh, it's only seven," she concluded. "We gained an hour last night." Cat put the book down and reset her watch.

Sis groaned as she rolled her wrist around tenderly. "How you feeling?" asked Cat.

"Besides being hung over, beat up, and sleep deprived? I'm fine."

Cat didn't believe her since she felt pretty terrible herself. None of them had reason to be awake yet, but the clear blue skies outside had flooded the window-lined room with light and pulled the three of them out of their much-needed sleep.

They had bunked down in a company town devoted to the production and exportation of salt. Nice hotels were in abundance—geared to the well-financed businessmen who frequented the factories for efficiency analysis. In the name of sodium glorification, the entire town was cast in white.

"Not much to see here," offered Rey, squinting with the one eye that wasn't sealed shut. Now that they were up anyway, Cat decided they might as well continue on to Loreto, where they could notify the authorities about their attack. Cat referred back to the Triple A guide. "The book says it'll take about six hours to get to Loreto. I assume it'd be better to file a report in person, but if you want me to call ..."

"What good will that do?" asked Sis, sounding pissed. She squinted and shook her head in a way that said Cat was being naïve.

"Rey said she got a good look at the guy." Cat looked to Rey for confirmation. Her one good eye looked back at her with the same *give it up attitude* that Sis expressed. The other eye was swollen shut, a painful shade of blue-black with a quarter-size spot of magenta under the socket.

"We were attacked—we survived. Ain't nothing the cops can do about it." Rey seemed resigned to accept her beating and move on. "The only thing missing is my jacket," Rey added, as if her brutalized look didn't count as a violation.

"What about justice?" asked Cat, feeling victimized.

"It's a wild goose chase," Rey explained. "The cops are engaged in a war down here—they don't have time for petty crimes."

"He almost broke Sis's wrist!" Cat cried.

"Close only counts in horseshoes and hand grenades."
Sis flashed a sarcastic smile. "The swelling will go down,
and my wrist will be fine. I don't want to waste another day
of our vacation. I promise not to place any more bets while
I'm down here."

"What does that have to do with it?" asked Cat.

"Rey said it was one of the guys from the pool game."

"They were standing at the bar when we left."

"Just drop it!" yelled Sis. Her anger was not to be
messed with.

The sun shone down as if nothing had shaken the barometer,
and the girls set out to have a pleasant cruise to the opposite
coast. This atmosphere was exactly what Cat needed to
resume her faith in the safety of this trip. The warmth of the
day meant she could have her bike back—Rey would survive
without the extra protection.

It felt great to be alive after enduring the crushing
fear she'd experienced the night before. Assured of Sissy's
integrity, Cat swore she'd never doubt her sister's good
intentions again. Rey was another story, but looking at her
pitiful face, Cat felt sorry for her and didn't suspect any
guilt on her part. Cat was ready to claim this tale as a hard
lesson about placing big bets against bad guys—as long as
things stayed calm from here on.

A short time into the ride, the paved road ended, and
they stopped for a quick pow-wow to discuss the next move.
Cat was impressed that Sis's injury did not affect her ability
to ride. Maybe it was because she was used to dealing with

discomfort after a crash, since races didn't wait for riders to heal. Sis had always been stubborn and impatient, two traits that were on full display as Sis announced she was prepared to endure the bumps on the dirt as long as it meant avoiding the traffic jam that was bound to back up along the main road that led to San Ignacio. Rey agreed since the open space would give her plenty of wiggle room to choose the optimal course using the only eye she could see through. Sis accepted a double dose of ibuprofen from Cat before they hit the dirt. She was raring to go to the volcanic cones that were reportedly scattered across this section.

"It's mind over matter," said Sis, swallowing her medicine. "If you don't mind—it doesn't matter." With a final "Yee-haw!" she gunned her engine and gave Cat a thumbs up in jubilation.

Soon enough, craggy brown boulders popped up everywhere, as if they'd been dropped from the sky. "Time for a little rock hopping!" yelled Rey over the sound of the engines as the women paused at the top of the first volcanic plateau.

Cat admired the view, but wasn't sure what to do with it. Primordial nuggets dotted the vista before them. Sissy revved her engine and tested her grip. She nodded to Rey like she was ready to grin and bear it, and off the girls flew. As Rey and Sissy maneuvered their machines up and over the numerous impediments, Cat came to see her companions as otherworldly, and she felt like an alien. Despite having the most expensive vehicle in the bunch, Cat rode like a fish on a bicycle.

The pros exploded with gusto, eating up the terrain like

a couple of hungry wolverines. Cat watched as they hopped, skipped, and slipped gracefully, while she pushed, tripped, and stumbled like an elephant trying to boogie around a disco ball. She felt as uncoordinated as she'd ever been, and the ineptitude wore on her. She felt judged with each glance Sissy offered, seemingly to keep track of her. Cat knew she looked wobbly and worried, and Sis as a witness hurt Cat's confidence more than the rocks did. Eventually Sis stopped to flip her helmet up and give Cat a rundown on how to level this beveled playing field.

"Use your hips to steer," Sis called out over the sound of their humming engines. "The engineers at Beemer put a lot of thought into this, so trust their wisdom. The clearest path is the one you're on—don't look at the rocks as obstacles. They're stepping stones for your amusement." Her words were poetic, but Cat still wanted to quit; leave the laughter to the masters, if this is what they call fun.

Sissy made a swoosh sign, like the Nike symbol that made their saying legendary. "Just do it?" jeered Cat inside the privacy of her helmet. "Fine," she sighed and with a "one, two, three," she turned off her brain and went for it. Standing on her foot pegs, Cat gave it some gas, aimed her wheel at the top of the hill, and set her eyes on the prize instead of the pebbled path. Doubt faded as the bike took charge and climbed the seemingly insurmountable mountain. In that moment, Cat realized it was her head that was her problem, not her gangly limbs. Her body had gotten her far in this world, but her head kept her stuck in the mud half the time. Better to turn caution off and go with the flow. Cat wondered if that would solve the problems she had with Chris. Sadly, amid the glory of this rousing vacation, he didn't seem worth the same risk.

San Ignacio came into view around two in the afternoon. An Easter egg-colored oasis in the middle of a pallid desert, it was made up of a short strip of pastel storefronts. The guide described it as "one of the most charming towns on the peninsula." Rey said the date palms that lined the streets would be the only greenery they would see until they reached the seaside towns again. A storybook wooden wagon, decorated with hand-carved pink and red dahlia blooms, provided a yummy appetizer of churros for Sis and Rey. Cat took pictures of the ornately painted cart while Sis and Rey stuffed themselves on four of the donut-like treats.

"Dessert before lunch?" asked Cat, raising her eyes at the rule-breaking duo.

"Don't want to take Advil on an empty stomach," Rey explained, rubbing her tummy sarcastically.

Cat ducked the jab as she noted the nearly empty bottle. She was surprised to find there were only a couple of pills left. "We'd better steer clear of violent criminals until we find more pain relief."

Backing her bike up to the curb, Sissy lowered her kickstand and pointed to a sit-down dining establishment a few doors away, saying she needed to use a restroom. Unfortunately, the snack shack did not allow "travelers" to use their bathroom.

"For locals only," the owner explained in Spanish.

"¡Pagamos a clientes!" Sis ranted, waving a dollar bill in

the air as an angry plea. Sis was desperate for a bathroom; she drew the line at squatting on the side of the road when it came to number two. The owner didn't budge, so Sis tossed a vulgarity and banged on the counter for emphasis. "*¡Gilipollas!*"

"Fudge packer!" she huffed as the women shoved their way out the door. "Hope they don't mind if I *poop on their stoop!*" Her loudmouth stunt was a front; she was already charging up the street to find another option. Rey and Cat followed.

"This is one of the nicer towns around. The guy doesn't want us shooting in there," Rey explained.

"Do I look like I'm *carrying a gun?*" asked an indignant Sis.

"Heroin, dummy, not guns. Transients will shoot up in the bathroom and leave their needles."

"How can these people afford *drugs?*" asked Cat.

"They do them to survive," said Rey.

"Do I really look like the kind of *schmuck* who'd *shoot up drugs?*" Sis asked.

"Do you really want me to answer that?"

Cat could see by the stone cold look on Rey's face that it was time to move on from this conversation. "A sign on the highway said the next rest stop is twenty kilometers from here. Let's just go there." Sis agreed to suck it up and wait for the public restrooms.

As they rounded the bend around the last of the volcanic mounds, the highway began a steep dip toward the coastline. Sissy had given Cat a few tips over lunch on how to deal with the "twisties."

"Switchbacks are a biker's dream, and acceleration is the key to staying in line." Using her plate to explain the physics, Sis had insisted that it was safer to accelerate into the turn, keeping your eyes fixed on the furthest point visible. "You'll wind up looking over your shoulder in the sharpest turns, while your bike heads a different direction. It takes a little practice, but it's safer."

Cat wasn't sure what Sis had meant until now, as her head turned to the right and her bike headed in the opposite direction. It was extremely disconcerting. Her eyes kept darting between the furthest point in the turn and the section right in front of her. It threw her off every time, and she jiggled her handlebars all the way around the first few switchbacks. Finally, she shut off her mind and looked as far as she could see, while her bike magically stayed on track in a smooth arc.

She practiced a couple of times at slower speeds, but got left behind by the racer girls. When she came around the fourth bend, they were waiting for her. Sissy yelled over the noise of the engines. *"Enter on the outside, close to the dirt. When you spot the end, cut in toward the middle of the road; it'll shorten your path and allow you to use the throttle more!"*

Cat was hoping to avoid the need for greater speed in these hairpin turns. It was all downhill from here, which made accelerating a bit tricky. Downhill, her bike picked up speed no matter what, so now she needed to judge how much brake to squeeze. She was getting pretty comfortable cutting across the lane at the end, until she hit a curve that banked inward. The slant toward the double yellow line gave her added momentum, so she hit the brake midturn, which screwed up her line.

As she tried to correct it, a truck flew out of a tunnel up ahead. The driver leaned on the horn and Cat swerved. It was an extremely close call and just about stopped Cat's heart. When her aorta returned to action, it was lodged in her throat.

"Holy shit," she gasped, sweating. At the bottom of the pass, the highway banged a right and began to follow the coastline. Cat's nerves were on fire, but the sight of the ocean seemed like a sign that the rest of the day's ride would be fine.

CHAPTER **13**

MULEGE

The first town they found on the west coast was Mulege. The trio exited the highway to find a restaurant and a place to refuel. Rey also needed a pay phone where she could use her calling card. The devil inside her had devised a wicked plan … she was ready to enlist the assistance of her Mexican connections.

Cat offered her cell phone, but Rey invented a fable about her father that involved hearing loss and a personal grudge against dropped calls. "Don't wait for me," said Rey as she headed toward an old-fashioned phone booth on the sidewalk.

"Don't worry—we won't," said Sis as the sisters headed inside to find a seat.

Inside the privacy of the booth, Rey persuaded one of her old pothead friends to arrange a pick-up in Loreto. The small-time deal meant she would pay full price, which her comrade doubted her ability to pay. Rey said she was flush and told him to rush it. She couldn't risk a mishap, insisting she would have all the cash by tomorrow evening. Playing Cat would be no problem. There was great diving to do in Loreto, so a day without riding would be an easy sell. Now she had to come up with a convincing story to get 25,000 pesos out of Cat's charitable hands—pronto.

"How's your dad?" asked Sis when Rey arrived at the table.

"He's not doing well—catheter's backed up." Rey gave her best impression of concern. "My sister's taking him to the ER." *Step one—done,* thought Rey mischievously. "He needs to keep working," she continued. "The holidays are his busiest time." Rey smiled inside at her quick improvisation.

"Let us know if there's anything we can do," offered Cat.

Step two, thought Rey. Grabbing a menu, she silently sighed in relief. *This is easy.*

As the trio continued down the coastal highway, the ocean vegetation offered Cat high hopes for finding her favorite underwater wildlife in Loreto. The Triple A guide promised some of the best diving in Mexico here, and Cat had already spotted half a dozen signs advertising scuba trips. She was super excited to get back to the world down under and planned to dive tonight if she wasn't too exhausted from the ride. As it turned out, the rest of the route was easy street.

The recently paved roadway along the coast had guardrails and enough space for the ladies to split lanes all the way to Loreto. It was dinnertime when the crew pulled into Nopolo, eight miles south of Loreto. Cat was happy to cover the cost for a luxurious room at the Stouffer Presidente. The extravagance extended beyond fancy accommodations to a full-service tourist desk that was happy to arrange a triple-tiered dive package. The fun would start tonight, with two day dives planned for tomorrow. That was all Cat needed to know before she made arrangements for a hearty dinner to recharge her before a midnight dip in the ocean.

Cat finished a brief call to her fiancé and was about to make dinner reservations for three when Rey stormed into the room. Sissy had mixed a cocktail from the minibar and was waiting for Rey to return before they headed down to the restaurant.

When Rey burst in and started jabbering, Sissy sat in the down-filled couch, and Cat scooted toward the back of the bed at full attention.

"My dad needs surgery—his catheter caused an infection, and they want to operate right away."

"Oh, no," said Cat, rising to her feet.

"We don't have health insurance," whimpered Rey. "And the hospital says they need payment up front—I don't know what to do." With unusual openness, Rey began to cry quietly. "I need to wire them two thousand bucks as soon as possible." Rey collapsed in a heavy heap on the couch next to Sis, and Cat placed her hand on her back.

"What about the money you brought for the silver?" asked Sis.

Cat had almost forgotten that Rey had a job to do while she was down here, too.

"My dad pays for the order quarterly," Rey said quickly. "It's a commodity, so he orders when the price is low. That's what makes coming down here worth it."

Cat shot Sissy a look that said *have some sympathy.* "Don't worry, Rey, I'll lend you the money."

Sissy's look was stern in return, as she flipped a message to Cat. *I don't believe her.*

Rey looked like a pound puppy begging for a bone. "Really?" she asked Cat with mock shock. "I'll pay you back, I swear—on my mother's dead body." Rey made a sacrilegious sign of the cross and smiled graciously at Cat.

"I just hope your dad's okay," said Cat, because that was the only thing that mattered.

⚜

Twenty minutes later, Rey was on her way to a Western Union downtown with 25,000 pesos in her pocket. Cat had given all her traveler's checks to Rey, but the hotel where they were staying accepted plastic for everything. She would have to get to a bank by closing time tomorrow.

"I cannot believe you gave her all that money," said Sis. She sounded a little jealous. "And I really can't believe you had that much on you. Jesus, Cat, we aren't in Saint Tropez, you know." Sis took a dig at the vacation Cat had taken last year, one that Sis was not invited on.

"If you get in trouble in a foreign country, money talks, so I keep a pouch hidden beneath my shirt. That's why the guy who attacked us didn't find it."

"So you actually believe the story about her dad?" asked Sis.

"Why would she lie?" asked Cat.

"I don't know," said Sis. "But I'm beginning to think that Rey isn't painting the whole picture here. She never said anything to me about coming down here to buy silver. I just thought she'd be a good wingman."

"What does that mean?" asked Cat, feeling as though Sis was picking on her for not being a good travel companion.

"I mean, you and I have had a tough time getting along for the last few years, and I thought it would be good to have a distraction in case we, I don't know, hated each other." Cat knew they'd had some heated discussions in recent years, mostly regarding their mother, but Sis's mere mention of hatred seemed extreme.

"So why did you agree to come with me?" asked Cat, feeling edgy.

"Because I really need a vacation. Living at home ain't easy."

"That's not my fault."

"Oh, no, you're just an innocent bystander in the mess that is our family. Do you know how many times I've had to fix shit between Mom and Dad after Mom went on one of her benders?"

"I was dealing with her drunkenness while you were still in diapers!" yelled Cat. "I practically raised you!"

"You and Mom were gone too often to even know what Dad and I were doing. *He* raised me. He's the only one who gave me the time of day while you were prancing around town in your tiara." Sis looked as though she might hit Cat now, for real. This was not what Cat expected when she offered her sister the vacation of a lifetime.

"All that time I spent on the damn runway," said Cat, trying to maintain a calm demeanor, "paid for your bikes and your races and your hearing aids. And in case you forgot, your *surgery*. How can you be so ungrateful?"

"Because you left me to fend for myself. I was thirteen against a mother that wished I was dead. You know she didn't want another child after Bobby died." Sis looked as if she might cry now.

"That is not *true*," said Cat, even though she knew Sis had been gypped by the birthing order. She had definitely missed out on the loving mother Cat had known before her younger brother died. "I know that Mom was not the same after we lost him—"

"We?" Sis interjected. "I never met him. He's not *my* brother. He's a ghost, a story, the boy who broke our mother's heart and who could not be replaced."

"You weren't born to be a *replacement*—"

"I was born out of mourning, to a mother who didn't have any love left. She already had one princess, and Dad hassled her until she gave him what he wanted. Dad wanted another son. And Mom wanted to be done with it. She was your manager and you made her proud. I was a big disappointment, a ragged little dirtball who moved like a mammoth and talked like a mongoloid."

"Sissy," Cat said gently. She desperately needed to stop Sis's train of thought, but as usual, Sis barreled on, gaining momentum.

"Dad wanted someone he could ride with. When I started

to win races, I thought I might be able to get out of El Paso, like you did. You know, travel the world and see what I could become outside of Texas. But no, by that time Mom had become so messed up that Dad needed me to stay and protect him. I swear to God, Cat, he would have had a heart attack a long time ago if I had left him to fend for himself with her."

"Dad is fine," said Cat, feeling suddenly out of touch with how bad things had become.

"Really?" asked Sis with a laugh. "Well, aren't we all then?"

"I understand that you're mad about me leaving you alone there. If you had told me, I could've helped you get out, too. I still can. How much do you need?"

"Right, because money solves everything. You don't get it. The only thing that gives Dad joy is seeing me win on the racetrack. My fate is sealed, and I'm actually okay with that. I just wish you would stop flaunting your star-studded shit whenever you come to see us, while eternally complaining about how hard it is to be famous. You know what? I'm done talking. Go ahead and save Rey. She is smitten with your bullshit. Don't worry. I'll still give you what you need: a first-class lesson on how to be me. Then you can go back to LA and shove it."

With that, Sis stormed out the door with an earthshaking slam, leaving Cat to marinate in the heap of fury Sis had flung at her. Sis was definitely flipping out, but Cat knew that she was right. And no amount of money could fix it.

Meanwhile, in the land of bread and honey, Rey was doing amazing things with Cat's money. First, she called her friend in Mexico City who had organized for her to pick up four ounces of pot tomorrow. Rey wired 15,000 pesos for that purchase. Then she contacted another buddy and secured an opiate addition to her package. Cat had generously offered her enough money to cover a half ounce of black tar heroin as well. Rey justified this naïve loan amount as a means to procure some much-needed stress relief. She hoped the heroin would ease her ongoing nausea, and she would surely find time to consume it all before they boarded the ferry.

The plan was good to go. The heroin would cost another three hundred bucks, which left her with five hundred Benjamins. Rey would repay Cat a portion of what she owed right away, as a token of her good standing, and would shave another two hundred off the top to replace her stolen jacket. As far as refunding the rest of the money, she would swallow that bullet when she got to it. For now, her plan was tight. The drugs were on order, and the length of her life was no longer at the mercy of the cartel.

CHAPTER  14

CONFESIÓN

There was nowhere to go but down after last night's confrontation. Cat was thirty feet below the surface of the sea, shining her flashlight on lobsters, urchins, and an electric eel who reeled back into hiding each time the beam caught him. Shining her light in the void made her swoon, since bioluminescence was in bloom. The moon was transitioning from full to new, but the muted ellipse offered enough glow to highlight the brilliant phytoplankton.

Cat waved her hand a couple of times to mobilize the neon green amoebas when all of a sudden, the effervescent movement of a tentacle caught her eye. An octopus peeked around a rock at her, then edged itself around and swam right at her, gliding like a nautical gypsy. After seven years of exploring this habitat without a single sighting, Cat could barely contain her excitement. *An octopus—wow!*

Now I can die satisfied. As the morbidity of that statement sunk in, Cat realized there were numerous things she had to fix to be satisfied with life, and, with all that Sis had said last night, Cat was beginning to realize that she could learn a lot from Sis's priorities. It was time to mend things between them, and Cat needed to tell Sis how much she really meant to her.

Having opted to give Sis plenty of space to cool off today, Cat had scheduled three dives; the first from the beach, the second from a boat, and the third would be a night dive—the perfect trifecta. The scuba group took a brief break to dry out on the beach after the first experience down under, before they loaded their equipment onto the boat and headed out to see the creatures that preferred to stay away from the swimmers and snorkelers close to shore. The captain announced the first place they would anchor was near an island off the coast that functioned as a salt source. The captain explained that salt had been a major export in here since the Spanish settled in Baja. Due to the lack of tourist attractions on the nearby mineral isle, the water around it was pristine and contained a colorful array of marine life. A one-man sailboat had crashed on the outlying rocks during a hurricane years before, and the vessel had become a reef that attracted mantas and sharks alike.

The sharks were harmless, since great whites never ventured this far up the gulf. "The waters are too warm and shallow for such huge fish," the captain assured them. "However," he warned, "man-of-wars are rampant." Cat had read about the devastating imbalance that was altering the ocean's diversity. As ocean temps increased, so did the number of shrimp that were staples in the jellyfish diet. She'd heard about the paralyzing effect that a man-of-war sting could produce and was not interested in tempting fate with a second attack by a "stranger" in three days. She'd had enough of getting beat up, so she agreed to stay close to the group. Cat paired up with a random partner and then boarded the boat for a bumpy ride toward Isla del Carmen.

After a late wakeup, Rey convinced Sis to head out for a walk around town. She would've preferred to go solo again, but she figured a little distraction for her urges would be good. As they wandered into the tourist trap area, Sis announced she needed to do a little shopping.

"I never thought I'd hear you say that," said Rey.

"Yeah, well, I've heard it can be good therapy." From the way Sis sauntered along as she walked, Rey guessed Sis was feeling a little off today.

"How's the wrist?" Rey asked as Sis stopped to try on a bracelet and had to ask Rey to assist her with the clasp.

"Fine, I mean, I'm glad I didn't break it. You know I'm going for the Triple Crown this year, and I can't afford to hurt myself like that again."

The Triple Crown was the "be all to end all" in racing. If Sis pulled it off, she'd be the first woman in the history of motocross to do so.

"You're definitely a contender," said Rey, a compliment that felt weirder to say than the more common ribbing she and Sis participated in on a daily basis. Rey wondered what her goals should be next year. It was a shoo-in that she'd win on her flip tricks, but she really wanted to think about the bigger picture. First place in a speed race continued to elude her, and she knew that was the only way to start making real money.

As Rey observed Sissy wandering through the crowd, picking up trinkets and handmade woven clothes, she could tell that Sis was thinking hard about something. It was as if each stop at a vendor was more about a pause in her thoughts than any purchase Sis considered.

"You okay?" asked Rey after Sis stopped to look at a papier-mâché figurine of a woman bearing a basket of fish. "You seem a little off today. I mean, we're *shopping*."

"I'm just thinking about getting something for my mom. It's her birthday soon." But her words were quiet, distracted.

"A dolly for your mommy?" Rey poked her playfully in the ribs, hoping to get a smile. Sis ignored her, continuing up the street at such a casual pace that Rey almost tripped on her heels a couple of times.

At the end of the long boulevard, the space opened up into a picturesque plaza that contained two enormous stone structures. The first was the Misión de Nuestra Señora de Loreto Conchó, a beige building engraved with the date 1752. An even grander building sat next door. Its ornamental facade imitated the church, but it had been more recently erected. The Spanish word for *museum* was carved in stone above its foreboding wooden door. Never before would Rey have guessed that Sis would set foot in a museum. A bar before noon maybe, but Rey had already proposed this when they left the hotel, and Sis said she wanted to take it easy today.

"You want to go inside with me?" Sis asked Rey. "I'll pay."

Now Rey knew something was wrong, so she shrugged a *maybe, I guess,* and followed behind Sis as she stepped inside the museum and asked about the fee.

"Admission to the church is free," the curator told them. He pointed toward the main entrance and invited them to light a candle at the altar.

Sissy entered the empty chapel quietly as Rey stood in the back. Rey had plenty of experience with this, but Sis seemed to need privacy, so Rey obliged and sat down in a pew. The light coming through the stained glass was radiant. Sis looked as though she felt awkward, hunching her shoulders down as she sat, as if she wanted to be smaller. Taking a risk, Rey got up and moved closer to Sis so she could tell her what to do if Sis changed her mind about lighting a candle. It seemed like the best way to ease Sis's mind was to go ahead and say a prayer herself.

Rey moved past Sis along the outer aisle and grabbed a tea candle from the box, moving toward the eternal flame to light it. As Rey set the candle down, she bowed her head, ready to ask God for help. There were plenty of troubles she needed help with, and heroin was numero uno, but that was not something Rey was willing to discuss with God. She didn't even think she would ever be able to confess her ever-increasing addiction. So she did something unusual: she made a request for God to help Sis instead. Rey did the sign of the cross and opened her eyes to find Sis watching her for clues on how to do this. "You can do it, too," offered Rey, "it doesn't matter what you believe in, God will listen."

"I'm out of practice."

"So?"

"I feel like a poseur. I haven't been to church since I was a kid."

"You can ask for forgiveness. Or help winning the Triple Crown." Rey smiled at her suggestion to keep things real. The trick worked. Sis grabbed a candle from the pile and copied what Rey had done. When she got up from her knees, Sis looked pleased with herself—the deep lines in her forehead that had said she was feeling remorse of some kind had disappeared completely.

"Let me guess," said Rey, "you asked that God give whoever is hot on your heels next year a flat tire at finals."

Sis smiled meekly. "I just asked him to help me see what I need to do to be the best I can be."

"Well, that pretty much covers everything," said Rey, suddenly wishing she had such insight.

Before Sis exited the old church, she ceremoniously kissed the gift she'd bought for her mother and promised aloud to do better. As the two of them stepped out into the bright sunlight, the church bells rang to announce the hour. "It's one o'clock," said Sis, acting distracted. "I think I want to walk around alone for a while, if that's cool with you."

"Sure," said Rey. It was the perfect time to connect with her drug-dealing friend and complete her mission to replace the drugs that had been stolen along with her jacket. She was about to hail a cab to save time getting back to her bike at the hotel when she spotted a store that had leather jackets for sale. She had almost forgotten that she needed to replace that, too, in the event of more rain or, God forbid, a bad wipeout. Rey was freshly outfitted a few minutes later when she hit the road to score in Puerto Escondido.

Cat was taking a nap when Sis entered the room, and awoke with a start, eager to share an overview of all the glorious things she'd seen during the island excursion. If only they were on speaking terms again. Cat knew that silence was not the way to go, so she decided to pretend everything was fine again.

"One more dive, and I'll be ready to leave tomorrow—if that's cool with you guys."

"Yeah," said Sis, looking sheepish. "Hey, I, uh, want to apologize for last night."

Cat could hardly believe her ears. Sis had never apologized for anything in her entire life. It made Cat want to hug her, but she knew that would be too much for Sis. "I'm just sorry you feel the way you do," Cat offered instead.

"I don't feel that way about you," acknowledged Sis. "I mean, some of what I said is true, but I have been looking forward to this trip since the day you asked me. I feel bad now that I invited Rey, and I'm sorry."

Cat was gobsmacked by this admission. It was the first time Sis had said anything remotely remorseful, and Cat almost felt bad for Sis's obvious discomfort. "I'm not sorry she came," said Cat, and she meant it. "I just hope we can spend some quality time alone together at some point. I think we need to talk a little more about some of the things you said last night."

"How about we go to dinner tonight—just the two of us," Sis proposed.

"Sounds perfect," said Cat. "I'll buy."

"I wouldn't have it any other way," Sis said with a smile. Cat was about to go for a hug, despite her better judgment, when Rey came through the door wearing a brand new Harley-style jacket.

Cat's next dive wasn't scheduled until three, so she offered to treat Sis and Rey to the lunch buffet downstairs; she figured she'd butter them up with a yummy lunch and then declare what her preference for the next few days was. Langoustine, quiche, and ceviche were a few of the selections. Cat had a taste of each, and the girls focused on the crème fraîche and cheddar cheese-smothered steak quesadillas.

The day was totally gorgeous: eighty-two degrees and sunny, with intermittent clouds. The breeze was just strong enough to billow the peasant skirt Cat wore on her leisurely stroll around town after lunch. Sissy and Rey had opted to stay at the beach and catch some rays. If Cat had been into that kind of thing, she would agree it was a perfect day to bask in the sun, but she wanted to do a little walking, a little talking, and purchase her first gifts. She reminded herself that they needed to be small, no room in the saddlebags for a big haul.

She'd forgotten about their mother's upcoming birthday until Sissy showed her the gift she'd bought. So her interest in shopping originated with the birthday girl in mind. Her mother was relatively picky when it came to presents. No clothes and absolutely nothing to indicate her age. Cat often bought her fancy booze; high-end brands she could not afford on the salary of her seafaring husband. Top-shelf bottles made her mom feel special, for their possession and her inebriated escape. But the more she thought about it, she felt a sneaking unease about contributing to her mother's fifty-year plus bad habit.

As she perused the numerous stands filled with pottery, painted gourds, and woven goods, Cat was disappointed by the selection of generic tourist crap. She turned over a potted bowl with an intricate mural to find a sticker that read "Made in Peru." She walked away empty-handed, feeling like her purchase power only weakened the needy who clearly bought trinkets from South America in an effort to make the most of their mark-up. Cat was about to retreat from the vendor haven when a child approached her with a backpack and offered a selection of toys for under a dollar. "One dollar, American?" quizzed Cat.

"Only if you can afford it," replied the three-and-a-half-foot cherub.

"*¿Qué tiene?*" she asked with her American diction. The boy rattled off the list, holding up the most appealing things. There was a dinosaur woven from reeds, a train engine painted like a taco, and a clear plastic box filled with what looked like black-eyed peas. "What are these?" Cat asked, pointing to the last item.

"*Frijoles saltarines,*" he responded. It reminded Cat of a nursery rhyme.

"What's that?" she asked.

"Mexican jumping beans," the boy said, rolling over his consonants. Cat had never seen them before and didn't realize they were an actual thing. She asked the boy if he had a box of three. "For a buck twenty-five," he said, puffing up with confidence as he proposed it. Cat handed him a fifty and told him to keep the change. He staggered dramatically, and then offered an exuberant wave as he disappeared down the street. It was the best-spent money she'd thrown down yet.

Cat returned to their room with little time to spare. She struggled into her damp suit, rummaged through her dive bag for SPF 50, and slipped into her sandals. Making her way down to the beachfront, she lugged her heavy gear across twenty-five yards of hot white sand to the new group of divers. The dive master paired them up in teams, and Cat turned her back to shuffle backward toward the sea in her floppy fins. En route to the water's edge, Cat spotted the girls on the patio in the distance. Sissy waved and flipped, *This is amazing.* She raised her cocktail as a salute to Cat and flipped again. *Thank you!* Then Sis blew an exaggerated smacker-oo toward Cat and signed, *I feel pretty rich for a small town Texan.*

Cat nodded and beamed. *Texas is best,* she flipped to Sis. Then she dunked down backward and slipped into the sea.

15

AMENDS

A s far as Cat was concerned, money was only worth the paper it was printed on if it wasn't buying a better life. So she spared no expense on dinner for two. It was the first chance the sisters had to speak freely, so they covered all the important stuff, beginning with a little contrition by Sis.

"Sorry about last night," she said as soon as they were seated. Cat knew apologies weren't her thing and could tell by Sis's hunched shoulders that her angry diatribe was weighing heavily on her.

"I'm sorry you've had to endure so much at home without me," Cat responded.

"It's not that," offered Sis, pausing as the busboy set two waters down.

"Can you bring a bottle of sparkling water as well," Cat

asked him, returning her gaze to Sis as the young man left their vicinity. Cat unfolded her napkin, placing it across her lap, and Sis followed suit.

"I'm just frustrated with Rey right now, and you happened to get the brunt of it. I don't regret coming, I wish I'd come alone, I mean, just me and you."

Cat grinned on the inside, raising her eyebrows to show she was both pleased and a tad surprised by Sis's admission. "I actually kind of like her, but it's nice to know that you and I can get some private time. It's been way too long since we hung out together—away from each of our intense vocations."

The server entered their space to deliver the bottled water and ask if they'd like to see the wine list. Sis shook her head, and Cat asked if she wanted a cocktail instead. Shaking her head again, Sis began to scan the menu, and Cat asked the man to give them time to decide. She considered Sis's refusal to drink an extension of her apology, and Cat was thrilled to get Sis's sober opinion on things. "Are you pretty hungry?" Cat asked. "The chef's tasting menu for two sounds good, but it'll probably be a lot of food."

"I'm always hungry," said Sis. "I also need to eat something quick since I've been popping ibuprofen like candy—last thing I need is an ulcer right now."

"The way you've been riding, I can't even tell you're injured. God, what a freaky situation the mugging was, huh?" Cat was resigned to the fact that robberies were par for the course down here, but without Sis and Rey having guided her to brush it off, she might have flown home two days ago.

"I was afraid I might be done for next season," said Sis, rolling her wrist slowly in a circle motion and shaking her head at the thought of being out of commission.

"You always bounce back," said Cat.

"I need to be in the best shape of my life if I want to take the Triple Crown next year."

"Winning races is what you were born to do."

"True," said Sis.

"I wish I knew what *my* calling was."

"Superstardom isn't in your cards?"

"It doesn't make me happy."

"What about motherhood and marriage?"

"I don't want to marry Chris," Cat admitted for the first time out loud. She looked down with a hint of shame at the opulent diamond on her ring finger.

"What'd he say about the mugging?"

"I didn't tell him." Cat snickered and rolled her eyes at the memory of her first call to him after the incident. "He started giving me shit about Slick Rick leaving messages on the home phone before I had a chance to tell him about us. That's the biggest problem for me; he's totally self-absorbed. If I tell him about the attack, he'll insist I come back—but only to protect his precious product."

"So you're burned out on Hollywood, *and* you want to end your engagement."

Cat nodded solemnly.

"Well, I may be living at home still, but I'm happy and still hungry to ride all the time. I think that's more important than making tons of money."

There was a long pause in the conversation as the waiter

returned to take their order. When he left again, Sis appeared to be lost in her observation of this upscale place. White linen was the theme of this scene. The high-octane color they'd been bombarded with in most of the restaurants was replaced by subtle lighting, soft guitar music over the sound system, and the murmurs of couples who were dressed to impress one another. Sis seemed more mature under this lighting, and she had combed her hair down in such a way that downplayed her crazy hairdo.

"So," said Sis, looking at Cat as if this were the million-dollar question. "What do you really want to do?"

"I want to live in a shack on some shore somewhere."

Sissy laughed. "Sounds like vacation brain is making you a little bit crazy. And what, you want me to fill in for you on Chris's movie?" Cat smiled. "You know I'll grab Hollywood by the balls—if the money's right."

Cat cracked up at Sis's gumption. "And have some artistic fool direct your every move?"

"Yeah, screw that." Sis took a sip of the sparkling water and burped quietly. "Here's to simple living then," Sis proclaimed.

"And doing what makes us happy," added Cat.

CHAPTER **16**

LORETO TO LA PAZ

The women hit the dirt as soon as they crossed the state line the next day. They were on a mission to find a mission, San Luis Gonzaga. It was next on Cat's list of cultural explorations, and Sissy and Rey seemed happy to oblige her whim. "As long as it means getting dents in our rims along the way," Sis added.

The direct route meant avoiding the highway entirely. Rey said she'd be able to tell where they were headed by the view on the horizon. But as soon as they steered clear of the coast, there would be fewer landmarks, no mountain range to guide them or rambling rivers to confine them. She admitted that they might be led in circles, since none of them had a compass. "I'll use my GPS," offered Cat, selecting the map app on her phone. It picked up the exact coordinates within minutes.

"Damn, I got to get me one of them things," Rey said in amazement. Now that they were set in the right direction, the plan was to give each other plenty of space to play and to seek out waterways for some soppy fun. Cat rode in the middle since she didn't need as much space to flaunt her tricks, Rey stayed to the right, and Sissy headed left in the lead position. In this staggered formation, they could slalom the copious cacti with ease. It was a breezy eighty-five degrees when they left Loreto, but Cat's phone reported ninety-five a short time later. The heat was oppressive without the ocean breeze, so the girls stopped for numerous water breaks, to drink as well as douse their torsos.

Their route was punctuated with continuous whoop-de-woos. They hit jump after jump, side by side, until the race bug bit Sis, and Rey was forced to fall behind into single file. Cat fell behind a bit as the mounds got bigger, while Sis and Rey launched faster and their hang times grew; up, down, uup, down, uuupupupup. During flight, Sissy's bike let out a high-pinged ring; it was the sound track to Cat's weekends as a kid.

As early as age ten, Cat watched her little sister whiz around their homemade track on Dad's days off. It was fun to see Sissy spinning her miniwheels around the banks of the turns, so aggressive and brave for a four-year-old. Now at the age of twenty, Sis was a dream on wheels, riding her bike like a beast, leaving hardly a mark on the ground. At times, it seemed that her tires were hovering, the lift-offs so smooth her Honda seemed to levitate. Sis was like a tiger about to pounce upon approach, but her loft and delicacy upon landing reminded Cat of a beach ball at a baseball game. At one point, Sis hit a very steep incline and flipped her bike head over tails, landing with a feather-light puff in the dust going thirty.

Inspired by the Cirque-du-Soleility of their tricks, Cat felt frisky enough to attempt a couple of bumps herself. It was easy to land on this hard-packed sand, and the smaller humps left enough view for Cat to plan her exit strategy. Much to Cat's amazement, Rey came off a jump and threw a nac nac, letting her KTM swing to the left while she swung her legs to the right in a pike. From Cat's viewpoint, this move seemed to slow her momentum, and the sudden drag made Cat think Rey might wind up on top of another cholla. Rey bailed midstunt and barely sailed past the dangerous cactus below.

Sissy, who was busy showing off up ahead, was unaware of the near collision, but Cat learned from Rey's mistake and took great care to aim for clear touchdowns as her jumps became more energetic. The ladies rolled up to the mission around ten thirty. "Right on target," exhaled Cat as she stopped to catch her breath. "Riding like this is a workout—no wonder you're so ripped, Sis. How's your wrist?"

"It's pretty good, happy to have those cushy landings."

"Dude, you were kicking ass back there—impressive riding," Rey said, removing her helmet. Cat noticed that Rey was tapping her jacket pocket nervously, as if confirming the whereabouts of something, and when Rey gazed up to see Cat looking at her, she abruptly stopped the patting and reached up to redo the rubber band that secured her now mussed ponytail.

Cat was ready to explore the church, but the young ones had another mission in mind. Sissy and Rey wanted to check out the dip in the distance that resembled a half pipe. Cat left to join the tourist crowd, and the girls rode over to check out the valley. Cat had not been a member of a congregation since she left home and followed no spiritual devotion outside her ethereal connection with the ocean. But she still held sanctuaries in high regard and felt especially respectful of any that had faithfully served worshippers for hundreds of years.

The San Luis Gonzaga Mission, in its simplicity, dissolved any misgiving Cat had about wearing dirty leather inside. Cat figured rustic gear was apropos for any worshipers who crossed the desert to get here. The stone structure offered respite from the heat. The cement pews were cool, and Cat indulged in the serenity despite the parishioners' whispers that echoed around the splendid chapel.

When she emerged from her peaceful time-out, Cat passed through the old wooden door to find a rabble-rousing crowd pointing at the deep gully that had transformed into a trick pit for the racer girls. Cat shaded her eyes from the brilliant sky and saw Rey flip off the lid of the pit, spin her bike around, and remount it before slipping gracefully back down again. Sissy flew up next and did a bucking bronco that would impress the most trophy-laden rodeo rider.

The onlookers edged closer to give a collective cheer with each impressive trick. Cat watched in total awe and disbelief that she could claim them as her riding partners. The swelling crowd whistled and hollered as Sissy threw her arms up after hitting another mind-boggling catapult.

"Who's that guy?" a young boy asked his father. The man shrugged.

"Her name's Sissy Lang," Cat piped in behind them. "She's a big star." Cat encouraged the little boy's amazement. "You ought to get her autograph—it'll be worth something someday." That's all she had to say to make the crowd hungry for a piece of Sissy. Having exhausted her exhibitionism, Sis pulled up next to Cat and was instantly besieged with requests for autographs, mostly on pamphlets from the mission. Inspired by her holy zeal, she scrawled, *Jesus saves, motocross rocks.* Sis beamed as she posed for pictures with the excited kids.

CHAPTER 17

LA PAZ

When they finally pulled away from San Luis Gonzaga, the GPS estimated the arrival time in La Paz as 2:00 p.m. It would have been faster if not for all the flowing water. The rain from the last few days had turned the dry creek beds into rushing springs of murky, reddish water. It was an invitation to remain cool and wet.

Sissy reassured Cat, through flipping, that all the important parts of her engine would be above water as long as her butt didn't get submerged. It was a riot to come crashing down the bank of a stream into almost three feet of water. Cat held on tight as her bike surged through the current until it could grip the sand and shoot out again. They were totally soaked within the first twenty minutes. It was the perfect finale to this last section of cruising across

Baja. The ride went by quickly and La Paz was before them in no time.

When they stopped for a quick snack on the road leading into town, Sis spontaneously blurted, "What do you say we try camping again?"

"Sounds good to me," Rey sang merrily. She was always game to slumber outside.

"Can we even do that here?" wondered Cat aloud. Despite the low-key appearance, she was under the impression that La Paz was devoted to sailing clubs and yacht slips.

"I'm sure we can find a campsite," said Sis. "It'd be fun to sit around a fire pit, roast some marshmallows, and drink cold beer."

"We could probably buy sleeping bags here," said Rey.

Cat thought this sounded like a safer way to wing it than the impromptu adventure they'd had the first night, but she planned to set some priorities if this was to be their last soiree on Baja. She had assumed La Paz would be one of the highlights of their trip, so it took her a minute to adjust to the fact that it could be fun at the lower end of accommodations. "I'm not really into hot dogs on a stick," she said.

"What about fire ants?" asked Sis.

Cat ignored the teasing. "Can we at least find a place with a bathroom?"

"I'm sure with all the yachts that dock here, we can find you a nice public shower," said Rey.

"Fancy enough for the super riche?" asked Sis.

"I just want to clean up a bit before we board the ferry," Cat retorted.

With that, the ladies set out in search of a ferry schedule and a campsite with upper-crust appeal. It didn't take long to discover that the ferry only sailed at night. They decided to camp for the evening, spend tomorrow exploring La Paz, and catch the ferry at 5:00 p.m. for the overnight passage to Mazatlán. Cat agreed to pay for a suite on the ferry, otherwise known as a bunk room, while Sissy and Rey anteed up for the expensive passes to transport the bikes. The girls tried to butter Cat up by helping pay their way. This detour would be the end of Cat's grand plan, so typically frugal Sis threw down cash for the campground and firewood.

Meanwhile, Cat went across the street to a hardware and camping supply store in search of sleeping bags. She figured it was better to be safe than sorry since the next leg of the trip would take them into territory that might not have any hotels available. The Day of the Dead was eight days away, and Rey said it could draw hundreds of thousands of revelers. Cat was happy to outfit each of them with a quality sack so they'd have the option to sleep under the stars if that became necessary. She prayed the festivities would not include rain.

"We booked a site at Aquamarina," announced Sis as soon as the women reconnected. "It's right on the bay and has showers *and* scuba."

Pulling into the entrance of Aquamarina made Cat think of home, as the wooden and white fee station was covered with ivy and resembled the Annenburg Community Beach House in Santa Monica. They parked their bikes like ducks in a row in front of the clean and ample seaside spot. As soon as they had peeled off their riding gear, Sis and Rey volunteered to join Cat at the shower house made up of private teak stalls.

After they set up camp, Rey went for a walk around the premises, and Sissy got busy constructing a "one-match" teepee in the fire pit. Cat stretched on top of her sleeping bag, doing minor yoga poses to get her hip to relax and the kinks out of her back. Cat was prone and feeling peaceful when she put in an obligatory call to her agent.

"Hey, Rick, it's Catrina. I'm just checking in...."

"Babe! Where you been? I've been texting you like crazy." Rick was a textaholic. Cat often skipped reading his messages when they came in clusters and called him directly instead.

"I just got in from a swim," she lied. "What's up?"

"There's a script I need you to read right away. Mel Gibson's attached. He's trying to turn his career around, and he needs an angelic costar to lighten public opinion about him."

"Gibson is *crazy*, Rick," Cat interjected.

"Yeah, I know. He's an asshole. But he's freaking famous—and you could use his star power. If we're ever going to feed you to the masses, this could be the perfect platform."

Cat pulled the phone from her ear and listened from afar to his babble. When he finally paused and waited for her response, she announced her next destination as the Marriott in Mazatlán. She had no idea if this was true, but surely there had to be a Marriott in Mazatlán. At the very least, she could swing by there to pick up a script. Settling him down, she thanked him for all his hard work, bid him goodbye, then pitched the phone inside her open toiletry bag and lay back to look at the clear blue sky for a while.

Cat was postponing a call to Chris when Rey moseyed into sight. She shined a hazy lazy smile, like she had been drinking. Having completed her preparation of the one-matchstick-fire pit, Sis seemed ready to imbibe as she stood up, clapped her hands, and asked, "Who's ready for a brewski?"

Cat rocked to a seated position and announced she was ready for a dip.

"Any takers?" Cat asked, hoping for once that her companions would join her and put off their binge for a bit. They shook their heads.

"Nah," said Sis.

Cat assumed her sister was about to indulge in whatever liquid fire Rey had procured for them, so she headed off to the restroom to change into her suit and to get away from it. When she returned a short time later to grab her towel and toss her clothes, Sis flashed a grin of bliss. "Well, look what the cat dragged in."

Sis had been cracking this joke for as long as Cat could remember, but today she sounded enthusiastic. Cat followed Sis's and Rey's gazes to look behind her. Three handsome guys were stopped dead in their tracks at the edge of the campsite. As Cat made eye contact with the tallest one, he timidly inquired, "Are you the girl from *Darkstar*?" That was all it took to hook the men.

The leader of their pack introduced himself as Brad before pointing out his comrades as Adam and Steve. Cat admired Steve's shy smile and passive attitude; he seemed less impressed with her fame than his friends. For the first time since they arrived in Mexico, it was a pleasure to meet a man who was taller than she was by a good four inches.

"Where ya'll from?" asked Sis, drawing out her own twang to match Brad's southern accent.

"Steve and I are from Texas; Adam's from Arkansas. We graduated from University of Texas last year and are just getting together for a long weekend before Adam here starts a new job."

"We're from Texas, too," said Sis. Cat could tell by Sis's hot-to-trot reaction to Brad so far that she was happy to have that in common. Adam offered a bright-eyed kind of stupid-looking smile, reminiscent of Jim Carrey. Steve hung back for the most part, occasionally making eye contact with Cat, before looking down at the ground. Each time she caught him looking, she offered him a smile, but it was clear that he was somewhat overwhelmed by her presence. Brad was not disarmed by any of them and began flirting with Sis almost immediately.

"Why don't you join us tonight?" he asked Sis, although his invite was aimed at all three of them. "We got steak tips marinating and beers on ice."

"Sounds like a plan," said Sis, speaking on Rey's and Cat's behalf.

"Okay, it's a date. We're at campsite ten—just around the bend. See y'all later."

⚜

Each of the guys spent quite a bit of time staring at Cat when they reunited, until Sis jump-started an in-depth conversation with Brad, leaving the remaining foursome to muddle through idle chitchat. Cat was back to pretending she was taken, or at least living up to her standard off-the-market level of engagement, and Rey sat rather quietly, seemingly uninterested in making new friends. Cat was pretty shocked when Sissy and Brad moved from making small talk to making out even before the steaks hit the grill.

Watching her little sister get busy with a relative stranger made Cat uncomfortable. It wasn't especially shocking, considering Sis's ever-aggressive attitude, but it made Cat feel small somehow, like a dud who always played things safe. The handsome man beside her was respectful and sweet, but watching Sis go for it with Brad almost made Cat wish she could fling off her ring and jump on him … oh, to have one day where she could quit caring what was polite and do something that felt goddamned good.

Adam was actually the most attractive guy in the bunch, and his broad shoulders and tight butt were hard not to notice. Rey was sitting next to him, but the faraway look in her eyes made Cat wish she could take Rey's place and cozy up next to Mr. Hotty McBody. The more she thought about breaking the rules, the more depressed she became about the man who was waiting for her at home.

The reason behind her commitment to Chris seemed suddenly shameful. Money, fame, and safety had been the aphrodisiacs that held them together, and neither chose to address what Cat considered a below-average sex life. As Sis did her best impression of a sex kitten, climbing into Brad's lap to share a beer with him, Cat felt envy, masked with the disgrace of being in the right place at the right time for a one nighter, but being too afraid of changing. So she turned away from all of it and continued to answer Steve's silly questions about *Darkstar*, while Adam managed the meat on the grill the same way Sis handled her new-found thrill—with gusto.

The group wound up dining in a boy-girl-boy-girl circle around the campfire. Cat finally loosened up a bit after Sis and her guy took a walk in the dark for more privacy. Without that distraction, Cat was able to focus on Rey who seemed increasingly uncomfortable. She fidgeted and used a stick to make lines in the sand, clearly thinking about something other than this coed barbeque.

"Everything okay, Rey?" Cat asked.

"I need to pee," Rey stated frankly. Before Cat had a chance to offer to go with her, Rey grabbed her jacket and said, "I'll be right back." She scrambled to her feet and charged down the path without a second glance. Her sense of urgency contradicted her previously zoned-out behavior. Cat was about to hop up and follow Rey when Sis and her man returned, trying to hide the sparkle of pure satisfaction in their eyes.

"That was quick," Cat quipped.

"Every second counts when you're getting to know each other," quipped Sis.

Cat suddenly wished she could fulfill her own urges for once, but pleasure was still a foreign emotion. Cat got to her feet and politely excused herself for a quick trip to the bathroom.

CHAPTER **18**

QUICKIE

In the dimly lit bathroom at the far end of the campsite, Rey sat in the handicapped stall with her pants around her ankles and her mind consumed with an urgent need that made her fingers shake. She'd come down hours ago from her first go around and was ready for a massive toot. Grabbing the baggie from her pocket, she dipped her pinky fingernail in and pulled out a bump to snort. She dove in again, but this time the edge of the bag snagged on a zipper at her wrist and caught her off guard. The bag tipped and tossed a large sum of powder on the ground.

"Fuck!" Rey spat.

"What happened?" Cat asked, having quietly entered the bathroom.

Hidden inside the stall, Rey swiped her shoe across the white mess trying to hide the evidence. "I just got sick."

"Sorry to hear that," Cat said, sounding slightly irritated, like a high school hall monitor accepting the excuse of a punk rocker late for class. "If you want to bail from the barbeque, that's cool with me."

"No," said Rey a little too quickly. "I'll be back in a minute, after I clean up this mess."

Cat entered the other stall for a quick piss, and Rey moved her feet to hide the spilled powder, just in case Cat could see under the stall at all. As soon as Cat flushed, Rey began to quietly shuffle her feet, trying to clear the smear without arousing Cat's suspicion. Rey could hear Cat washing her hands for what seemed like an eternity, followed by the sound of paper being pulled from the metal box on the wall.

"I'll tell the guys you went to call your dad, but I'll call in the cavalry if you're not back soon," Cat said kindly.

"Don't worry about me," Rey said in a way that sounded more demanding than she intended. Softening her tone a bit, Rey tried to sound subdued to hide the fact that she wanted to scream *Fuck* again. "I'll be fine." Rey muttered a bunch of whispery expletives as soon as the bathroom door closed again, confirming Cat's departure. She inventoried her loss. The heroin on the damp floor looked like lumps of misfired toothpaste. She left it for the janitor, who would likely be none the wiser. Rey's goodie bag had lightened up significantly, and her rage about the sloppy mishap made her anxious to chase the dragon. She filled her fingernail four more times before she felt good enough to face the group again.

By the end of the night, Rey had gotten her high on, Sis had gotten her guy off, and Cat made a big ol' melted mess of the marshmallows. The girls returned to their campsite alone, and the boys went home with a really big fish tale from Mexico.

🔱

"That guy was amazing," Sis confided to Rey the next day as soon as Cat was out of earshot. Sis had no regrets about her one-night stand, but she really didn't care to hear Cat's opinion about it. "That is the fastest *O* I've ever had ... I mean, the guy was a master. He leaned me against a tree and made me come so hard, I almost lost feeling in my legs. And he didn't even ask me to return the favor!"

Sis glowed with excitement as she described the expert handling of her nether region. "Okay, okay," Rey interjected when the details became too explicit.

Sis quit filling Rey in on the sexy details and got down to the heart of the matter. "He wants to see me race sometime," Sis whispered. Her eyes were bright and her forehead lifted to the sky; she sounded giddy and hopeful, like a girl who had just asked Santa for a very special gift. "I *really* hope he calls me." Sis practically pranced as she continued to clean up the campsite. It was the most girly gait Rey had ever seen on her tomboyish teammate.

"Don't tell Cat about this," warned Sis. "She's a total priss when it comes to this shit."

Rey nodded, having felt the same way last night when Cat almost caught her in the act. By the time Cat returned from primping, the gear was rolled up and tied to the back of the bikes. Sis and Rey were roaring to go.

"Let's *eat!*" hooted Sis. She seemed ready for a long day

of eating, tanning, and nonstop girl talk. Spring break had sprung in October.

They made a quick trip to a beachfront restaurant, where boating folks dressed in preppy sailing gear filled the patio while mostly kids took a dip in the ocean. Rey sat next to Sis, where she had the perfect view of the water. Cat sought cover under an umbrella to their left and spent a fair amount of time making phone calls. It was the first time Rey had seen her disregard the sea, keeping a close eye on the sun's angle and adjusting her position to avoid it. She later admitted that a major audition was on her horizon, and she needed to heed her agent's rule about proper skin care.

Rey watched as dolphins and pelicans swarmed around the ocean in front of them, while Sis took charge of ordering for all them—appetizers and fizzy drinks came in rounds from the waitress who frequented the patio. This time, none of the beverages had booze in them.

Sissy pounded sparkling water instead of beer in an attempt to battle dehydration and prevent the insidious seasickness that often affected her. A dose or two of Dramamine would be key as well. Rey steered clear of alcohol because she felt like throwing up, but nothing happened whenever she excused herself for the bathroom. Even the thought of food made her gag, so Rey avoided the fruity juice that the sisters kept raving about and prayed her discomfort would be over soon.

It was a day devoted to recovery and the chance to plan out their mainland strategy. The three amigas agreed to spend the next few days exploring the opposite coast on their feet instead of their seats. Cat booked home base at the Marriott. She confirmed with the front desk that a script would arrive for her soon. Rey arranged for a supposed meeting at the silver mine outside Mexico City. "We'll drive by it on the way home; it won't take much time—they'll have a package waiting for me."

Rey had one more assigned pickup, and it had nothing to do with silver. She would grab the last of her assigned pick-ups on the way out of town and head straight for the border. Oddly enough, the border worried her less than the ferry ride. She kept telling herself that this was just another crossing. She had committed plenty of daring acts in the two years she had been muling. Swallowing a bunch of drugs would be another notch on her mule harness, but the belt was squeezing her tightly these days.

Rey was beginning to think this might be the last of her drug-carting adventures. She wondered wistfully what she could do instead to earn such a pretty penny. Her efforts to coach Cat on the bike had switched on a light, and Rey wondered if teaching at the race school might offer her safer income. Anything would be better than being worried about a bust and trying to muster up a bit of willpower to resist the constant call of the drugs in her pocket all the time.

"Hey, Sis, I've been thinking—does your coach ever take on apprentices?"

Sis looked at her, a thoughtful expression on her face. "I can ask him—why?"

"You want to teach racing?" Cat asked. "I think you'd be great at that."

"I want more outta life, you know?"

"Yeah," said Cat. "I do."

In spite of Cat's uplifting encouragement, Rey was being dragged down by a sinking feeling that she was setting all three of them up for a high-risk situation; one that could get all three of them in major trouble. As the time to hit the deck approached, Rey wanted to toss the drugs, toss her lunch, and toss her ferry ticket in the trash. The approaching departure was testing Rey's bravado. Pretty soon she was going to have to excuse herself to the bathroom and choke down twenty-three balloons of heroin. She already felt like hurling, and this certainly wasn't going to help.

Carlos told her that mules could ingest as many as 150 balloons, so Rey knew she could swallow twenty-three of them, but the bigger problem would be keeping them down. Carlos had clearly explained how to regurgitate the balloons on the mainland—Rey hoped they could wait that long. What if she packed the balloons too full? Would they get stuck coming up? Or worse, could they burst? And what about the replacement marijuana that was vacuum-sealed by her friend? Would that pass the test and mask the scent? With only an hour left to mull it over, Rey decided it was time to act.

At three thirty, as Cat paid their tab, Rey wandered off and did the deed. She was only able to swallow sixteen balloons before she started to feel scared about what they might do to her insides, a thought that almost brought some of them back up. With her gag reflux in full swing, Rey was forced to abandon the plan to swallow any more of them, stuffing the last five balloons in her jacket through a hole she haphazardly tore in the lining of her sleeve at the seam. They were wrapped up tight—it'd be impossible for the dogs to smell them, right?

She snorted the contents of the last two balloons up her nose in a desperate attempt to suppress her rising fear. It was quite a lot to take in each nostril, and her entire nose all the way up to her sinuses was completely numb when she was done.

Fuck it, Rey thought, feeling immediately braver. *Better to be wasted if I'm gonna get arrested.* The possibility of getting busted seemed real, but Rey wasn't going to back out now. She was feeling quite euphoric as the high kicked in, and nothing ever mattered when that was the leading sensation in her brain

The ferry began boarding at four for the five o'clock departure. The ladies had VIP tickets, which meant they could board first. Cat had them on the dock with plenty of time to spare, and plenty of time for Rey to break out in a sweat. As they walked up the plank toward the ship, Rey felt the balloons turn into butterflies in her stomach, but when they passed the federales and their machine guns with ease, she heaved a sigh of relief. There were no dogs to be seen anywhere.

The bunk room was barely big enough for two, let alone three people. It was difficult to turn around, and Cat could see it would be tough going to sleep. She figured the space would be small, considering the size of the ship and the bulge of the crowd during boarding. It took a while for folks to get settled, and a lot of people simply had seats.

"Least we have a place to lie down," Cat remarked, trying to make the most of it. Rey was visibly shaken, which seemed odd since she was the slimmest by far.

"What's the matter, Rey?" asked Sis.

"You look like you're in pain." Cat added.

Rey swallowed hard, coughing slightly. "Yeah, I think I need to lie down."

"Suit yourself," said Sis, "but that's the worst thing for me. I'm usually better on deck. The smell of the engine is making me queasy." Sis grimaced and popped a Dramamine. She motioned for Cat to accompany her outside and signed, *We'll check on her later.*

"Let's go watch the launch," Cat said out loud, "and let Rey get some rest."

"See you soon!" the sisters said in unison.

The first thing Cat did up on deck was check the weather for the next five days. It said there'd be smooth breezes and clear skies, with day temps in the eighties and nighttime lows nice and mild. "Looks like perfect weather," reported Cat.

Sissy held on to the railing, and Cat noticed her knuckles were looking a bit white. Her grip was tighter than Cat had ever seen Sis grip her bike. Cat assumed Sis was just nervous about the possibility of waves on the open ocean. Luckily for Sis's grip, the captain spoke over the loudspeaker to welcome them aboard and to relay the reassuring information that it would be smooth sailing all the way to Mazatlán. They were scheduled to arrive at ten the next morning. "I feel great," said Sis, beaming. "The Dramamine is already working."

"So you got lucky last night?" Cat asked quietly.

"I was *born* lucky," said Sis with a smile. "Last night was just another example of that."

Cat smiled back at her sister. They kicked back on the bench seat behind them and watched the sun go down, and Cat suddenly remembered the present she had in her pocket.

"Oh, I have a gift for you," she said, retrieving the forgotten box from her pocket. She cracked it open and spilled beans onto Sissy's palm. "Close your hand so they don't get away," Cat playfully warned. Sissy cupped one hand over the other.

"They look like seeds ... but they're wiggling," exclaimed Sis.

"They're Mexican jumping beans," announced Cat with glee. "It's you, me, and Rey!" she proclaimed.

Sissy peeked at the jiggling beans and grinned like a kid. She carefully opened her fingers to expose the collection. She and Cat watched as the beans bobbled.

"The bugs feed on the bean and eventually die inside it," Cat explained, recalling what she'd read on the Internet about the beans. "You'll know when the beans quit moving. I got them to remind you of our trip. Even when the bugs are done, you can keep their caskets as a memento. Consider it a sliver of entertainment for a limited time."

"Kind of like your last movie?" Sis quipped.

Cat put her arm around Sissy and said, "Or a token of my appreciation. Thanks for getting me back on the bike."

"My pleasure," said Sis. Cat waited for something more sentimental. Instead, Sis said, "I am *one* hungry hippo."

"May as well feed the need," said Cat, "since we're stuck in *this* seed for the evening."

They worked their way back to the resident side of the ship to ask Rey if she wanted to join them. The thrum of people and the hum of the engine drowned out all other sound, so they didn't hear Rey until they entered the room. She was curled up in the fetal position on the floor.

"Ahh," she groaned. "My stomach ..." Rey was writhing in pain. Her face was ashen and her forehead was shiny with sweat. Cat was stunned. She glanced at Sis to see that she was equally alarmed. There was barely room to squeeze around her. Sissy stepped over Rey's legs so Cat could enter the room and close the door. Facing Rey's backside, Sissy pointed at a smear of dark brown blood on the ground underneath her.

"You're bleeding!" Sissy knelt down to get a closer look at the crimson red leaking through the black thread of Rey's motocross pants. "Are you on your period?" Rey didn't answer, so Cat leaned in to look.

That's a lot *of blood*, signed Cat, her worry mounting.

Rey didn't say anything, and Cat assumed she would if she could.

"Are you pregnant?" Cat asked tentatively.

"What?" hissed Sissy, glaring at Cat.

"Ahhh," moaned Rey, "my stomach, it hurts...." Rey curled in more tightly around herself. The blood spread beneath her.

"You're bleeding a lot, Rey," said Cat, trying to sound calm. "Let's get you out of these pants so we can see."

The two knelt down to straighten Rey's legs. Cat squatted

next to Sissy and pulled at Rey's boots, then gently worked her pants down past her hips. The pants gave way and the sisters gawked. Blood gushed, dark and clotted. "Rey," Cat said knowingly, "it looks like you're having a miscarriage." Rey started to tremble and speak in rapid-fire Spanish. Sissy tried to decipher what she was saying and relay it to Cat through flipping while Cat stroked Rey's head.

She says she had sex a few months ago and hasn't had it since, flipped Sis. Cat shook her head, the memories of her own experience flooding her brain. "She doesn't want her family to know," said Sissy.

"My *father* will *kill* me," cried Rey, clinging to Cat's wrist.

"She doesn't want to call anyone ... no doctors, her family, *no* one." Sissy was doing her best to translate quickly as she shifted her position to get away from the steady stream oozing onto the floor. Sissy was beginning to look pale, too, so Cat told her to grab a bunch of towels from the staff.

"Tell them you need them for a sick kid or something." Cat fought to think straight. She was distracted by the flashbacks that crowded her throbbing head. "Hurry!" Cat ordered. "And don't say *anything* about blood." Sis slipped into the hall.

Rey was shivering violently. "I'm *pregnant?*" Rey looked like she might cry as she covered her mouth with one hand while fear shot out of her wide eyes. Then she buckled over again and moved her hand to her abdomen, shaking and seemingly resisting the urge to scream. Cat asked if she could sit up, but Rey jerkily signaled no. So Cat squatted down in the miniscule floor space closest to Rey's head.

Cat spoke as calmly and kindly as possible. "I had a miscarriage a few months ago. It'll probably go on all night. We'll clean you up as best as we can, but tomorrow we'll need to find a doctor in Mazatlán. To make sure it's all ... gone."

"Please!" Rey begged. "No one can know about this!" Rey sounded petrified, so Cat reassured her by stroking her hair and whispering, "It's okay ... you're okay," over and over.

That is what Cat had longed for during her loss, someone to swear she would be all right. Chris hadn't managed such kindness. Cat's pregnancy had also been unexpected, yet she welcomed it as the weeks went on and cried for days over her spontaneous abortion. Who knew what Rey really thought about this unplanned baby? Maybe it would be simpler— never having sensed its presence. Cat assumed this was the situation, since there was no way Rey could have been aware of her pregnant status and still ridden so wildly or gotten drunk so much. Tonight would provide a quick end to a complicated situation.

Hopefully, Rey would see it as a clean break. Cat *wished* she could see her own loss as a relief, since it had become an out for her engagement at least.

"Ahhhhhhhh," moaned Rey.

"You're okay, I'm here for you," Cat murmured. In the midst of witnessing Rey's terror and turmoil, mothering her was easier than Cat expected.

CHAPTER 19

LA PAZ TO MAZATLÁN

When the clock struck midnight, Rey was dozing fitfully, resting between contractions. The sisters had established she was about three months pregnant, based on her last period having been "sometime during the summer," and her last sexual encounter about the same time. Rey didn't offer much when it came to answers, but angrily exhaled "a crossing guard" when they asked who the father was. Sis and Cat tried to fill in the blanks as Rey lay resting.

"She had sex with a guy who helps kids cross the street?" Sis said.

"Or the border," Cat concluded. Both sisters raised their eyebrows.

Sissy grimaced at Rey's chaos. "Was yours this ... *gory?*" she asked.

"Yeah, it was bad, but I was too sad to see it like that. I had already pictured life as a mom, and it dissolved in one night."

"I thought the pregnancy was easy come, easy go, you know? I would have called, if I had known."

"I was really sad for the first few weeks, but then I began to see it as a reason to end things with Chris, and that sort of made up for the pain of losing the baby."

"So what are you going to do about that bling?" asked Sis, her ring finger raised like an expletive.

"I'm waiting for the right time to return it," admitted Cat.

"Give it to me!" Sis conceded. "That shit would fund my next five seasons."

"Then you'd have to marry him." Cat smacked Sis's knee.

"That rug rat couldn't handle me. I'd insist on a honeymoon like this," said Sis.

"This is *hell*," Rey gasped as she shivered under the poncho that Cat had retrieved from her bike. They had each brought a single saddlebag up as luggage, but they had used up all the available linen in an attempt to clean up. So Cat snuck down to the belly of the ship and begged the parking guard for temporary access to her vehicle. She told him she needed some "feminine toiletries" from her saddlebag. As Rey awakened, the sisters filled her in on their plan.

"Just pretend you're really, really seasick," Sis suggested. It seemed like a reasonable idea after Rey's nausea all week. Morning sickness explained it, but they would blame tonight's drama on a Dramamine failure instead.

"If anybody asks, you spent the whole cruise puking. We'll wrap all this crap in the poncho—and toss it on dry land." The blanket that had doubled as a sleeping bag was their first line of defense in this cover-up. It would be tossed along with Cat's long johns, riding socks, two cashmere sweaters, and three of Sissy's shirts, all of which had been used and abused in the name of cleanup. Each could be replaced in the States.

Hard-hearted Rey seemed shattered by her situation. She cried off and on throughout the night and spoke with surprising honesty as Cat sat alongside her and listened without expressing judgment. Rey lamented her mistakes without much explanation: spontaneous and unprotected sex with a crossing guard, overlooking her missed period, disappointing her family, these were the faults she spoke about openly.

In an attempt to ease Rey's guilt, Cat focused on the fact that miscarriage often happens when there's a weakness with the fetus. Rey nodded meekly in response to Cat's kind words.

In the predawn hours, Cat escaped their crowded quarters onto the empty deck. As the crescent moon glowed on the horizon, she sucked in the ocean air. It had been a very long night. Rey was holding back, fighting the urges her body had to expel. Cat feared that the worst was yet to come and worried Rey would attempt to exit the ship walking tall but slip into labor pain and fall. There was also the matter of trying to unload a bundle of bloody clothes on the mainland. Blood was the kind of stain that got attention from anyone with a heartbeat.

I may have to pay for another emergency surgery, but at least she'll be safe. Suddenly, a buzz in her pocket told her to check a text. Pulling out her phone, Cat read, *Paging Dr. Lang!*

I may play a doctor someday, but I am not cut out for this shit, Cat wrote jokingly.

HELP!! Sis texted. That was the end of Cat's playful response. She spun around and starting jogging.

The screams became audible before Cat had rounded the last corner of the corridor where their hideaway lay. She barreled through the door, brainstorming ways to muffle the sound that would soon draw a crowd. Cat stared helplessly at a panic-stricken Sis, who was trying to keep Rey from thrashing in a fresh pool of blood. Sissy was green, and Rey looked gray as she haphazardly swiped drool from her mouth.

Cat knelt beside Sissy. She offered Rey her last pair of clean wool socks to chomp down on. "I really think we need to find a doctor," said Sis with a tone of fear that was out of character for someone who had raced with serious injuries innumerable times.

"No doctors!" blurted Rey, whose resistance seemed bigger than a girl who was simply worried about her father's reaction.

Cat knew in times like this, a woman's emotion didn't always make sense, and she was determined to go along with whatever Rey needed. "Listen, you're going to okay, Rey. This isn't an emergency—we've come this far, and I know you don't want to worry your dad. So keep cool and let's just get off this ship." Cat glared at Sis as a means to say *bear with me*. A knock at the door silenced all of them. The women froze. Cat held her breath.

"UhhhHHHH!" Rey exploded as another gush of blood worked its way out of her.

"*¿Hola? Cómo estás?*" A man on the other side of the door started to fiddle with the locked handle, and the girls huddled together as they heard the jiggling of keys. "*¿Hola? Eres bien allí?*"

"*¡Sí!*" said Sissy in Spanish. Cat put one hand on her hip trying to block as much of the inside scene as she could before she cracked the door a bit and asked the man for a bunch of towels, explaining that her sister was sick and too embarrassed to let him see her like this. The man nodded suspiciously, then backed away slowly, pausing as Rey emitted a low moan. Cat cut her off with a boisterous, "*Gracious*, Señor," hollering down the hallway at the man who was on his way to grab towels.

"Rey," Cat whispered forcefully now. "You got to keep it together—if you want us to keep your secret, then *shut the hell up!*" She felt bad for being mean, but it was a petty threat compared to the risk of disclosure to the obviously wary ferry guy. The man returned moments later with a stack of fresh towels. "*Gracias,*" said Cat.

For a moment, she thought she caught a look of recognition in the man's eyes, so she shut the door before he had a chance to say, "Are you that girl from *Darkstar*?"

When the ship finally docked an hour and a half later, the turmoil had subsided. The miscarriage was over, and Rey seemed comfortable again. She was wearing a very strange wardrobe, but she was clean and calm now. Sissy had the bundle of wet, red rags tucked under her arm. She was less likely than Cat to draw attention from the crowd as she kept her eyes peeled for an extra-large trash bin.

Cat tried to impart upon the crowd that Rey was in need of sympathy, telling her repeatedly, "I've never *seen someone so seasick*!" The elevated tone was meant to bring attention to Rey and away from Sissy's bloody bundle. All the while Cat kept her arm interwoven with Rey's for support. She was undeniably exhausted, and her legs looked like they might give out on her.

Doing their best impression of intrepid tourists, they posed as friends who were both relieved and excited about their arrival in Mazatlán. The crowd pushed against them as a bottleneck formed at the exits. Cat was praying that they'd find a place to dump the evidence before they got within visual notice of the federales that lined the dock at the bottom of the ramp. Cat had noticed their presence while boarding and found their heavy artillery foreboding.

Rey was praying quietly and in such a way that made Cat think she was about to pass out. "Oh, God," she said after a sigh, and Rey's eyes filled with tears. Cat stopped for a second to ask if she needed to sit. Rey bit down on her lower lip, and her head drifted back like she might fall that way.

Instant sweat formed on Rey's head, and Cat grabbed her arm and whispered, "It's the sweater." The cover-up was cashmere and hung halfway down Rey's thighs, but the only thing they had that was clean and long enough to hide Rey's blood-stained midsection.

As they neared the open air on the ship's port side, Sis squeezed her bundle tight to minimize its visibility. Cat spoke inaudibly in hushed desperation, trying to encourage Rey to keep going. They made it through the exit door and past a row of ship employees only to spot a group of federales who were toting AK-47 machine guns. The police presence was heavier than what they had seen on the west coast.

Cat's left leg felt wobbly as she flashed a smile, trying to cover for her own nervous disposition. As Sis moved ahead, Cat shortened her stride and tried to distract the uniformed men from Sis's scheme. Sissy approached an open trash bin and turned to face Cat and Rey, pretending to ask them a question so she could back up to the bin and block the view of the disposal process. Sis laughed gaily and tossed the package like it was no big deal. Cat caught Rey as she stumbled, paying close attention to the men in fatigues.

"My baby," whispered Rey, stumbling a bit. Cat fought to keep her upright, but Rey fell to her knees reeling. Rey bowed her head and paused on all fours, seemingly distraught at the loss of her fetus. Then in a flash, she collapsed and threw up everything she had to lose.

Sis moved around the bin to rush over and help Rey stand up again. She bent over, reaching under Rey's shoulders and then paused to see what it was that Cat was looking at. Lying at Cat's feet in the morning heat, a cluster of white balloons rested in a puddle of bile. The cops moved quickly, looking ready to help an innocent civilian, but their attitudes changed when they spotted the crime sitting on the ground in front of them. The Lang sisters had little time to react to what was actually happening, as the federales lifted Rey from where she lay, then wrestled handcuffs on all three of them, brusquely rushing the women to a nearby SUV. The plastic cuffs had been wrapped around their wrists with zero regard for the heavy jackets the sisters were wearing. Breathing heavily from the insane amount of heat inside the cop car, Sissy tried to muster a decent translation for "My sister and I are innocent!"

Despite her frantic plea, all three of them were suspect according to the driver who radioed a call about the bust. Cat was overwhelmed, but her anger was edged out by astonishment. Sissy was livid. She glared at Rey. They had been told by the cops in no uncertain terms not to talk, but Sis flipped a message to Cat by turning her back to expose her tie-wrapped hands. Signing blindly she flipped, *Where's your cell phone?*

"In my pocket," whispered Cat.

"*¡Callado!*" an officer commanded from the front seat. Cat shrunk back like she'd been wounded. Whatever he said meant *no talking*. Considering her limited language skills, Cat was terrified of being separated from Sis and vowed to comply with whatever the federales wanted, as long as she understood their directions. She hoped her captors had a better grip on their second language than she did.

CHAPTER 20

GUILT BY ASSOCIATION

During their intake at the detention center, the ladies were whisked away in separate directions, and Cat assumed Rey would be taken to a hospital. The sisters were brought into a room that was segregated from the primarily male scene so female officers could search them. Cat might have balked at the humiliation of stripping if she hadn't spent so much time modeling. After getting dressed, the sisters were placed in a cell together. Cat assumed she and Sis would be exonerated soon, but her hopes were dashed when the sisters were called in separately for questioning. The preliminary interviewer spoke excellent English as he asked about the events of the preceding week. Cat figured the clean floor tiles, kind vibe, and respect she detected from the officer was a sign she would be fine if she cooperated. She recalled as much

187

of the truth as she could, focusing on the assault at the motel and the disappearance of Rey's jacket.

"We all wanted to leave the scene, but Rey said we shouldn't report it," Cat conceded. "Seemed strange to me, but the town was so wild I chalked it up to bad luck for the out-of-towners."

"How did a woman of such … refinement wind up in El Rosario?" Cat realized her squeaky-clean image would be rewritten once Hollywood got word of this situation.

"I'm doing prep work for a film," she said "Speaking of which, I really need to call my agent."

The seemingly kindhearted cop stopped to jot down something when she made that request. His demeanor changed. "I am not at liberty to assist you. I'd advise you to keep your requests at bay for the rest of the day. We do not take kindly to folks who bankroll our drug problem down here." The man stood up to leave, and Cat interjected.

"I didn't know about the drugs!"

"That's what they call a cliché in storytelling." This remark came from somewhere outside the room and fed through an intercom attached to the wall. Cat recognized the voice vaguely, and her instinct was confirmed as a second man waltzed through the door. Cat's eyes widened at sight of the man she thought was the owner of the Horny Toad bar in El Rosario. She sat looking up at Paolo Cruz in uniform. The medals on his chest and the manner with which Cat's interviewer stood at attention when he entered the room indicated that this chisel-cheeked Romeo was a high-ranking government official.

"What are *you* doing here?" Cat asked in complete confusion.

"Hola, Ms. Lang." The commander walked slowly in a 360-degree circle around her. "You're even more exquisite when you're caged." Cat's breath caught. Don Juan was still appealing, despite the fright he aroused in her. His silver beard shone under the incandescent light of the single bulb above them, and Cat had no doubt this fox was her foe.

"I'll be friendlier when I'm free," cooed Cat, trying whatever she could think of to get on his good side.

"I owe you an apology," the commander said. "I'm sorry for *any* pain we caused you or your sister. We were trying to save Ms. Abella from herself and catch the cartel in an act of revenge." Cat fought to place the puzzle pieces as she listened to his story: "It was not my intention to hurt you."

"*You* were the one in the motel room?"

The man admired his manicured hands. "I always outsource my dirty work."

"You *had* us *attacked*?"

"Ms. Abella was the target. The two of you were—how do you say—collateral damage."

Cat couldn't believe what she was hearing. The law had been on her side until now. She opened her mouth to speak, but could not conceive her next question. Taking her confusion as his cue, Commander Cruz continued.

"Reyna is a guinea pig. We removed the drugs so she'd run, helping us reel in the bigger fish. We were right on track to trail her safely. But then she refinanced a replacement cache—or shall I say *you* did."

"I had nothing to do with it!" Cat cried. Her defense was denied as the man threw down the traveler's check Cat had signed for two thousand dollars. They had recovered it from the Best Western in Loreto. Apparently, it was suspicious even by Mexican standards for a black-and-blue-eyed Latina to wire a huge amount of money from an American movie star. For all the shock of Rey's behavior the last two days, Cat was most repulsed by the exploitation of her dad's handicap. She shook her head. Rey had lied time and time again to them. Cat couldn't wait to confront Sissy about her idiotic decision to invite a lunatic on this trip.

"Can I make a phone call?" asked Cat. She yearned to speak to Chris.

"American rules do not apply here." He stood up to leave. "Your sister may be your only ticket out of here. I hope she has change for the pay phone."

However, Sissy was not as informed when they reunited in their cell, so Cat filled her in as quickly as possible. "Why the *hell* did you *bring* her?" Cat demanded.

"She said she knew the best routes," explained Sis. "And I thought a girl like Rey would toughen you up."

"Oh yeah," said Cat, "I'm feeling real tough now." She scowled as she looked around their sorry cell.

Cat's disgust grew as they waited for news. It was all she could do not to knock Sis down and pull at her crimson highlights. Cat was furious that Sis had brought Rey along for *levity* on this otherwise idyllic reunion. But she couldn't lay all the blame on Sis's stupidity when she remembered her own generosity, which now implicated her in an illegal drug trade.

"I'm sorry we're both so naïve," Cat admitted eventually, trying to unify their accidental plight. Hair pulling wouldn't solve the problem. The last thing they needed was dissension between them.

Their loyalty and Cat's royalty gave the sisters an edge, but Rey knew she had nothing to lean on in the face of isolation. The little esteem she had left waned in light of the indignity she was served at the far end of the hallway. Battered and bruised from her interrogation and severely depleted from the loss of blood the night before, she still grasped what was happening. The man from El Rosario was not the proprietor of the bar or the town. He was President Calderon's chief drug officer. Commander Cruz had recently been threatened when a helicopter he was supposed to fly in was downed by members of a drug gang. Everyone on board perished, including Mexico City's police chief, who worked directly below him. Commander Cruz made the news with his commitment to avenge the death of his friends. He was aggressively pursuing the offenders and directed his anger at Rey.

"I tried to *help* you!" he growled. Cruz's right-hand man slapped Rey's face. The commander leaned both hands on the table and got in Rey's space. "We took the drugs to set them off. We wanted to catch your boss when he came to assassinate you. But you, you stupid little punta, went ahead and replaced them!" The cohort slapped Rey again, and her entire head whipped back.

"Tell me what you know about Pedro Escondido!" the commander roared.

Rey's cheek stung, but her mind was retreating. She drifted in and out of listening, praying that all this pain would go away. Knowing that an X-ray would be used on her soon to detect any remaining balloons, she had tried to regurgitate the last of them during the short time she was privately confined to her cell, to no avail. If she could get her hands on the goods, a megasnort would give her immediate relief. Seemed like a reasonable option to avoid further questions. As Rey returned to reality, Commander Cruz awaited her response. He grabbed her head as it rolled back on her neck.

"Give me names!" he demanded.

She tried hard to focus on the task at hand. Rey thought about who she could sacrifice, when suddenly the image of a newborn, covered in blood and bleating loudly in a trash can, flooded her brain like a hurricane, drowning her in vile self-hatred. She could not destroy any more lives today. Her lips were sealed, or so she thought.

Out of the blue, Rey hurled involuntarily. One balloon landed in her lap, the other in her hand, and she stared at them, yearning for escape. Commander Cruz gave a look to his goon, who promptly confiscated the evidence. Then the penguin, as Rey began to see him, lowered his pointy beak and glared at the puke on his shoe. "You are disgusting," the Commander hissed. He ordered Rey to be returned to her cell. She collapsed as the deputies dragged her facedown by the armpits, so the tips of her toes left long dark marks along the cracked cement floor of the hallway.

⚜

It was dark by the time Cat awoke from an unplanned nap. The glare of the fluorescent lighting gave her a headache, or maybe it was the harsh realization that the nightmare she'd been having was real.

"What time is it?" she asked Sis. Sissy was slumped on the floor with her back against the cot that Cat lay on. Cat nudged Sis gently with the toe of her boot, leaving a dusty imprint on her shoulder. It was a sad reminder of the dirt bike ride that was over.

Sissy startled, then popped up. She breathed a sigh of relief as Cat came into focus, only to yell *"Fuck!"* as she bolted up and put a palm against her ear.

"What's the matter?" Cat asked.

"My processor's beeping, the batteries are done." Cat glanced at the door and wondered if anyone out there would be willing to grab a pack from the confiscated saddlebag that held the key to Sissy's hearing. A little *fan*fare would be welcome right now.

"How long will they last?" asked Cat. She stood and looked through the steel-barred window in a fruitless search for someone who might be willing to help them.

"That's it," Sis said, dejectedly removing her earbud. Cat was about to holler for some help when an announcement blared across the sound system: *"¡Apague las luces!"*

With that, the room went black—not a hint of ambient light. "Sissy?" But her sister didn't respond.

Cat managed to relax again sometime after midnight. She lay down behind Sis on the cold hard cot and hugged her body for comfort. The scene was too surreal for sleep.

Miss American darling was in a Mexican jail, with no money, no food, and charges that could end her career.

Then something amazing occurred to her: *I didn't pick up the script!* Cat never missed an assignment, no matter how much a potential role upset her. Slick Rick was probably going nuts after her missed check-in at the Marriott yesterday. She imagined her phone was blowing up by now, and she couldn't wait to get that kiss ass on the phone again. Lucky for Cat, there would be no sassy retort from Sis about Rick's annoying rhetoric. Without light or sound, Cat's most opinionated critic was officially incommunicado.

CHAPTER 21

MEXICO CITY

C at stirred at the jiggle and clank of heavy keys unlocking the door. The guard stared down at them on the cot, sneered, and said something Cat could not understand. She straightened her legs on the way to waking, and the left one seized from inaction. The hamstring cramp made her jerk, and she bumped Sissy's bum in the process.

Sis jumped to a seated position as the guard repeated what he'd said, but lip-reading in Spanish was a whole other ball game. Since neither woman understood what he was saying, they relied on his gesture, which brought them to their feet. They continued to follow his signs out to the long hallway, where Rey was being wheeled on a gurney by two men.

Is she dead? flipped Cat.

She'd be stiff—and hidden, Sissy signed back. Cat breathed a sigh of relief as the men squeezed through the narrow pass, and the back of Rey's hand brushed her own. It was dirty, but warm. As soon as Rey was ahead of them, the officer commanded them to follow her.

Where do you think they're taking us? flipped Sis.

I suppose the airport is out of the question?

The guard pointed and motioned for them to walk. Moments later, they got their jackets back, right before they were ushered out to the police van. The sisters were allowed to sit freely, without restraints, an indication in Cat's mind that they were close to being released. The first thing Cat went for was her cell phone, but it had been removed from her jacket. Rey didn't require restriction either. She lay unconscious on the metal floor of the truck, her body shrunken, eyes gaunt, lips blackened. Rey looked horrific, but she was better off in a blackout. Cat prayed that Rey would just stay down, so Sis didn't knock her out.

After ten minutes of bouncing on the rough road, Rey was roused. She opened her eyes and gazed mutely, squinting at the two women sitting above her. She didn't move or speak for a time. Her mouth looked really bruised, and Cat wondered if she could talk at all. Finally, licking her crusty lips, Rey managed with raspy breath: "Do you know where we're going?"

Sis could not lip-read with all Rey's swelling, so Cat spoke for both of them. "We were hoping you could fill us in."

Rey pulled herself to an uncomfortable seated position. "We're probably going before a judge," she explained.

"You better tell him the truth," said Cat, fuming.

"I will, but they claim to have proof against you, too."

Cat flipped this info to Sis, who shouted at Rey, *"You'd better get Cat off the hook!"*

"You'll both get cut loose by the truth," offered Rey.

"What'd you say?" asked Sis, who still couldn't hear without her ears turned on.

"I'm the only one headed to prison." Rey made a move to lift herself onto the bench next to them.

"I can't *hear* you!" hollered Sis, losing patience.

"Her hearing aid died, so speak clearly," Cat said. "And stay down where you belong. No telling what Sis will do if you come near us."

There was a pause as Cat gauged the situation, suppressing the temptation to scratch out Rey's eyeballs, but Sis couldn't contain her surge of anger. "I hope you *rot* in that prison. If I *ever see you* on the street again, I'm going to *run. You. Down.*"

When the relatively short ride ended, Rey muttered, "It's good to have friends in low places." Flabbergasted by Rey's outrageous flippancy, Cat stared at the fiend that sat before her. Then the guard yanked open the door and shuffled all three of them into the high court of Mazatlán.

Rey faced her reckoning first. The judge, who spoke English, said she was guilty until proven innocent, for the transportation of class A drugs across Mexico. He said Rey would be subject to a maximum sentence of six months in prison. The final verdict would be decided at the trial, and the trial date would be set at the end of the hearing.

Next, the judge sentenced Sissy to time served for

"criminal association." Cat politely informed the court that Sis was deaf and could not understand the proceedings. Given permission to intervene, Cat signed a translation for Sis, adding her own interpretation at the end: *We'll be out of here soon!*

Her optimism faded as the judge referred to Cat as an "accomplice," and her face fell as he listed "La Pila Penitentiary" as the place she and Rey would stay until sentencing.

"I'm innocent!" Cat cried as the cuffs snapped onto her wrists again.

Sis shot a look of shock at Cat before turning to face the judge. "Do you know who this is?" Sis flexed an open palm in the direction of Cat's famous face.

"Yes," the judge confirmed. "So does the photographer who followed you. Thanks to his telephoto lens, we have evidence of Ms. Lang's link to an extremely dangerous drug gang." No longer concerned with Sis's ability to read lips, the judge returned his eyes to the page before him. "Bail is set at three million dollars," he announced coolly. "The trial will be set for September."

But that was *last* month, Cat thought confusedly. As a deputy led her to the door, Cat mouthed one last message to Sis: "Call Chris!" That was all she got out before she was removed from the room.

⚶

The transport arrived after dark, and Cat was nearly comatose with hunger. The glaring lights of the prison made Cat squint to establish her surroundings. Glancing up at the looming cement wall, she read Reclusorio Del Norte. There was no identifying label that mentioned La Pila or San Luis Potosi. Cat's mind began to spin, and the only person she could turn to for reassurance was enemy number one.

"I thought we were going to a place called La Pila," Cat said nervously to Rey. Cat's suspicion had been piqued when the eight-hour drive Rey said to expect was extended by nearly two full hours.

"We're definitely not at La Pila," Rey confirmed. She had noted signs along the way that indicated they were entering Mexico City, which was much further south than the town of Potosi. Rey decided to ask the guard what was happening. The conversation lasted several minutes as Rey gathered facts from the one guard who was willing to answer her. After what seemed like an argument, Rey confirmed that the women had been rerouted to one of the most notoriously corrupt prisons south of the border.

"There was a riot at La Pila today. Thirteen prisoners died. So they brought us to Mexico City."

"Shit! How am I supposed to tell Sis about the switch?"

"Just go with the flow tonight," Rey insisted. "And tell them you can afford the best of whatever they have to offer. We'll figure out how to contact Sis tomorrow. Until then, don't make waves." With that warning, Rey was whisked away.

Cat didn't know what to make of the new arrangement, but dutifully remained as polite as possible during processing. The fact that she was left to casually stand around outside, without cuffs, made it clear that a famous face promised certain advantages. The guards chatted nonchalantly as Cat awaited her "check-in." Gazing up at the whitewashed walls against the purple sky, there was nothing much to note about the sterile exterior. It seemed oddly serene. The silence of the desert that loomed beyond the fortress made Cat think she might actually get a good round of sleep tonight.

As the guards continued their Spanish conversation, Cat focused on the moment and tried to consume as much fresh air as she could before the next step began. Trying anything to calm her mind, Cat focused on the incessant buzz of nocturnal bugs. I *am* fine, she affirmed as she welcomed the crickets' sonata into her brain. As Cat got lost in peaceful thoughts, a nursery rhyme came to mind:

```
Rock-a-bye Sissy, inside your crib,
When the day breaks, you'll be free to skip,
But until then, you must settle down
Or Mom will blow up, and she wears the crown.
```

If Sis could thrive in the confines of their childhood homestead, Cat could endure a night in prison. She listened to the grasshoppers again and was brought back to a conversation she'd had on Sissy's twentieth birthday, a week after the implant operation.

"What's the coolest thing you've heard so far?" Cat had asked over the phone.

"The sound of the flame on the stove," Sis admitted. Cat had been amazed at the subtlety of her observation.

Focus on the little things, she reminded herself now, adopting some of Sis's pluck for good luck. When the officer indicated it was her turn to enter the building, Cat nodded at his Spanish mumbo jumbo and marched strong and tall into the penitentiary.

22

RECLUSARIO NORTE

Wen daylight came, Cat sat hunched in the corner of her cot, her eyes on the floor as she fought to keep the walls from closing in. The eight-by-ten-foot space had crushed her resolve. Any strength she walked in with was overshadowed by insomnia, fear, and depression.

She and Rey had been brought to a coed prison; a fact that had only come to light when the guard brought her to her cell last night, and she made brief eye contact with the man in the cell next to hers. His expression showed his recognition of her, at least she hoped that was what made her eyes go wide with excitement. The only thing that gave her peace in the face of this crazy and possibly dangerous development was the fact that everyone in this place was allowed to interact during the day, so Cat assumed that rape was not high on the list of things she would have to worry about. She figured she could choose to stay within the confines of her private cell and endure this hell alone for however long it took Sis to get someone in LA to rescue her.

When the guard locked the gate last night, ensuring both security and seclusion, Cat prayed she would be okay inside one of these cells for the elite inmates. "You'll be safe," the warden promised as he received her cash in exchange for reassurances. The five hundred bucks that was tucked in her sock bought a weeklong slot in D block, a segregated wing for those who could afford it.

The cell next to hers was outfitted with a television, apparent from the applause blaring through its bars. The sound of the canned laughter from a sitcom filled the hall until the Spanish command for "Lights out!" rang out, ending the familiar sound. It was the one time Cat missed Chris's habit of watching TV into the wee hours of the day. Craving some connection in the dark, she tentatively uttered "Hello," but received no response. Even so, she took comfort knowing that *Seinfeld* was available in Mexico. Cat had had a bit part in one episode. *Least I can still earn residuals,* she thought, accepting the end of her acting career.

Losing her income wasn't the fright that kept her up all night—it was losing her life at the end of a knife. Imagination was her enemy, projecting any number of violent ends to this vacation. Reality intruded when the Mexican guard appeared at first light, rapping on the bars and placing a rusty cup in her meal slot. She graciously accepted the breakfast until she noticed lumps that resembled wet dirt.

The guard didn't like her look of disgust and reprimanded her prima donna behavior.

"Do you want to wind up on the top floor?" he threatened. "The only way down from there is to soar—right over the railing." He laughed maniacally.

"I'm allergic to gluten," Cat lied, feeling spooked.

"You want green eggs and ham?" he asked with a snort. "Doctor Seuss *es para las locas.*"

When he offered her a second cup filled with watery gray milk, his look said, *Take it!*

The scent of curdled dairy aside, Cat clanked the cups together to express *Cheers* and *Thank you,* setting them down as soon as the guard left. She could not bring herself to taste it. The absence of appetite was a relief. Dinner last night had been a similar mystery substance, but she had choked it down, not having eaten in two days. Now the fist in Cat's stomach promised to punch the slop up if she swallowed a single glob of it. She slunk back to the cot to conserve energy.

To her right, a tattered trunk served as a nightstand for her personal items. Burberry-scented lotion was an absurd notion now. She wished she had Kleenex instead, to catch the watery snot that had already spotted her jumpsuit. Wiping her nose with her sleeve, Cat noticed that the bulk of the XL coverall, required by her long limbs, made her look like a clown in a not-so-fun house. She pulled up one pant leg to scratch her unshaven shin and noticed the effect of dehydration. Those crocodile lines had no time for expensive lotion; a tongue-moistened thumb and a hemline tug would have to do the job.

Next to the trunk sat the toilet, a battered bucket that said *Hold it*. Opposite that sat a desk and a chair, also bolted to the floor. Three concrete walls connected by iron bars faced the narrow hallway and provided full exposure. Terrified to pee in plain view, Cat held it in.

As morning wore on, the hall outside her cell began to hum with activity. Prisoners in varied states of slovenliness cruised past Cat's cage. Gawking at the newbie inspired an air of festivity, increasing Cat's anxiety. This was not the kind of popularity she wanted.

"Hey!" announced Rey, standing just outside Cat's cell. The sound of a familiar voice pierced the haze of Cat's misery, but the sight of Rey left Cat speechless. "Cat got your tongue?" Rey joked as if nothing bad had happened.

"Funny," said Cat flatly, imagining a bulls-eye on Rey's head.

"Nice place," continued Rey, "looks like they take your fame seriously."

"It'll suffice."

"I bought you a taco," offered Rey. "It's better than the mush they brought. I got it from a cart in the courtyard."

Cat wanted nothing from Rey. "I'm not hungry."

"You'll be fine dining soon—Sis will be here by noon." Rey sounded eager to make amends.

"Only if she can find me," Cat argued. "She's on her way to La Pila. There's no way she could know about the switch."

"She's a smart bitch."

Cat let that slide. She was itching to kick Rey's hide, but thought she might need her help in here.

"Do you have something important to say?"

"I'm on the move to make some friends—preparing for an extended stay. You want to check the place out with me?" Rey pushed Cat's gate as an invite.

"I need to wait for Sis." Cat pushed back with more force than intended. The door banged against the frame with a clang.

"Bring your wallet if you leave. We're surrounded by thieves, and you'll need a couple of bucks for the food carts." Rey looked at Cat apologetically.

Cat wanted to add bruises to Rey's cheeks, but the prim and proper pageant girl in her just stared at the floor until Rey retreated down the corridor.

After Rey left, Cat sat for an hour with her arms around her knees, thinking about "The Biz" and the loss of her place in it. She wondered if damning pictures and the truth of her whereabouts would be on *TMZ* by this evening. For the last week, she had embraced her misgivings about Hollywood and all that came with it. Now that she was trapped in an even worse reality, Cat missed Los Angeles. She had felt a different kind of trapped in Beverly Hills, but in the face of this incarceration, Chris and Slick Rick looked like the best friends a girl could want. Cat could not wait to tell them how she realized that.

"Hey," the neighbor guy next door interrupted. He was a shaggy-haired, white guy—definitely not a Mexican. He was blond and looked well fed, so Cat assumed he was American. "Are you that chick from the movies?" he asked, looking intrigued.

"Excuse me?"

"I'm about to grab a bite to eat, you need anything?"

Cat had the sense that he was trying to butter her up. She smirked. "I'm all set."

"Okay, well, my name's Billy Ray. Now that we're acquainted, can I ask you to keep an eye on my stuff while I'm gone? My last neighbor stole my DVDs—guess he couldn't afford his own collection. You can watch whatever you want on my flat screen."

"Um ... I guess I could. Am I allowed to hang out there?"

"You can wander wherever you want during the day. The guard will keep an eye on you."

Without words, he pointed behind her at a watchman who stood to the right of her enclosure. The guard gripped his gun but didn't join the discussion.

"You look familiar," the neighbor admitted. "I'm from Canada—we only get lame flicks. But you do look like the girl from *Darkstar*."

"Guilty as charged." Cat put her hands up.

"Don't say that in here." He winked.

After a brief exchange, Cat agreed to watch a movie at his place while the Canadian went on a walkabout. He assured her she could breathe easy in block D, before he left her marooned on his atoll.

⚜

At half past one, Cat gripped Billy Ray's bars as she heard the all too familiar twang of Sis announcing her arrival.

"Have no *fear*, Sis is here!" Sis, who was being escorted by a guard, dashed ahead of him as Cat pushed her face against the bars.

Cat beamed as she rushed through the cell gate to embrace her sister. "You're a sight for sore eyes." Cat half-laughed from nerves.

"And this place is a sight to behold," Sis observed, waving at the surroundings. "I would have been here sooner but ..."

"Yeah, sorry about the mix-up," Cat interjected. She pushed on her unlocked gate and ushered Sis in.

Sis raised her brows at the open-door policy. "This place is pretty relaxed."

"Did you talk to Chris?" Cat got down to business.

"I left to come here at 3:00 a.m. and called him before that. He wasn't pleased, and that was *before* I got into the whole prison situation."

"Is he freaking out?" Cat sounded worried.

"He's freaking self-centered, if you ask me."

"Did he book a flight?"

"He said it was 'bad timing.'"

"He's not coming?"

"He wouldn't commit." Sis rolled her eyes at this tidbit.

"I don't believe you." Cat shook her head in denial. "Did you bring my phone?"

Sis nodded and flipped, *They didn't even* frisk *me*.

"Give me," Cat demanded. She retreated to the bed and dialed. Chris answered right away. "Hey," she purred. "You heard about our snafu?" Sis looked pissed about the de-emphasis. "I'm sorry, hon—I love you, too," Cat oozed. "Guess I'll be home sooner than expected." There was a long pause as she listened on the other end. "Okay, I'll call Rick, I'm sure he has time to deal with it." She rolled her eyes as Sis flipped him the bird. "But—" she persisted before a long pause. "Okay, I'll keep you posted. I hope to be on the first plane tomorrow." She paused again as Chris cut in. "Forget the rest of the ride—I'm ready for the quiet life." She laughed uncomfortably. "You better include a stunt woman in your script's budget."

Sis scoffed at Cat's wimpy declaration.

"Okay, thanks. I love you so much. I'll call you when I have better news." Cat hung up and speed dialed Rick. "He thinks Rick is the better connected for this," she whispered, waiting for her agent to answer.

"Chris needs a stuntman, too."

"Shoot!" Cat barked when the call when straight to voicemail. "Hey, Rick," she cooed sweetly. "Can you call me? I'm in a little trouble and need to speak with you." Cat's chipper tone clashed with the facts, and Sis looked appalled by her bullshit.

"Who's protecting who?" asked Sis. "You need immediate assistance—it's okay to admit this is urgent!"

"Don't yell at me!" Cat burst. "I need to be calm when I talk to Rick so he doesn't flip out on me."

"This is an emergency! They say they have proof against you. We need to get the authorities involved. I realize your connections are the best bet—but get them to move, quit trying to schmooze them!"

"I cannot *wait* to get home." Cat dramatically started tossing her toiletries into her saddlebag as if she had somewhere to go. "At least life in LA is safe—this is *way* too wild for me."

Billy Ray, who had returned during their argument,

turned up the volume of the local news. Almost immediately, Sis caught a news flash in Spanish and pushed past the bars to catch the report from his fort. An image from *Darkstar* splashed across the screen, followed by her sister's mug shot.

As Cat snuck in to investigate, Sis paraphrased in English. "Catrina Lang," Sis translated, "arrested on drug charges." The newscaster used the term *contraband*, and a close-up appeared of Rey grabbing a vacuum-sealed package from Carlos the cowboy. The Sangre de Cristos were in the background. The second picture was dim and out of focus, but it showed Cat holding a similar item. Flat and green, it looked suspicious. Sis squinted to decipher the picture, but Cat knew exactly what it was.

"It's a cactus paddle," said Cat.

"Well, it looks like they caught you red-handed," said Billy matter-of-factly. "It's not cool to have evidence—true or skewed. I got screwed by some pretty weak proof, and I'm serving an eight-year sentence." The ladies flinched at his report: "Thought I'd be out in a month or two ... sixty-six weeks ago."

"But she's innocent." Sis turned to face an ashen Cat, setting a hand on her shoulder. "We'll get you out by the end of tomorrow—I promise." Cat nodded, unsure.

"I'll do whatever it takes," Sissy swore.

"Just buy her a get-outta-jail card," the guy suggested.

"If it's so easy, why haven't you done that?" asked Cat.

"I got busted with ten cases of oxy—bought in Mexico, shipped from Canada, and sold to America. Three countries want to piss down my neck, so I can't check out yet. I got nowhere to go, and life in El Norte is better than a hideout in the desert."

"Let's go for a walk and talk alone," urged Sis.

"There's no such thing as a legitimate release," Billy continued. "It's a lawless place; money writes the rules. But I know who to talk to," he added arrogantly. "I'll get you connected immediately—for a fee. Come with me."

CHAPTER 23

DEAL WITH THE DEVIL

The sisters reluctantly followed the Canadian as Sis asked this virtual stranger his name.

"Sorry," said Cat. "It's Billy Ray."

"Like Eddie Murphy, in *Trading Places*," he added randomly.

He better not pretend to be blind for a dime, flipped Sis.

Billy Ray? Nice name, Cat flipped to Sis sarcastically.

"Okay, Billy," Cat said. "I'll go along with your game, but don't take my fame or my money for granted." Cat did her best impression of a badass. "You better not *cross* me," she threatened. "I've got connections stateside."

Sis smiled at Cat for showing some cojones. As the trio ventured into the belly of the abyss, the sisters were shocked by what a metropolis it was. Prisoners on the first two floors were milling around their zones freely, and the courtyard was filled with both men and women engaged in various open exchanges. Bookies, barbers, and baristas were earning a dime off dice, lice, and iced coffee.

Sounds of madness emanated from floors three and four, testimony to the bleak conditions on the upper decks. "The fourth level is A block, reserved for the kooks," Billy explained. "The third level is B, for violent offenders. Those floors are locked down all the time. The level above us is C. They have the same freedom we do, but there's no fee, so conditions are shabbier. The ground floor is D block. You and I are in the VIP section. The oxycontin craze in the States allows me to afford it."

Cat could tell by the Canadian's upscale cell and his comfortable manner that VIP advantages included access to outside goods and the benefit of respect from fellow prisoners—besides the guy who lifted his DVDs. Sissy looked up at a skeletal woman leaning over the railing. "Do the people upstairs get to *eat?*" she asked before flipping to Cat: *She's begging for handouts.*

"The standards in here are no worse than on the outside," Billy added. "Some inmates have kids living with them; better to be together than let them fend for themselves."

Cat looked up. The second floor seemed ratty, but its inhabitants looked happy enough. Many of them leaned over the rail to talk to folks below. Cat understood why Rey had been so impressed with Cat's accommodations. The rest of their floor housed twenty-by-twenty cells jammed with five sets of bunk beds each.

"They're short on space on every floor," explained Billy. "It's why they let us out during the day—fewer fights that way, if you can believe it." Cat could not believe any of this. It was impossible to fathom her red-carpet status in this otherworldly fantasia. She felt like Alice in La-La Land, a role she thought she had developed to deal with Los Angeles.

In the courtyard of El Norte, the walls seemed to expand. It was an independent universe with alien creatures following unwritten rules. The writhing populace bustled about, bumping into her like she was a point guard in a pinball machine. A man across the room shouted Spanish poetics like a prophet. A bloated woman floated by them, flaunting bulbous breasts in a low-cut dress. And Billy Ray moved like he owned the place, offering coins to filthy kids who called him "Señor Beelee" when they thanked him.

Though guards were constantly visible, any threat from their presence appeared unlikely.

"Seems like an easy place to escape," Sis muttered.

"They expect everyone to try it," explained the Canadian. "It's actually considered human nature. The guards are ripe for extortion, so it's easy, but not free. The guards need to feed their *familia*, so the more pesos the better when it comes to negotiations."

"How much do you think I need?" Cat inquired.

"Depends on speed of the deal," he said.

"How about today?"

"That'll cost you," Billy stated. "Let me see what I can do." Without further warning, he rushed away, heading in the direction of a stocky guard in the distance. As the sisters stood alone, Sis established a plan of action. "You look exhausted, Cat. Want a coffee?"

Cat shrugged. Grabbing her hand, Sissy edged toward a coffee cart. She retrieved a few bills from her pocket. *"¿Cuánto?"* Sis asked him. The man sneered as he glared at Cat, and then Sis.

"For you?" he asked. "Or the pretty one?" Cat shrunk at his presumption.

Sis ignored his discourtesy. *"Por un café, por favor."*

The little man adopted a hushed tone as if peddling something illicit. *"Cincuenta."*

Sis didn't balk at the 400 percent mark-up. "Gracias," she said, handing him an extra ten pesos as gratuity. Giving Cat the cup of joe, she noticed her sister's shaking hand. "Have you eaten today?" The beauty queen, who'd lost her glow, shook her head no. Sis ushered Cat to a taco cart, but any interest in food waned when Rey appeared before them.

"Hey, strangers," she joked.

"Hey, ho," Sis quipped, looking ready to choke her. Cat tensed, expecting a melee, but relaxed at Billy's quick return.

"I talked to a high-ranking guard named Manny. He says for enough money, he'll get you out ASAP."

I got ten thousand bucks, Sis flipped to Cat, patting her jacket.

"What?" cried Cat.

"Cash advance from your credit card."

"How did you get that?"

"I stole your ID a long time ago. You can thank me when you're free."

"He wants fifty," corrected Billy.

"Grand?" asked Sis.

"A release this quick is unheard of."

"Guess I need to get some more cash," Sis conceded.

"Don't leave me," begged Cat.

"Give me your phone—*I'll* get in touch with Rick. Don't worry ... I'll be gentle." Cat grudgingly returned her cell. Sis glanced at the watch on her wrist. "It's ten to four. I'll go straight to the bank."

Billy shook his head knowingly. "They often close early ... there's no guarantee."

"Listen," Sis said to Cat, "I'll be back." She handed her cash. "Just get through one more night."

Sis turned to address the Canadian. "Make sure she eats, please?"

Billy nodded. "And you." She pointed at Rey. "Stay out of her space, or there'll be hell to pay." Then Sis rushed out and Cat crumbled.

"You want a taco or a taquito?" Billy asked.

Zombie-like, Cat headed toward her cell. "I'm not hungry," she said with a sigh.

"Fasting won't help," Rey called.

"I feel sick," Cat whined.

"Suck it up," Rey chided.

"I feel faint," Cat cried. She began to rush toward the VIP wing as the Canadian and the derelict followed her. Entering home base, Cat fell to her knees and cupped her hands to her face before dropping her forehead on the ground. "I'm going to throw up."

"You do look clammy," Billy remarked.

Cat's breath grew rapid, her heart pounding in her chest. Within seconds, her palms were soaked in sweat and damp hair clung to her temples. She raised her flushed chin, fighting to maintain consciousness, but the air felt heavy and hot. "My heart is *racing*." She was scared.

"You're wigging out," Billy said.

Cat looked more than a little concerned. "My *life* is *over*!" she screamed. "I feel like I'm having a heart attack!"

"It's a panic attack," he explained.

"What do we do?" Rey asked worriedly.

"Give her something," Billy responded.

"Like *what*?"

"What have you got?"

"Drug wise?" Rey asked.

"She's an actress—check her pill box."

"I only have ibuprofen," Cat panted.

"I got oxy," he said matter-of-factly.

"You want a pain pill?" Rey asked.

"What *for*?" Cat implored.

"For your *stress*," Billy said.

"To help you relax," Rey explained.

"Will it make me high?"

"It'll make time fly," Billy said with a smile. "No pain, all gain, I like to say."

The anxiety had Cat shaking uncontrollably—she was desperate to end this dread. She got up and started to pace the tiny space. "I am totally *freaking out*," she wheezed.

Billy left Cat's place and began rummaging under his mattress. "Give her two of these before she drives us *all* crazy." He handed a couple of pills to Rey, who presented them to Cat.

"They're sedatives," Rey explained. "People take them all the time."

"I think I'll have a few, too," Billy said and popped three. Accepting their assurance, Cat collapsed on her cot to get her bearings. Her head spin lessened as she closed her eyes. She tentatively placed the tablets on her tongue and slipped into free fall. Worry seeped from Cat's brain as the noise in her mind dampened. This growing calm was inversely proportionate to the increased assembly of inmates. During the next hour, prisoners began to pass through the hallway in droves, seeking a view of the newbie before lockdown occurred. When a man with a coffee cart approached, the vendor paused and asked Rey, "*¿Uno café?*"

"No," she answered. "Gracias."

"*¿Un autographo?*" He gazed at the motionless movie star.

"Not today," Rey explained.

"Hey!" a man called as he rapped on the bars. Cat's eyelids fluttered as she struggled to regain wakefulness. "You are verrrrry bea-u-ti-ful!"

Cat inhaled deeply, battling sleep, as a third man wooed her in Spanish.

"She's *resting*," Rey called, seeming desperate to protect her.

The second guy whistled to wake Cat up. In a stupor, she scrambled to her feet, dreaming of a roll call. Realizing it was still the jail scene, she told Rey she needed to pee.

"I have to go to the bathroom," Cat slurred, not wanting to use the potty in the corner.

"Whoa," warned Rey. "Let's wait a bit."

Cat stumbled through the gate, but wavered as the men surrounded her.

"*Está borracha,*" the slimy guy exclaimed.

"She's not *drunk*," Rey said, peering down the hall. She called out to Billy, but the oxy high held him captive.

As Rey scoured the area for assistance, the hands on Cat's back grew in number. Dizzy with fear, Cat screamed, "I can't *breathe!*" Like a terrified feline, she crouched on her haunches.

"Leave her *alone!*" Rey yelled, as the crowd closed in.

"*¿Esta bien? ¿Esta bien?*" The coffee vendor seemed ready to defend her, but Cat could not read his good intentions. She flailed as he reached in to help, and then her eyes rolled back in her head.

CHAPTER 24

STUCK

Bumps in the mattress pressed Cat's ribcage as she struggled to consciousness. There was a mist in her brain. She wanted to be vigilant, but the pills lulled her back to a sleep, where the word *escape* would take on new meaning.

As REM kicked in, Cat the crusader raced through a dream state. Red and blue lights flashed in her peripheral vision as the California Highway Patrol followed closely behind her. Popping a wheelie, she created a shield against the bullets that flew out of a rusted blue pickup filled with gun-toting banditos up ahead. Dead set on catching the villains, Cat leaned forward. The plastic puck on her knee grazed the concrete, and she careened her race bike sideways to avoid getting pulverized.

Adrenaline was a high-speed hazard as she slalomed

across the freeway, dodging bullets and veering around innocent drivers caught in the crossfire. Her black leather suit resembled her skintight garb from *Darkstar*. She hit the throttle, rocketed past a camera truck, and the director yelled, "Cut!" As the crew applauded the perfect take, Cat smiled at all the adulation. *How I can I live without the ovations?* she thought wistfully.

Darkstar II, albeit fantasy, brought her back to a place where she felt coddled by subconscious optimism. The idea that she would get out alive and thrive in the aftermath of this horror show was renewed faith. She was beginning to see a beam at the end of the tunnel, when a piercing scream and heart-pounding *thump* pumped paranoia through her veins again.

Within seconds, chaos erupted inside the prison. Cat bit her lip to confirm her abrupt wakeup, and conscious pain updated her status. She sat up, attuned to the cacophony of distress, and noticed that Rey was curled up like a dog on the cement floor nearby. Cat had no recollection of the night before and wondered why Rey was here, but the presence was a welcome surprise in otherwise grim circumstances. The overhead lights flipped on as guards barked orders in the distance, drowning out the coyote-like baying of the female inmates.

"Rey!" Cat whispered, feeling freaked and craving camaraderie.

"Rey!" she repeated. The critter in the corner remained inert, and Cat cursed her worthless compadre. She draped the prison-issue blanket across her shoulders like a shawl and snuck toward the hall, tentatively pressing her face against

the bars to get a look down the causeway. Guards rushed toward the courtyard, babbling in Spanish. Cat was taken aback by the unnerving cries of a very young boy crying "Mama" and the whine of an ambulance rushing past.

Pushing her nose through the bars again, she caught a glimpse of a dilapidated gurney being pushed hurriedly down the hall perpendicular to hers. Ten minutes later, a broken body was wheeled in the other direction with an ambivalence that said *dead*. The cries of the toddler pierced the slowing pandemonium until his wails sailed away under the hushed insistence of fellow prisoners, and the guards commanded, "Lights out!" again.

Cat sat on the lumpy bed, trembling with agitation. She'd felt safer dodging the bullets in her dream.

Rey looked pretty brain dead when Cat finally opened her eyes the next day.

"What time is it?" Cat rasped.

"I don't know," Rey slurred.

Cat spun her watch around and saw 6:15 on her Rolex. Her head throbbed as light hit her eyes, but recollections of the late-night calamity hauled her out of her muddy slumber.

"Do you know what happened last night?" Cat asked.

"You were freaking out, so we gave you a bunch of oxy and put you to sleep."

"Yeah, well, I was wide awake when someone died outside."

Rey didn't bat an eye as she rolled from her side to lie

flat on her back. "Sure you weren't dreaming? It could have been a bad reaction to the downers." Rey reached into her pocket to grab what was left of the heroin she had smuggled inside up her sleeve. "If you're feeling stressed again, you should take a zip o' this."

"I said somebody *died*, and you want me to get high?" Cat leaned in and snagged the bag of heroin, pitching it toward the pit and scoring a three-point shot into the latrine.

"What the *fuck*!" Rey scrambled toward the toilet, gaping down at the drowned narcotics. "Bitch, you better—"

"Good *morning*!" Billy sang a salutation that doubled as a warning.

Suddenly a watchman appeared to unlock their doors. Cat opted not to tell the guard about Rey's drugs, for fear that she'd get in trouble for them, too. But she almost regretted that decision after the guard departed, and Rey started in on Cat again. "Bitch, you better git...."

"What happened last night?" Cat asked Billy, ignoring Rey's threat.

"When you lost your head?" Billy asked.

"*No*," Cat corrected in exasperation. "When someone lost their *life* in the courtyard!"

"Whoa! I think you need another chill pill."

"I need to get away from you people!"

"Come on," Billy said to Rey. "Let's let her cool down a bit." He pushed on Cat's gate, coercing Rey to walk away from the lost heroin. Before they disappeared down the hallway, the Canadian cautioned, "Don't bite the hand that feeds you—we're the only friends you've got here."

Cat was stewing. The fog in her brain fueled her fury, and she was ready to take her anger out on Rey. A girl fight in prison would likely go unnoticed, but she wondered if she had the strength to hit her. If push came to shove, she wouldn't know what to do. A fist in the face would injure Rey, but would it damage Cat, too? What if the Canadian stepped in, and the two of them ganged up on her?

Cat sighed. Premeditation was stressful—she wished she could plan an impromptu attack. *Well, that's an oxymoron.* Cat laughed at the play on words and considered the fact that maybe her anger was part of her hangover. She had no idea why people indulged in these drugs; the oxy was making her stupid *and* bloated. When Cat sat down to relax, a sliver of silver caught her eye.

Lying next to the gate were the dual crosses Rey swore she had worn since she was three. Moving toward the door, Cat leaned down, hugging her stomach and snagged the necklace, noting its broken clasp. In a momentary lapse of restraint, Cat stormed toward the toilet and tossed the dual crosses in the foul water. It made her feel powerful and vindictive, feelings as foreign as the local language that continued to elude her.

She stood for a while, staring down at the bottom of the metal bowl, wondering whether she could, and would, pull the flush string. *Passive* was Cat's middle name, always had been, and tears of anger squeezed onto her cheeks as she pondered why she couldn't knock Rey's teeth out instead.

"Damn it!" Cat whispered angrily. Then she squatted down, placed her arm inside the bowl, and grabbed the chain again. Coughing to suppress the urge to vomit, she pulled the charms to safety, flushed the drugs instead, before tipping back onto her butt as she held her contaminated hand as far away from her face as she could. This was a new low; she never would have imagined sleeping so close to such a vile basin, let alone reaching inside it. She flashed back to her early days on the runway, when she had modeled for months in France. She had been horrified by the bathroom practices of the French. If only a bidet was available today, she would power wash her hand.

Au contraire, Ms. Millionaire, she thought candidly. Putting on airs with a French accent lightened Cat's spirit.

"It's only shit." She swore at the smell of it. Then she wiped her hand on her tan jumpsuit and took care to polish the tarnished crosses. Cat sighed, closing her eyes to imagine the big blue sky that canopied Sis, on her way to save the day.

🜨

When she actually burst on the scene, Sis was hollering like a hotdog seller at a ballgame. "I got *wet* wipes, *tooth*paste, and forty thousand bucks. Let's clean you up and get outta here!"

Cat was drowsy but awake and at the sound of Sissy's voice she came to, albeit in a haze.

"What's a matter with you?" asked Sis. "You looked wasted."

"I had a panic attack last night. Billy gave me pills to help me sleep."

"What pills?" asked Sis.

"Oxycontin," muttered Cat.

"Are you serious?"

"I have no idea *what* I am or *who* I am right now. So don't look at me that way," Cat said in a gruff and monotonous tone.

"That shit's *addictive*," Sis pressed.

"It's not like I was shooting up," Cat protested.

"Same thing, dip shit. It's morphine in a pill. I got some for my wrist and couldn't handle it."

"Well, it definitely made me spacey—and *constipated*," Cat whispered.

"You need prune juice?" Sis whispered.

"Caffeine will do," Cat countered, "but give me some of those wet wipes first."

Sis handed Cat a bag filled with wipes and stuffed with money. "A farmer's bath is my kind of cleanup. I'm usually fine with a spit shine."

"Where did you get this?" Cat asked, regarding the money.

"From Chris," said Sis. "He sends his best—*not*. He's pissed … thinks your little stint in prison will make it hard to get funding for his script." Cat looked down at the ground and shook her head. "I told him, 'Least your leading lady will be outta the clink,'" said Sis.

"There'll be hell to pay in LA after this run."

"Cross that bridge when you come to it. Let's find that guy Manny, and get this deal *done*."

Sis was exiting through the gate in front of Cat when an armed guard approached the two of them. "Visiting hours are over," he said harshly.

"What?" asked Sis, flipping her palms and making a face.

"Come with me," he insisted. Sis backed up and put her hands up in resistance, so the guard held his gun across his chest.

"Please let her stay. I'm leaving today." Cat flashed him a hopeful grin.

The guard sneered but seemed to consider the request. *"En tus suenos."* Then he herded Sis in front of him with the end of his gun and told Cat *she* was free to stay, but her "brother" would have to leave.

"Oh, that's funny," Sis scoffed as the guard ushered her away. "I'll be back!" Sis hollered to Cat. Cat clung to the bars of her cage and hollered "Wait!" to no avail. Knocked off her axis once again, Cat nervously spun the diamond ring on her finger. Its hundred-thousand-dollar clarity revealed the transparency of Chris's priorities. *He bought my love and now my freedom; what does that make me?* She felt dirty, like a whore, and wished she could give the diamond to Manny and mail the cash back to Chris. The Canadian said that American money went a long way when it came to feeding the guards' families. *Greenbacks are where it's at,* Cat remembered, clasping the bag of them tightly.

As Cat gazed down at the ostentatious diamond, a ray of sun cast a constellation of rainbows across the ceiling, sparking a recollection of the theme song from one of her favorite movies.

Someday I'll wish upon a star,

And wake up where the clouds are far

Behind me.

```
Where trouble melts like lemon drops
Away above the chimney tops
That's where you'll find me.
```

"There's no place like home," Cat said aloud. Then she closed her eyes and imagined herself at six, pumping her heels toward the sky on the swing set her dad built with callused hands. She could picture Sissy watching from the stroller, itching to get out of its bounds and fly high like her big sister. How far they had come, and yet Cat couldn't wait to reverse directions. But it was clear that the yellow brick road would never intersect the starlit path she'd been pursuing. With the wind of Sis's courage at her back, Cat put on an imaginary pair of ruby shoes and headed out of her cell and straight into the storm.

CHAPTER 25

DICEPTION

The noise of the crowd in the courtyard bounced off the walls as Cat rounded the corner. This space had the acoustics of a gymnasium. Her eyes were drawn to the loudest bunch near the hall entrance where a group of men were throwing dice and waving money, their raucous cheers a stark contrast to the misery written on the face of a young woman in their midst.

The timid teenage girl sat between the legs of a man who looked forty years her senior and appeared to be the leader of the crew. Cat wondered if she was his daughter until he wrapped his arm around her neck and set his hand on her breast. She smiled meekly, accepting her role as concubine. The smell of refried beans yanked Cat's attention from the shameful scene toward a taco cart as her battered brain said, "Feed me."

Moving briskly through the crowd in the direction of food, Cat nearly ran over a small boy chasing after a ball made of twine. He stopped as she paused, then zipped around her legs to retrieve his plaything. "Excusee," Cat said, putting her hands up. The boy grabbed his toy and gazed up at her. "Can I have a piece of your string?" she pantomimed.

The boy offered the ball to her. Cat unraveled a sixteen-inch section and paused, wondering how she could clip it. The boy dug into his pocket and produced a key ring that held a small bottle opener. He motioned for Cat to return the ball to him, then thread the twine through the hole and rubbed the straight edge back and forth against the filament until it broke. He handed the freed bit back to her.

"Gracias," she said. Then she motioned for the boy to follow her to the taco cart.

"Hola," Cat said to the squat woman manning the stand. *"Una papa y dos de pollo, por favor."* If nothing else, she could effectively order a snack in Spanish.

The woman stuffed the corn tortillas generously, topping each with a dusting of cheese. The cross-eyed cook behind the lady smiled as Cat handed a taco to the kid. Then, with a wicked, toothless grin, the female vendor said, *"Diez dólares."*

"Ten bucks?" asked Cat. "I'll give you eight—American." The woman took the money without pause, stuffing it inside her brown bra.

"Muchas gracias," Cat said, turning to thank the boy again, but he had been swallowed by the undulating mob.

Rey had been following Billy, but his faster pace was not aligned with her hung-over shuffle, and she lost sight of him as he beelined through the hive of swarming people. She slowed her pace to deal with a throbbing headache, and as she reached up to receive a daily dose of comfort from her crosses, she discovered their absence. Time stopped, and the room began to spin. Rey was overcome with anguish multiplied by the five hours of her "come-off" from heroin. She crumpled to the ground in despair—losing that necklace in here was like riding out an earthquake on a sandstone foundation. She was about to let the tears roll when Sis appeared, wearing a prison suit.

"Where's Cat?" she demanded, looming over the little Latina and standing only a foot away from her to emphasize their height difference in the name of intimidation.

Don't cry, don't cry. Rey looked up at Sis and whispered, "Piss off."

"Fuck you. Where's Cat?"

"I don't know," Rey said.

Sis unzipped her pocket. "Here," she said, tossing Rey's motorcycle key on the floor. "They accidentally included your bike in the transport from impound—I tried to trade it on the street for a churro, but the guy said it smelled like dead rat."

"Nice jab."

"You worthless scab. Where's the Canadian?" Sis's eyes bore down on Rey for a second, but looking over her head to see if she could spot Billy.

"He's in here somewhere," said Rey with the casual air of someone who could care less about threats.

"I'm about to flip out on you. You want to live? Help me find him."

Rey was too sick to counter an attack from Sis, so she begrudgingly came along. The former teammates pushed their way across the room, looking for Billy. To Sis's obvious relief, they found Cat instead. Rey could see that she was collecting a bunch of wrinkled pesos from one of the guys who'd been playing dice yesterday. Sis rushed toward Cat, who had turned to the adolescents on the sidelines and was redistributing the pesos among them.

"Hey!" said Sis, placing her palm on Cat's shoulder.

Cat spun around quickly, backing up as if she was on guard. The sight of Sis softened her face, and she hugged Sis with gusto. "How did you get back in? And why are you wearing that outfit?"

"One of the guards is a big fan of Motocross, so I signed my name on his BMX magazine. He gave me this getup and let me in the back door."

"I guess we're both pretty good at *Diception*," said Cat. "That's the name of the dice game I was playing." She pointed to the crowd of dice guys.

"Finally learning the lingo," mumbled Rey. Sis snagged the plastic cubes from Cat and delivered them to the nearest hombre before corralling her sister away from the gamblers. Children scurried behind them like rats following the Pied Piper.

"No mas," Cat offered apologetically, holding up her

empty hands. Over the heads of the dirty cherubs Rey spotted the gloomy young woman in the older man's clutch. The bleak teen seemed enamored by Cat, but as she caught Rey's gaze she lowered her eyes, as if her admiration was somehow shameful.

"When did you decide to roll with the tide here?" asked Sis with surprise.

"I'm trying to rise above difficult circumstances. Most of these folks are trying to enjoy life a little bit. So I decided to spread a little butter on their bread."

"Taking from the poor to give to the poor ain't exactly charity."

"I threw a hundred bucks in the pot at the end. That ought to pacify the haters."

They continued to walk as Rey trailed behind them. "I feel so sorry for these kids," Cat continued.

"They come here to live with their parents—better than being an orphan," said Rey.

"Well, did you hear about the mother who committed suicide last night? I guess she had been complaining about the conditions in B block and got sent up to D. She was forced to leave her toddler behind, and took a swan dive over the railing. Having your kids live in prison is outrageous."

"Maybe that's why they told me to leave earlier," said Sis. "There were a bunch of stuffy-looking officials outside when I arrived."

Cat looked grim at the thought of it. "Hey, Rey," she said, sounding surprisingly kind. "I got something for you." Cat grabbed the twine from her pocket and exposed the lost crosses. Rey didn't speak as she sheepishly reached for them with shaky fingers.

"Thank you," she murmured.

⚜

By the time Sis's illicit visit ended, the Canadian had sealed the deal for Cat's departure. Catrina Lang would be pardoned in the morning, and the sisters would be headed to Texas by noon. Cat knew she needed time to heal, and seeing her family would bring much-needed relief from this ordeal.

"A couple days away from this nightmare, and you'll be fine," said Sis. "Then you'll get sick of the quiet Texas life again and leave." There was a painful truth behind this dis.

"What would I do without your snarky remarks?" Cat crooned as she opened her cell door and sat on her cot for some much-needed rest.

"And who would I be, without the queen as my sister?" Sis had walked in behind Cat and without a pause to consider the exposure, sat down on the toilet in the corner to pee. "At least I'm in line for the throne, although I'd prefer to take a piss in your Beverly Hills bathroom."

"Well, let me throw you a bone while I decide if I'm ready to retire to a place that's somewhere in between jail and Hollywood." Cat offered her engagement ring as a gift to Sis. "You said this could sponsor how many seasons?"

"That depends. If I spend my downtime taking trips with you, I'm going to need a per diem. You're a bit of a liability. This *might* cover one more jailbreak. After that, you're on your own."

"I've been on my own for a long time now. I want to ride alongside you for a while." Cat spoke as if they'd never had a falling out in the first place. "I love you, Wild Child."

"Yeah, well, I love public displays ..." Sis stood and hauled her pants up. "But not when it comes to PDA." Sis held her hands up, lest Cat move in for a hug. "Now *stay* outta trouble, you hear?"

And with that they said goodbye, one last time.

26

ESCAPE FROM EL NORTE

Rey shuffled along behind Cat as two young guards at the rear of the group spoke under their breath. Rey started to pay more attention to what they were saying when she heard one of them mutter the term catch and release in Spanish.

"The Starfish *es muy magnifica*," the second guard responded.

Rey turned, ostensibly to look at a handicapped inmate on wooden crutches struggling with his heavy cell gate. She glimpsed one of the guards casting an imaginary fishing line toward Cat, who was oblivious to their remarks.

"Face forward!" he demanded.

Rey jammed her hands in her pockets and hunched her back as the guard kicked at her heels.

"The chum has it coming to her," the first guard said to his comrade, loud enough to annoy Rey.

"*You're* a chump," Rey snapped.

The second guard informed Rey that his pal had said *chum*, not *chump*, and she would get a swift kick in the ass if she didn't shut her mouth and walk faster.

"*Chum?*" Rey asked, questioning the reference.

"You are lucky to be so *chummy* with a movie star," one of the guards said to Rey, before turning back to his amigo to say: "*Una estrella de mar, y un cubo de chum, por treinta mil American.*" As their conversation continued in Spanish, the guards scoffed at the thousands of dollars Cat was about to pay to get her and Rey out of here. Rey wondered why the guards were including her in their chitchat. Her heart raced as she contemplated this major mistake on their part— were they about to include Rey in the jailbreak? And why were they referring to her as chum or shark bait?

Sissy arrived at 9:00 a.m. and parked her Honda around the corner from the prison entrance. This was her second arrival of the day. The first had been on Cat's Beemer, which she parked next to Rey's KTM. As the bikes nestled side by side one last time, Sis resisted the temptation to spit on Rey's. She had respect for it, if not Ms. Piece-of-Shit Reyna.

Sissy pressed her palm against her left breast pocket to confirm the bulge of cash was still there. She felt out of her element when it came to game time; she was sweaty, short of breath, and had flutters in her stomach, everything she had trained herself to squelch on race days. Today's win would be sweeter than any other. Negotiating with the authorities successfully meant saving Cat's hide and getting back to the ride.

Sissy cleared her throat as she neared the external security station. "I'm here to see Catrina Lang," she said. The guard pushed a clipboard through his half-drawn window and said, *"Firme aquí."*

Sis scrawled her full name, failing to hide her wobbly motor skills. Men with machine guns stood on either side of the window; look-alikes for the guards who had busted the girls straight off the ferry. Sissy's nerves began to fire as she fought to maintain her composure. Her knees buckled, so she placed her hand on the shelf in front of the window, and the guard on her right gripped his weapon as a warning. She explained her strange behavior as heat-related, small-talking her way out of the tension.

"It's hot as blazes today," Sis said, unzipping her nonventilated, solid leather race gear. "Muy caliente." She fluttered her collar for emphasis.

"They're expecting you," the guy behind the window said. "Take her to the loading dock," he told one gun-wielding guard. Sis's reunion with Cat could now commence.

⚜

As Cat worked her way down the corridor, she slowed to walk in step with Rey. "Thanks for getting me out of here," Cat whispered with an innocence that made Rey ashamed.

"De nada," Rey said, still reeling from the feeling that her own luck was about to turn.

"I left some stuff in my cell for you to use," added Cat.

"Shampoo and some creams—I told the guards to hold it. I didn't realize I'd see you at the exit."

Or through it, Rey thought. "Sis has the money, right?"

"She better," Cat replied. "I made her take it with her for safekeeping. I'm still unclear if this is a break-out," Cat whispered, "or a legit release."

"Well, fifty grand ought to be enough for them to call off the hounds, if it is an escape. But I'm sure they have a plan for you to get out of town safely. Manny mentioned something about an escort—I assume he meant security, not a plan to sell you to a prostitution ring."

"You have a strange way of looking at the bright side of things," Cat scoffed.

"You'll be fine," Rey clarified. "And lucky me, I get your fancy toiletries." *Or a piggy back discharge.*

⚜

All three women arrived simultaneously, at opposite sides of the same back door. Sis shook with relief as the egress opened and Cat was standing before her, a woman on the verge of freedom.

"*¿Donde es Señor Manny?*" the gun-toting guard standing outside in the sun asked the silver-haired man guarding Cat.

"He's coming," retorted one of the young guards standing beside Rey.

Cat smiled slightly at her sister and discreetly flipped a message to Sis to confirm she had brought all the money. Sis nodded.

Suddenly, a potbellied man appeared from the bowels of

the basement and the younger guards straightened. Señor Manny spoke in English as he addressed the crowd.

"The commander has verified your release, as soon as we get the money."

Sis hurriedly snagged the thick envelope of bills from her pocket. "Here," she said, handing it to him. Manny took a quick peek and handed it to one of the guards who had been antagonizing Rey. "Count it," Manny told him in Spanish before turning to Cat to give a rundown on the proceedings.

"You are free to go now. I have been assigned to accompany you to the border to ensure your safety. All your belongings have been released to me. I will follow you to your next destination and return your possessions when we get there. I've been hired to act as a bodyguard and will stay in an adjacent room any place you decide to reside overnight. That is, unless you plan to head straight back to Texas."

"That's a long ride," Sis interjected. "I made a reservation in Morelia, so we can freshen up and have a meal before we leave. Is that cool with you, Cat?"

Cat nodded with a look that said *thank you.*

"It's all here," the young guard said when he finished counting the money.

"Okay then," Manny continued. "I'll meet you around front in an unmarked car, and we can head straight to Morelia. The commander is adamant about getting you back to the States safely. If there is anything you need, let me know. I'm here to serve you. I just ask that you steer clear of trouble."

He glared at Rey with a look that said *Got it?*

"Excuse me," Sis interrupted. "There's been a mistake. *Rey's* not part of this, is she?"

"The payment covers both Americans, and includes my protection. Is there a problem?"

"Yeah—" Sis contested.

Before she could argue, Cat interjected. "That's *very* generous, sir." Cat smiled broadly as she sent a message to Sissy that said *shut it.* Her instant charisma was an effort to counteract Sis's fury. "Please tell the commander we appreciate *all* his consideration, and I promise we'll obey the law from this point on." Cat flashed a look to Sis that mixed shock with coercion.

Rey nodded and uttered, "Absolutely."

Sis nodded dutifully, too, as she mentally prepared to beat the piss out of Rey at the first opportunity.

An unspoken treaty bonded the trio as they made their way to their bikes and got ready to ride again. Cat was as relieved as she was peeved, but anger turned to pity as a police van filled with fresh convicts rolled past. She wondered how many innocents were about to be confined to the cage she had narrowly escaped, and how many guilty ones had already paid their way out of doing fair-and-square time. It was a shame that alternative rules applied to people with money and the celebutantes who followed them through VIP doors. Cat was conflicted by Rey's release, but now was not the time to discuss it. She only hoped the poor souls heading to the flipside had enough dough to buy benefits on the inside.

Manny pulled up beside them, and Sis shared a clandestine message with Cat.

I am going to kill this bitch, she flipped, looking heated.

I don't think that qualifies as staying outta trouble, Cat flipped.

"I'll wait 'til we get to the States again," Sis growled.

Cat felt a ping of empathy as the sun shined on Rey's wretched face. *A little vitamin D would do this leech some good,* she thought mercifully, suddenly missing the pricey lotions she had left inside for Rey.

As the women started their engines, Rey could hardly contain her excitement. Her mind was moving a million miles a minute, and she was caught in the whirlwind of luck that had struck her. In a surge of self-preservation, she brazenly asked for another favor.

"Hey, the silver mine's south of the city, and they're expecting me. Mind if we do a quick pick up?"

Sis looked like she might explode. "This is not what I bargained for!" Sis raged, but Cat seemed pretty content with accepting the situation.

"Let's just stay cool and get out of here, please." Cat gave a look to Sis that said *Can we discuss this later, please?*

"We need to make a quick stop on the way to Morelia," Cat told Manny, who was standing by his car.

"For silver," Rey added, so Manny would not mistake it for an illicit errand. "That's the real reason I came down here, *es para mi padre.*"

"*¿Donde esta?*" Manny asked.

"*Peñoles,*" Rey stated, chomping at the bit a bit. "It's an hour southwest of here."

"Best pozole I ever ate is there," he remarked.

Sis looked ready to lose her composure. "I cannot take this bullshit. I'm seriously about to *beat* someone," Sis spit, kicking her foot into the ground without any concern for raising suspicion by the nearby guards.

Rey knew she was safe from Sis by the way Cat flipped a nervous message to her. It appeared she was telling Sissy to calm down.

"Lead the way," Cat told Rey after she seemingly defused Sis's objection. And just like that, Rey was free from her incarceration, en route to satisfy her father's needs, and exempt from Sis's fury. Today was going to be a great day— and it just so happened it was Rey's nineteenth birthday. Back on her bike, inside the privacy of her helmet, Rey said aloud: *"Feliz cumpleaños para mi."* As the officially freed jail mates steered merrily off the property followed by Sis on her Honda and the bodyguard in a Corolla, Rey made a birthday wish that had nothing to do with freedom.

CHAPTER 27

EL CARTEL

As the foursome rolled down the street, Cat soaked in the heat of the landscape. It felt great to be back on the road again. The magenta hues of the cactus blooms seemed dreamy in comparison to the insipid walls of El Norte. Cat swooned at their Technicolor radiance, in spite of the fragrance of the dusty brick-and-mortar stores that lined the dirty avenue. Unlike the musty air of the penitentiary, the atmosphere on the outside was alive and dry, and the vibrations from Cat's engine made her feel free and ready to ride. In contrast to her breakdown in prison, she no longer felt like a victim.

The last few days had been trying, to say the least, but the experience had given Cat a kind of strength she had never known before. She felt oddly superior to Sissy, like she might actually be the tougher one for once. The new and improved disparity gave Cat confidence and left her with the unshakable sense that healing her family was way more important than raking in movie money. She knew that her unexpected trip to Texas would have to trump her return to the place she'd been calling home for the last ten years. Movie making could wait.

Cat was brought back to the task at hand when Manny honked and waved at them to follow him. Cat gripped the clutch, downshifted into second gear, and pulled into the parking lot of Elvira's Taqueria with a surge of delight that stimulated her appetite.

"Platos des carnitas con mole, y nopatlitos con pepitos, por favor." Cat smiled wide as the waitress took her order.

Sis's brow arched at Cat's improved pronunciation. Then she turned to the server and said, *"Un Milanesa, con arroz y frijoles."*

Manny and Rey ordered tortas before Cat requested the check be brought to her at the end. Manny made a face that said his machismo was being challenged by this role reversal.

"It's the least I can do," Cat explained. "I'm sure you have better things to spend your money on than lunch with a bunch of chiquitas."

"You've gone bananas," Sis cracked, proving her humor was still intact.

"Remember," Manny noted, "I'm getting paid for this."

"Hope they make it worth your while," Cat quipped.

"Two thousand dollars is enough to cover my rent for six months."

Cat flinched at the fact that two thousand bucks wouldn't cover her car payment.

"Wow," offered Rey. "That's enough money to buy six months of silver. Maybe my dad should become a coyote."

Cat read this as an insult and switched the topic quickly. "What kind of stones does he work with?"

"Turquoise sells best when it comes to tourists," Rey said. "But he prefers Mexican fire opals."

Sis seemed to zone out as the discussion turned to jewelry. Cat knew that girl talk was not her cup of tea. Sis had zero patience for pleasantries, so when Manny piped in, Sis completely checked out.

"We have the rarest fire opals in the world," Manny added. "The redder, the better, they say. I gave one to my wife when I asked her to marry me. They stand for hope, faith, and confidence." He grinned.

"An opal ring might be the perfect thing for you," Cat goaded.

"It's my birthstone," Rey admitted. "I have a bunch of them."

"What month is that?" asked Cat.

"October," Rey confided.

"When's your birthday?" asked Cat excitedly.

"Today," admitted Rey.

Cat could not believe Rey's humility and, despite the animosity between them, was driven to celebrate the surprising anniversary. "I can't believe you didn't say anything!" She raised her water to toast Rey. "Here's to a year filled with hope, faith, and confidence."

Manny lifted his beer as Sis stood and asked the host

where the bathroom was. Cat watched her go. "That girl can hold on to a bike going ninety, hands-free, but she's *never* been able to hold her pee."

"Well," said Manny, "here's to all of us getting what we need."

And that's all it took to reignite Rey's cravings. *Wish I could get high,* she thought longingly.

"Anyone else want a cerveza?" Sis asked as she plunked back down and hailed the waitress.

"Let's skip the booze today, okay?" Cat glared at Sis.

"What's one beer going to do?" Manny asked.

Sis smiled at him, but Cat just shook her head. "Let's just say we're no strangers to the danger of intoxication."

"Lemonade it is," Sis said reluctantly. When Cat asked Manny about his background, he happily admitted he was a family man trying to earn a decent buck. As Cat's questions evolved however, it became clear that Manny was an expert in the underworld and knew more about the drug biz than Rey did.

Manny shared what he knew about Rey's boss, the head of the most dangerous cartel in Mexico. According to Manny, the commander-in-chief of the Morales cartel, Pedro Escondido, had been born into a life of poverty and struggled as a day laborer during his early adulthood. "Dumb luck" allowed him to become the right-hand man to Escobar Morales, the original leader of the dangerous gang that continued to wreak havoc on Mexico's security to this day.

As his story had it, a young Pedro Escondido was hired to lay brick on a villa that Señor Morales had built in the early days of his drug fortune. In need of additional protection, Morales handpicked a few of the workers to continue on as personal aides and bodyguards, and hard-working Pedro moved up in the ranks as one of the chosen few. The villa quickly became Mexico's biggest marijuana factory, providing more than half of the marijuana to the southern states of America by the late nineties. Around that time, Señor Morales died, and Pedro Escondido, who had become as loyal as a son to him, took over the "family" business. Under Pedro's reign, the Morales cartel gained momentum through heavy use of firearms and a total disregard for Mexican authority.

"Until recently," Manny explained, "the cartel was seen as the winners of the drug war. Then President Calderon stepped in and upped the stakes when it came to police retaliation. I'm sure you've heard Mexico is considered the largest war zone in the world right now." Cat raised her brows and turned toward Sis, her face held a look of surprise and regret.

"Nowadays, the federales wear civilian clothing and masks to avoid identification and to blend in with the bad guys. They've successfully turned up the heat on the gangs, so a few years ago the cartels smartened up and hired thousands of 'soldiers' to run very small amounts of drugs. The 'army of ants' has allowed the drug trade to divide and conquer. They focus on smuggling hundreds of minor packages through hundreds of different entrance points to the US."

"So I'm at low risk for retribution," concluded Rey. "One in a million losers."

"She's right," Manny agreed. "With some exceptions—after the commander lost his top officers in a recent attack, he decided to set up a bunch of drug soldiers to fail by stealing their packages and waiting for the cartel to come looking for them. If enough of the army ants screw up, the head honchos take notice and try to make examples out of them."

"So I *might* be a target, *if* the cartel can find me." Rey spoke with the singsong of an adolescent.

Manny stared at her for a long moment. "You were initially tagged as a pawn by the commander. Now he's backtracking a bit because of your connections." Manny turned to Cat. "You are too well known to become a casualty. In the name of Catrina Lang's fame, I have been ordered to keep *all* of you safe." He turned to speak to Rey. "Consider yourself blessed."

"Why would an American movie star matter to Mexico's administration?" Cat asked. She'd received special treatment for her fame in plenty of foreign countries, but she assumed that it was simply the huge payout that had gotten her out of trouble down here.

"Your saving grace is all about saving face for el presidente. Nothing would destroy tourism faster than an incarcerated American movie star."

Sis looked from her sister to Rey to Manny. "So why'd they bother to release Rey?"

Rey sunk in her seat like someone who deserved to be referred to in the third person.

"Politics," explained Manny. "He wants the situation to look like a misinterpretation. The gangs need to know who's in charge, and a blatant arrest of one of their soldiers should not be ignored, but Calderon is stuck between a rock and a hard place. Rey gets the benefit of your publicity. A prisoner release in *less than a week* is unheard of—a prime example of the president's vow to maintain good relations with our wealthy northern neighbors."

"God Bless America," Rey quipped.

"Better thank Cat," Sis snipped. Then she kicked back from the table and waved to the waitress. "*Check*, please."

CHAPTER 28

MORELIA

Rey slept like a baby at their next five-star accommodation. It almost hadn't been an option as Sis continued to rage against the situation yesterday. She had nearly convinced Cat that they should head directly home, nonstop. To Rey's relief, Cat said she needed sleep if she were to make it back safely, and she insisted on staying at the finest hotel that nearby Morelia had to offer. Since Cat was still paying the way, her say mattered more than anyone's, and a quick read of Cat's Triple A manual convinced her that the Mansion Real sounded like the opposite end of the spectrum from Cat and Rey's previous three days, in terms of accommodation.

Unfortunately for both jailbirds, Cat had blasted past the pictures of the open courtyard dining, an architectural tidbit that was unfortunate in its similarity to the open space at the prison. Cat was so impressed with the rest of the place that when Rey joked that the courtyard reminded her of El Norte's courtyard, it didn't even faze her.

Security was tight, starting with the bikes that were safely stashed in the underground parking lot behind an iron gate. At least that quality guaranteed that their transportation would be waiting for them in the morning. None of them was about to risk letting anything happen to their main transportation out of here. The Mansion promised a night watchman in the garage.

When they had arrived yesterday in late afternoon, preparation for a major parade was underway. Cat thought that seemed like a great way to begin again, and enjoy a little fun Mexican-style, before they headed home. None of the women wanted anything to do with the police in the street or the guard in the garage, because they too reminded the women of all the darkness they had faced due to law enforcement. Sis nearly flew into a fury again when they woke to discover that all vehicles behind the hotel gate would be out of commission for the entire day due to the parade, a notion that would stir up varying degrees of emotion in all three women when they realized they were stuck in Morelia. For Rey, this delay meant she could try to make the most of her time in Mexico and do her best to pay back Cat for everything she had done to save Rey's ass.

The first indication of the unwelcome extension of their stay came as the sun peeked through the split between the copper-colored, velvet curtains. The windows were soundproof and the drapes were dense, so the moment that Sis peeled the drapes back to peer outside was the moment the ladies came to see that the only road out of the hotel was blockaded.

"It's a parade," explained the woman at the front desk over the speaker on the phone when Sis called to inquire. "It's the annual human rights march. We're expecting record numbers this year," the hostess bubbled in English. "It coincides with the Day of the Dead this time, so the theme is Zombies." Sis rolled her eyes and shook her head in frustration as the young woman continued. "You know how popular they are with the kids these days, with all the American TV? Organizers expect ten thousand participants. It should be quite a sight to see!"

"I don't suppose we'll be able to drive down the street while it's happening," asked Sis flatly.

"Oh, no, Señora, you are restricted to walking until later today. We assumed all the guests knew ... it's been all over the news."

"We've been away from TV for a few days," Cat called from across the room. She moved closer to the phone to address the woman with a quieter tone. "Can you direct us to the nearest breakfast place?"

"We serve a lovely breakfast in the courtyard," the woman offered.

"Uh," said Cat, glancing at her jail mate, "we want to get out and see the scenery." Rey could care less, but Cat was determined to avoid a closeup of the courtyard at all costs. "Any old place will do," Cat added. It was a nice improvement from her formally stuck-up standards.

"Guess we're destined to sightsee in Morelia," Rey said when the phone call was over. She thought that aspect might please her benefactor. It would give Rey time to hatch a plan to repay her in some way.

Cat seemed pleased with this development and looked to Sis for her opinion, when her cell phone vibrated from inside her saddlebag. "Shit," Cat proclaimed, looking down at the vibrate switch and flipping it off. "Thirteen missed calls," Cat read. "Damn, I forgot to turn it back on yesterday. Chris is going to kill me."

As Cat scrolled through the list of text messages, Sis said wryly, "And here is our first exposure to the zombie apocalypse." Rey was relieved to hear her sense of humor again. Things would not be easy if she had to keep watching her back to see if Sis was about to slug her.

"I really need some privacy to make a phone call," Cat said. "Can you step outside for a bit?" Sis looked pissed at the prospect of spending alone time with Rey, but waved her toward the door in respect for her sister.

"Let's go see what Manny says about the delay in our departure," Rey suggested, assuming Manny would break up a fight if things got heated between them. Rey exited the room first to find Manny walking down the hallway with a bag of breakfast burritos and four hot cups of coffee.

"Guess we'll have to hunker here for a while," he said, handing Rey the tray of jet fuel.

"Cat's on the phone, she'll be out in a minute," explained Sis. "How's the crowd out there?"

"It's an even mix of tourists and locals from what I can tell." He handed Sis a bulging burrito and opened the door to his room to invite them in. "Nicest room I've ever been in." He beamed.

"Yeah, it's amazing what a hundred bucks will get you," Sis remarked, thinking what a steal of a deal it was until Manny reminded her how much money that represented to him.

"The government's paying my way—if not, I'd be sleeping in my car." Like a good Catholic, ready to thank the Lord for his good blessings, Manny suggested they all take a quick trip to the cathedral after breakfast. Rey cringed at the thought of going to church after all her recent mistakes, but Sis looked surprisingly intrigued. "I might be up for that, but we have to wait for Cat," said Sis.

"If it's okay, I'd like to head out now for morning mass—I'll be gone for an hour, tops," he promised.

"That's fine with me," said Rey, hoping to skip the field trip.

"We should ask Cat that, too," said Sis. "She's the one paying for all this." Now Manny was one of Cat's benefactors, too.

Back in the room, Cat listened intently as Chris railed against her. "Do you know what you've put me through?" he cried on the line. "I have zero time to deal with this, and Rick has conveniently left the country. Why did you ignore my calls all night?"

"I don't want to fight," Cat said. "The last few days were a mess, and when we finally got released, I couldn't focus on anything but my immediate need to get away from that place. I'm safe and sound in Morelia now, and we'll be heading out as soon as the street is reopened."

Cat didn't have time to apologize before Chris blasted her for all her insensitive behavior.

As soon as she hung up, Cat rushed out into the hallway to join Sis and forget about everything she owed Chris now.

"Manny wants to pray," Sis announced. "What do you say we head to the famous cathedral with him?" Cat was surprised at her sister's seeming willingness to visit a house of worship. "You want to go to church?" asked Cat.

"I hear they have wine," Sis joked.

"It's cool with me," Cat admitted.

Manny handed her a tightly bound burrito. "It's one of the most beautiful cathedrals in the world."

Rey looked itchy and sullen. "I can't," she said to the ground. "It would be … inappropriate. I'll stay here."

"Don't show your face downstairs," Sis growled. "No animals allowed." Sissy moved threateningly toward Rey, who stepped back quickly.

Out on the street, Manny joined the Langs as they squeezed onto the bustling street for the one-block walk to the Cathedral of the Divine Savior. Cat had grabbed a pamphlet on the historical landmark in the lobby of the hotel.

"Built in the 1600s," Cat read, "the cathedral features various elements of architecture as well as a German organ made up of 4,600 pipes." Cat held the brochure high above the crowd and hollered the words toward Sis's sound processor, trying to be heard despite the cacophony of mob noise.

The mass was a sight to behold. As one of the biggest cathedrals in the state, it drew a crowd of over a thousand. In honor of La Dia de los Muertos, the congregation was privy to a special guest priest. At the end, he reminded the congregation about the Saturday night sound-and-light show that happened every week, and which would be exceptional tomorrow.

"That sounds cool," Cat whispered, increasingly drawn to the Day of the Dead ceremonies. Sissy seemed rapt during the entire service. "So you actually enjoyed going to church for once?" Cat asked as they filed out of the Cathedral.

"For all the douche bags in the world," said Sis, forcing Cat to shush her, "that Mass just reminded me there are a whole lot more who are decent."

As the sisters and Manny descended the stairs into the mild, cloudless day, the streets were teeming with folks getting ready for the official march. Having seen posters around the area, Cat had learned that today's human rights parade in Morelia was actually a spin-off of a movement that had begun in Mexico City. The zombie theme seemed strange, but she was moved by the major effort to bring attention to the plight of this country's citizens. Cat had been painfully aware of the sad situation in prison and made a beeline for a flyer about how to donate to the cause.

In addition to foodstuffs and colorful trinkets, there were hundreds of flower vendors offering colorful Mexican marigolds for sale. "They're the flower of the dead," explained Manny. "People use them to decorate altars in their homes or gravesites." The plethora of orange and yellow gave a shade to the afternoon that was beyond brilliant.

As they paraded through the crowded streets, the theme of zombies really began to bloom. "I didn't know costumes were such a big part of this," said Sis. "It's like Halloween."

Manny explained that this charity event started five years ago in Mexico City. "They always march through the downtown streets, but I don't ever remember costumes."

When they entered a shop selling zombie paraphernalia, Cat asked the shopkeeper what she could tell them about the zombie theme. The woman was more than happy to fill them in on the fun hysteria. "Here in Morelia, we are trying to break the world record," she said with mucho enthusiasm. "The costumes will hopefully get them on TV. I have a few left if you want them. Better hurry though, the party's about to start."

That was all Cat needed to hear before she ordered Sis to pick out a costume, agreeing to pay for everything. They skipped the march, however, and watched from the sidelines … the last thing Cat needed was to be "caught" on live TV dressed as a zombie.

The parade only lasted an hour, but the ensuing party in the streets relieved pressure to depart before tomorrow.

"This is incredible, I wish we could stay for the weekend," admitted Cat wistfully.

"What, are you crazy?" asked Sis. "Two days ago you were ready to quit this trip and hire a stunt woman for the movie. Now you want to dress like a zombie and stay?"

"Seize the day," said Cat, knowing that Sis would never skip a chance to party.

As they made their way back to the hotel, Cat made a few purchases: a small altar, a bouquet of flowers, and a colorful string of beads that seemed perfect for a small shrine. *Time for Rey to say goodbye to that baby.* Cat hoped to offer her a chance to engage in the spirit of the holiday.

Cat thought Rey's mistake needed closure and figured she, too, might find a bit of solace in one special goodbye to her own lost offspring. Manny followed behind her, remaining politely detached as Cat inquired about appropriate toys for a child's shrine.

When they got back to the hotel, Manny excused himself, telling them he wanted to change into cooler clothes.

"No need to hover over us," said Cat. "We are incognito now. Why don't you take a break, and we'll come back and grab you in few hours."

As Manny walked ahead of them, the sisters took a minute to flaunt their shredded clothes and ghoulish makeup, cartoonishly posing in the decorative mirrors that lined the hallway. Cat scrunched her face up, trying to distort it as much as she could. She stuck her tongue out to the side and crossed her eyes. Taking the cue, Sis peered in the mirror too, pulling her lids up and rolling her eyes so only the white parts showed. "I'd love to see this on the pages of *People*," Sissy said, noting Cat's unusually ugly presentation.

Cat turned and put her hands around Sis's neck as a silly threat, then moved in as if she might bite her. "That's a vampire, you dork. Get your demons straight."

"I kind of like the idea of never posing with a pretty smile again," said Cat, presenting crooked lips.

"You wouldn't worry about the tabloids obsessing over this new look?" asked Sis.

"Maybe I could use this diamond to buy eternal anonymity."

"I don't think the paparazzi are bribable—they seem to be chasing some kind of fame, too."

"Money talks," corrected Cat. "Chris just told me this morning that he shelled out fifty grand to bribe the guy in San Diego for the pictures he took of us in the desert."

"What?" Sis's mouth fell open.

"No guarantee the pics that got into the hands of the Mexican media won't surface, but at least *TMZ* is hampered for now. According to Chris, that bastard followed us all the way from LA to Mexico, just to get pics for *TMZ*. They offered him forty K, so Chris beat their rate."

"No way," said Sis as the cost of maintaining a good image sunk in. Cat shrugged her shoulders and finished walking up the hall. "So what do you say we just hang down here and enjoy the end of our getaway?" Cat asked. She unlocked the door to find Rey sitting on the bed. She hadn't left the room, as promised.

"I really want to stay," argued Cat. "It's only one more day!"

"Who the hell are you?" asked Sis. "And what have you done with my worry-wart sister?" Sis was done joking around and placed both hands on her hips with a look of concern, which Cat attributed to their safety. Sis was not one to admit vulnerability, but it seemed that she wanted the conservative Cat back. "I dig this new lease on life you've got," said Sis, "But this is not the place to run free."

Rey pulled herself to a seated position, listening.

"It's a once-in-a-lifetime experience," Cat said. "Halloween was our favorite day as kids. The costumes will keep us incognito, and we have a round-the-clock bodyguard to watch our backs. What are you afraid of?"

"Death by mutilation," Sis confessed. "Least we have

bait we can sacrifice." She glared at Rey on the carpet. "You mind leading the way, Rey? My sister wants to take a jab at this Day of the Dead bash."

"I'm happy to hang, if you guys want to stay," said Rey.

"As long as I don't have to hang with you, I'm in," said Sis. She stared at Rey as if to say *You worthless piece of shit.*

Cat glanced down at her Rolex. "Let's get back out there, the parade's about to start."

As Sis followed Cat's wave to leave, she gave Rey one final direction: "Just pull the fire alarm if the bad guys come to get you. So we'll know to come back and bury you."

CHAPTER 29

DAY OF THE DEAD

The next morning the women got up long after the sun did. The blackout curtains made nighttime eternal, and they were shocked to see the midmorning street filled with zombies again. The sisters were ready to leave right away, having slept with their makeup on, causing zombie-like pillow smears. Cat joked that their mother would be appalled to know she hadn't washed her face before bed.

"You're breaking all the rules now," said Sis as the sisters headed out the door without so much as a goodbye to Rey.

A quick knock by Rey on Manny's door confirmed that he was MIA, leaving her free to enact her latest scam. She would race to the drug store to buy rolling papers and cigarettes, then sneak in the garage to retrieve the last pack of pot hidden inside her gas tank. Besides gas fumes, the only issue might be a nosy parking attendant. But she had pulled off so many fast ones lately that one more sneaky move would hardly be challenging.

She made it on her quick errand and back in less than twenty minutes, a relief since she expected the sisters could come back any minute and knew that Manny would report back to Cat if he bumped into Rey in the street. She returned to the room with the half ounce of weed, reeking of gas and deception. She unraveled the liquid-proof casing and flushed the stinky plastic down the toilet. Then she emptied her pocketful of Zig-Zags, opened two packs of Pall Malls, and set out to roll as many joints as possible before Manny came knocking. Cutting each one with tobacco meant she could sell enough singles to earn back some of the money she owed Cat.

Revelers would be looking to party today before they adopted a more spiritual attitude. Rey figured if she worked furiously, she could buy back the sisters' trust a bit. If she sold it all, she could cross back into the US, break away from the chains of the cartel, and start a drug-free existence.

When the prep work was done, Rey had rolled forty joints like a pro. At five bucks a pop, she had the potential to earn two hundred dollars this afternoon. There would be plenty of college kids and foreigners lining up to buy as soon as she could get out there and pound the pavement. She would be safe as long as she was draped in zombie gear and kept the dealing on the down low. As she rounded the corner of the hotel lobby, Rey spotted the sisters coming through the front door. Ducking inside the lobby bathroom, she gave them time to get to the elevator. She hated hiding her motives from them again, but it was all for the greater good.

The sisters had brought the makeup-stained pillowcases for their booty and were bouncing them around as they dug their way to the bottom. Cat never ate candy, but now she wondered why. Had she really not liked it, or was it her fake model life that didn't allow for truth? After years of low-carb diets, Cat felt high as a kite and happier then she'd ever been.

"This is the life," she sighed.

Sissy smiled at the stick of the lollipop Cat sucked on, smeared with the black plum-colored lipstick she wore. Feeling like a kid again, Sis stuck out her own blue tongue to show off its hue.

"Nice," said Cat. "Maybe it's time we head back to check in with Manny. I wouldn't mind brushing my teeth—it kind of feels like they're wearing fuzzy slippers."

"What's the point? We have a full day of sugar intake ahead," said Sis.

"You don't think we should ask him to shadow us?"

"I don't know, I feel pretty freaking safe today," said Sis. "I mean, he's not a bad guy, pretty honorable, for someone who takes bribes."

"You sound like your old self again," observed Cat. "I was beginning to think this trip was turning you into a wimp."

"Well, you're the one who said let's stay and enjoy the party. This Day of the Dead shit is better than Halloween: no trick-or-treating required. But I would like to head back to the room for a sec to change my underwear. Too much candy gives me gas, and I think I just—"

"Too much information!" said Cat, who laughed while trying to look disgusted.

When they returned to an empty hotel room, Sissy hissed, "Where is that little cunt?"

"Nice mouth," Cat snapped. "She and Manny are probably out looking for us."

Cat turned on the flat-screen and sat on the floor to watch the news about the events around town. She lay down and pulled her knees to her chest; all the walking with her short leg was taking a toll on her back. Underneath the bed was a cellophane wrapper from a cigarette pack. "Manny must've been here," said Sis, grabbing the trash and holding it up for Cat to see. "Someone opened a pack of butts."

"I don't think he smokes," said Sis as she watched the newscaster interview a mob of zombies. She opened up a box of skittle-like candy and dumped them in her mouth. "This place is great. I wish we could stay."

"It's almost one, morning Mass should be done. Let's go find him."

"Shouldn't he keep track of us?" asked Sis.

Cat ignored that, since she had essentially given him free range today when she told him yesterday they really wouldn't need his services much until they hit the road again. She did want to offer to buy him lunch, though. "I can't believe he doesn't own a cell phone," Cat said. "We'll have to find him the old-fashioned way." She and Sis touched up their makeup and headed out again.

Cat and Sissy waited at the bottom of the cathedral stairs to see if Manny had attended a later Mass instead. Taking in the neoclassic façade, Cat was impressed by the ornamental pillars, while Sis seemed more taken by the wooden sculpture of Jesus that hung above the enormous entrance.

"Nice miniskirt," Sis observed, noting the colorful embroidery that covered Christ's loincloth. "That's one fashion piece that survives the ages, huh?"

"Looks like fabric. They must change it from time to time."

"That'd be a sight to see ... Jesus in his skivvies."

"I guess Manny will just have to fend for himself then," Cat commented, ready to move on. "I should've given him spending cash." Sis tsked at this.

"Stop trying to fund everyone—the only person who needs your money is me." Cat rolled her eyes at Sis's self-serving way, and the two moved on from the church to start sightseeing again. As they passed the cemetery just beyond the cathedral, Cat noted how nice it was to see smiling faces behind the fence. Children ran around playing while adult family members decorated the headstones of their dearly deceased. Such celebratory behavior would be considered sacrilege inside an American graveyard, a fact Cat knew first-hand from the annual trips they took to her baby brother's grave when she was a kid.

Beyond the iron gates of Morelia, brown-haired babes flounced around with strings of yellow flowers, the occasional petal drifting behind them. The images sparked playfulness in the sisters; they were reverting back to childhood, complete with bellyaches from the candy, torn clothes, and dirty feet inside their flip-flops. The Langs had spent more quality time on this vacation than in the last nine years. It would become one of Cat's fondest and most monstrous memories.

As the afternoon sun beamed over the citywide party, Rey was halfway through her collection of "Js." The first twenty-five had gone quickly. The hard part was keeping her pockets from overflowing. She wasn't prepared to handle a thousand pesos on a holiday weekend. All the banks were closed, so she'd been asking everyone for big bills. Though making change was risky, it did relieve the bulge in her pockets. The crowd was bustling like bumblebees. Hundreds of adolescents ambled around, arms askew, limping, their faces painted ashen white with sunken eyes. The skeleton crew was multiplying—everywhere Rey turned she saw ornately painted skulls. She was itching for quitting time and hustled like a hippie at a Dead show to pawn off the rest of her selection. When the last deal was done, she scurried back to the Mansion Real to hide the cash under her mattress.

Once again, Rey was alone in the hotel room. She had rolled one uncut wacky-tobacky fag for herself. She had been off heroin for almost six days now and hoped to continue this trend, but a measly joint was nothing when it came to drugs. Rey smoked a fatty as a means to stay clean, cracking a window in the bathroom to blow the smoke through. She kicked back on the bed to enjoy the mild ride and to wait for Manny and the girls to return. It was an hour before she put her feet on the floor again—they were as heavy as lead, and her head felt foggy. She left the Mansion and pushed her way through the crowd, like a real life version of the living dead.

Rey slinked her way through the crowd toward the aqueduct, where the parade was headed for the end of day finale. After hours of fruitless searching, she hoped the Langs dragged their asses this way. As long as they stayed put to watch the sunset festivities, she would be able to spot their blonde crowns above the crowd ... if she found a good vantage point.

She settled under one of the aqueduct's baroque arches, admiring the immensity of the ancient structure. She knelt down to tie her shoe when a firm palm landed on her shoulder and a man told her to stay down. Gazing up through the haze of the limited lighting, she found herself looking into the eyes of a federale. He was dressed in civilian clothing and wore a Santo Muerte mask over his face. Despite his costume, his voice was a dead giveaway. Commander Cruz, the asshole who sent her to prison, was standing above her with an M16 and seemed pretty pissed off.

"Is there a problem?" Rey asked, shaking his weight off her shoulder.

"I'm here to help you, and I need you to help me." Rey recognized the stilted English of the guy who had beaten her and sent her to prison. The man leaned over to help her up, then guided her outside the stone structure where they had more privacy. Rey's hair stood on end as she recalled her last interaction with him. His calm demeanor was scarier than his brutal berating at the jailhouse.

"I want you to bring me the cartel," Commander Cruz demanded. "I promise to keep you safe."

Rey could've run if she wanted, but her defense was pure defiance. "I'm not an idiot."

The commander grabbed her arm and got right in her face. "Call your boss and offer to return the drugs to him.

Tell him you had too close a call and don't want to be involved anymore. I'll arrest them when they come for you."

"That's a suicide mission," Rey spat. Then without a second thought, she kicked him in the groin, darted under the arch, grabbed a skeleton mask off an unsuspecting woman, and dissolved into the crowd. She heard one shot fire into the sky and assumed it was her only warning. She needed to find the Langs before the commander caught up with her again.

CHAPTER 30

ANTE LA MUERTE

S issy and Cat were taken aback by the beauty of the decorations that adorned gravesites around the city. The cemetery back home had always been a sad place for the sisters. No longer part of her parents' annual visit to her brother's grave, tonight's ceremony on Lake Patzcuaro would allow Cat to honor him. When they decided to stay another day, Cat had researched the mountain lake they would visit this evening.

"Smack dab in the middle of the Lago de Patzcuaro," she read to Sis as they wandered, "sits the tiny island of Janitzio, where Day of the Dead festivities are known for being especially spiritual. Rituals have been celebrated there for three thousand years. During the pre-Hispanic indigenous period, it was common to keep skulls as trophies and display them during rituals to symbolize death and rebirth. Dead children were considered little angels, so All Soul's Day on November first is also referred to as *Day of the Angels* or *Day of the Innocents*." Cat had joked about the fact that she might no longer be innocent enough to attend.

With their departure plans firmly set for tomorrow, their final plan for sightseeing was to hitch a ride to the island at midnight on one of the small winged boats called mariposas or "butterflies." There they would share in the memorial services, leaving trinkets for their dead sibling. "He would've been twenty-five this year," Cat said reflectively, lost in the thought of what a tall and handsome man he might have been.

"I want to buy him a toy," said Sis as they breezed out of the cemetery. "The parade passes through the downtown area, and the news guy said the finish line is at some aqueduct. Let's head over there."

Sissy made a selection from a vendor near the grand fountain in the center of town as the parade made its way around the corner. There were acrobats, fire jugglers, dancers, and wagons filled with scaled-down gravestones, decked out like the real ones. Performers wore glittered black-and-white masks, but the attendees were mostly in zombie gear. It was a wild and raucous group, singing and caw-cawing in Spanish.

Sissy translated intermittently for Cat, but most of the fun was in watching the acrobatics. They raised their zombie arms above their heads, boogey-man style, and swayed to the music as the square became crowded with people. They had a great view of their surroundings and could see the aqueduct ahead. It seemed as though the arches to the far right had fewer folks milling around them. Sissy grabbed Cat's hand so she wouldn't be swept away in the torrent of people, and they pushed their way through the madness.

As the sisters approached the outer edge of the crowded open space, it became clear that the crowd had thinned due to some police activity under one of the arches. Cat stood up on tiptoes to try to see. Sis, generally unperturbed by crash scenes and gore, pushed her way toward the circle of bystanders. The two of them reached the inner ring of onlookers at the same time, and gasped together. Cat's hand flew to her mouth. Manny was slumped on the ground, his throat cut from ear to ear.

"Oh my God!" whispered Cat, immediately feeling like her legs would collapse underneath her.

"Let's get outta here!" Sis hissed. She yanked on Cat's hand to haul her away. Cat began to cry as they made their way toward the safety of their hotel.

⚜

Rey hurried across the town square toward the hotel, glancing over her shoulder every few seconds. She prayed she would find Cat and Sis back at the hotel, but figured she would at least be safe there until the sisters returned.

She heaved a sigh as she entered the empty room. The sun was beginning to set, so she decided to wait for her companions inside, even though the solitude made her nervous. Then, like a miracle, she heard a friendly knuckle rap on the door, *bump-ba-da bump-bump*, and a familiar voice say, "Anybody in there?" Rey rushed to open the door for Manny.

Taking the stairs two at a time, they bounded down the hall and nearly slid to a stop at the door. Cat fumbled with the key, hating herself for insisting they stay here and wishing she could transport them back to Beverly Hills in an instant. She was crying too much to see what she was doing, and Sis's hands shook so hard she couldn't help. After a sloppy slip of the key through the lock, they were in. Rey was passed out on the bed.

"Looks like she found some more heroin," Cat said flatly.

"*You're on your own now, Rey!*" Sis leaned on the bed and yelled in Rey's ear.

The pressure on the bed caused the jacket strewn across Rey's chest to slip. Cat shrieked. Reyna had been eviscerated. Cut from sternum to pelvis, her insides were out. Her intestines looked like shiny gray balloons, the kind clowns use to make balloon animals. Her heart was exposed, and the twine that held the silver crosses around her neck was encrusted in sticky blood.

The sisters held their stomachs in the face of such gore, and Sissy nearly back-flipped off the bed, landing on her ass. She scrambled back toward the door, her eyes fixed on Rey's lifeless figure. Cat felt like her heart would burst. A pain shot down her arm, and she was having palpitations. She tried to scream, but a raspy peep came out of her dehydrated mouth. She had no words. She couldn't take her eyes off Rey, and it felt like she was fading. There was a flash of silver, and everything went black.

She was roused by the sound of Sissy's voice. "Cat, wake up!"

Cat felt her head rolling side to side. "Don't do this to me!"

"You fainted—now get *up*." Sis helped Cat up. They were breathing heavily as they stumbled in one clumsy unit toward the door.

"Shit!" breathed Cat once they reached the hallway. She leaned forward, resting her palms on her knees. She wiped her hand across her forehead, fighting to regain her breath and balance.

Sis started to haul her away, then she stopped and exclaimed, "We need our keys!" She returned to the door and jiggled the handle furiously, but it was locked. Cat fumbled the electronic card through the slot again, and Sis ran into the room. Fixated on Rey, she grabbed their jackets from the closet. Sis moved toward the bed to arrange Rey's jacket on top of her again, hiding the grisly scene. Cat watched from the doorway as Sis glanced once again at her dead comrade before she exited the room.

The girls confirmed their keys were where they should be, zippered inside their breast pockets, before they ran full tilt toward the fire escape.

In the shadows of the garage, Cat lifted the edge of her zombie garb so she could throw her leg over her bike, while Sis stood, messing with her sound processor.

"It's beeping," she explained. "The batteries are done; I've been sleeping with it on." Sis patted her jacket, aimlessly feeling for her wallet. "I left my wallet upstairs, the spares are there." She pounded her fist on her saddle in frustration, then shook her head in defeat and mounted her bike. Flipping off her ineffective hearing aid, Sis unlocked her helmet from its storage place on the handlebars, squeezed it on her head, and turned the ignition. She gunned her Honda and signed to Cat: *Follow me.*

She drove toward the door that allowed pedestrian access, hopped off the bike, and propped the door open with a heavy trashcan. Then she hopped on the bike and eased through the door, climbing five cement stairs in a controlled but bumpy set of wheelies. The entire effort took less than a minute, during which Cat lost her breath watching Sis do the maneuver, knowing that it was another first for Cat— and might be her last.

Cat was well aware that the lack of momentum in the tiny space meant she'd have to climb the stairs by doing wheelies with her 450-pound bike, a trick she had never tried and wasn't sure she could handle. She stood up on the pegs as she cleared the door jam, leaning forward and then back, struggling to lift the front end without tumbling off her machine.

"Trust the engineers at Beemer," Sis had said during a much simpler climb up the rock-dotted desert hill. All trust had flown out the window at this point, and Cat knew that this climb might save her life, if it didn't take it.

As her bike bucked and reared up the impediment toward the street, Cat held on to the handlebars with a death grip and nearly toppled over at the top as the bike landed on the flat sidewalk. She was sobbing now and choking on her panic as her throat felt like it was closing. Completely overwhelmed and shaking with fear, Cat barely had the sense to keep her bike upright as she set her left foot on solid ground and looked helplessly at Sis. The late afternoon sunlight was super bright for Cat's tear-stained eyes, and the fact that it was setting directly in front of them made it especially hard to see without the aid of shades.

Sis dropped her head and shook it back and forth, clearly relieved to see that Cat had negotiated the extremely advanced trick of stair climbing. She gave Cat a harried thumbs-up before turning to look ahead at the completely packed street filled with families. Cat was pretty sure Sis would know how to safely get the crowd to part for them; she just hoped Sis went slowly enough for Cat to follow her exact path.

The sisters carefully dodged the living obstacles until they reached a less congested part of the city and slowed to establish their plan. The lights were dim and infrequent, and the autumn sky was dark despite the city lights. There was no moon in the nighttime sky, and the early evening stars seemed farther away than normal.

Sis pointed to the end of a side street where civilization ended and the desert began. It suddenly seemed safer to flee into the black and empty desert. The human threat was worse than any sand pit could be. The girls turned onto the dirt again. Cat felt the warm wind blow up her legs as her zombie costume worked its way toward her hips. The soles of her flip-flops were much softer than boots, so her feet drooped over the foot pegs, making her feel much less connected to the bike whenever she stood.

Sissy had told Cat at the beginning of the ride that learning how to crash safely would be an important lesson, but one that would be better reserved for a later date, when the risk of injury wouldn't hamper their ability to get home again. Now everything threatened their safe return; both of them were wearing cheap cotton sheets, the only cash they had was the change from their candy binge. At least they had their jackets and their passports for the border crossing. Cat had taught Sissy a few things about international travel. They had consistently worn them beneath their clothing, with the exception of the time Cat spent in prison.

At first, they followed the edge of the desert, taking advantage of the light coming from the sporadic shacks that dotted the outskirts of Morelia. Sis motioned for Cat to follow her into the desert when a red light began to spin in the neighborhood to the left of them. When two more emergency vehicles appeared behind the first one, Sissy flipped cops and pointed her left index finger over her helmet toward the right.

I don't trust them, she signed quickly.

The sisters hung a swooping right turn and took off into the pitch-black night. Their headlights gave away their escape route, so Cat hit the gas to let Sissy know that she was prepared to outrun the authorities. Sis got the message as the ground became hilly. Fighting slippage on the dunes, Sis went into jump mode, hitting only the soft tops, picking up speed as she hopped. Cat was slower, but determined to keep up. She turned off her mind, looked as far into the distance as she could, and prayed that her headlight would give her ample warning about possible obstacles.

As Sis's eyes adjusted to the lack of light, she flipped off the switch on her aftermarket headlamp, opting to follow a less visible, more intuitive guideline. Sis only wished Cat could do the same, but street bikes were designed to have their light on all the time to make them more visible. They had to reduce the chance of detection and rely on Sissy's sixth sense to direct her.

Cat's headlight shined brightly, giving her ample warning as Sis's bike suddenly dipped below the horizon. A second later, Sis shot up and landed on the other side, her back tire touching down in slow motion. Cat approached the ravine slowly and saw the dip was sharp and deep. She glanced over her shoulder to see the flashing lights approaching, and could not believe the four-wheel vehicle was able to handle this terrain. Knowing the ravine would surely slow the cops down, Cat decided it was now or never as the thought of jail time kept her motivated. She eased over the downward lip, leaned back as the front end hit the bottom, and then gunned it quickly, controlling her bike like a goddess over the lip. Cat stopped her Beemer next to the Honda.

Looks like we're out of their reach, Sis flipped. The ditch did not appear to be passable for anything bigger than a bike, and Sissy looked relieved. She motioned for Cat to follow her again, then scanned ahead for the best path.

Cat craned her neck to look back and spotted the lights moving toward them. She steered her bike to the left to stagger the line and give Sissy a rear view. All of a sudden, Cat spotted a cow carcass ahead of her. She swerved hard to the left, letting out a gasp as she accidentally ran over one of its hind legs. Sis didn't notice the near miss—she was too far ahead now. Cat slowed to get a handle on her surroundings. A fence post appeared on her right. She swerved left again and strained to spot Sis, who was crouched low as if ducking below something.

Suddenly, Sis's helmet popped off and bounced on the ground. Cat watched in terror as Sis and her Honda wobbled fiercely. Cat could see she was slumped forward. Cat's stomach lurched when Sis and her bike tipped over. *How did she manage that?* The answer flooded her brain as blood spewed like a geyser from the neck of Sis's headless body.

Cat released her hand from the throttle, and her bike began to wobble. She flipped her face mask up to get air into her hyperconstricted lungs. Gazing through the open air, no longer muted by the dusty visor, gave Cat an absolute view of the nightmare before her. Sis's body had fallen off the side of her bike, which was lying on its side now, a few feet ahead. Like the sister who would not quit, Sis's helmet rolled on in what appeared to be super-slow motion, like a sailing stone.

Cat stumbled as her own bike tipped over, landing hard on all fours as gravity and shock brought her down. "Oh God, oh God, oh God," Cat repeated. Her mind could barely contain the horrible facts. She got dizzy and then sick, puking into the sand so hard she thought her eyes would explode. As Cat's body shook and heaved violently with distress, the most courageous person she had ever known lay dead. Sis's epic existence had been snuffed out by a measly wire, strung across an otherwise empty desert.

CHAPTER 31

DAY OF ANGELS

What is real, asked the rabbit? This child's fable played in a loop in Cat's mind as she cradled Sis like an infant, rocking her body and whispering, "It's okay, it's okay" as if to convince herself. Copious amounts of sticky, dark blood created a seal between them. It reminded Cat of the Elmer's glue the adolescent Sis had used to make Popsicle-stick motorcycles for Cat's hand-me-down Barbies.

What is real? Cat wondered as the flashing red lights illuminated the late afternoon sky. Five Mexican federales stood above her, asking *"¿Esta bien, esta bien?"* incessantly.

As one of them cajoled Cat to let go of her shattered sister, the zombie inside carried her to a place that was safe, where she could answer their questions. She did as she was told: *State your name* ... check; *show your passport* ... check; *come with us* ... check.

The zombie kept Cat's feet on the ground as facts came to light. Sis was gone ... check. The trip was done ... check. Cat followed the officer's guide as he wrapped her in an emergency blanket and used a sheet to cover Sissy ... a redundant costume considering her zombie gown.

Cat ducked as the officer put his hand on her head and helped her into the back seat of the jeep that had trailed them. Now she would see firsthand how this machine handled the supposedly impassable ravine. With the seemingly evil commander riding shotgun in the front seat, it was a miracle she survived his monologue, let alone the bumpy ride.

"Your little escapade led to the death of your friend," he said condescendingly. "She and Manny are two of the casualties in this war. If I hadn't followed you, there could've been two more."

"My sister," Cat whispered, taking it in.

"Her death is not in vain," he said. "You will be on the first plane tomorrow." Turning to Cat, he said coolly, "As for your sister's unfortunate demise, I will have Escondido's head soon enough. I'm glad we found you alive; the press would be breathing down my neck otherwise."

Cat slumped against the chest strap of her seat belt, and the sensation of intense pressure against her racing heart reminded her that she was, in fact, alive.

The morning light was painful to her swollen eyes. All her life, Cat had been told that her tourmaline greens sparkled like jewels in the sunshine. Now her lids felt like the heavy metal doors that jewelers rolled down at night to protect their precious inventory from would-be thieves.

Cat felt sick and hazy from the pill they had given her to sleep, because nothing could quiet her mind as nightmares replayed the horror show. *Sis is gone,* Cat thought over and over again, staring up at the corrugated white tiles of the hospital room ceiling. A quick visit from a nurse temporarily interrupted the broken record of Cat's mind for a minute. The young nurse was tender with her touch as she described in soft-spoken Spanish what she was about to do before she did it. The woman checked Cat's pulse, which Cat could have said was through the roof. Then the nurse held her head while she gagged on a shot of water to carry a welcome sedative down her throat. Sip ... check. Breathe ... check. The nurse snuck out as the officers entered.

Cat could not understand them, Spanish or English; her ears were not working. She relinquished control to the zombie-mode she had clung to in the back of the jeep, feeling no emotion as the officers presented crime-scene pictures of all the victims in front of her. *Can you identify these people?* Check. *Would you like us to notify their next of kin?* Check. *Sign here then.* Check. Cat signed "Catrina Lang" and listed the date with painful clarity: Day of Angels.

Her name had taken on new meaning. The Day of the Dead fell in the ninth month of the Aztec calendar and was dedicated to a goddess named Catrina, or Lady of the Dead. Now Catrina Lang's identity lay where the barrier between life and death was thinnest.

It was hard to tell which side of the line Cat resided in

now. But the doctors couldn't know that, so Cat performed the motions. Don't lose your head ... check. You can't go home without it ... check. She needed to leave the hospital today and find a private place to pray while the experts handled the arrangements.

Bringing a body home from a foreign country was an experiment in bureaucracy. Sis was stuck in the Mexican morgue until the t's were crossed and the i's dotted. What else could Cat do but wait? All Saint's Day offered some reprieve; it was a sacred holiday, and Cat had a job to do, one last honorable mention before she faced the horror show at home. She needed to say all the right things and get out of here, so she let nursery rhymes from her childhood ring on repeat as a means to seek comfort amidst this insanity.

One-two, buckle my shoe, three-four, shut the door, five-six, pick up Sis, seven-eight, sorry we're late, nine-ten, we're home again. Cat could see her mother waiting for the news ... she hoped she had enough booze.

CHAPTER 32

ALL SOULS' DAY

The deal was real, her zombie act had passed, and Cat would be forever altered by the facts. She'd been mugged, arrested, and witnessed suicide, murder, and death. No matter what Cat tried, be it sedatives or sleep, she could not delete the horror show that played on repeat in her mind. Practice Makes Perfect was one of her parents' favorite sayings, and Cat was building immunity to it as the recurring images of gore became almost boring.

"Pop Goes the Weasel" began to infiltrate her brain after twenty-four hours of seeing Sis's helmet pop off over and over again. Cat wondered how long this could go on. She had been understandably upset by her brother's death, too, but she hardly ever thought of him anymore.

Bobby died when Cat was two; she had no memory of him outside of pictures. There was a photo of the two of them as toddlers that resided on her mother's bedside table. The snapshot captured them rolling a ball in their sun-scorched yard in what was probably October, based on the jack-o'-lantern in the background. Bobby sat shirtless in a diaper, while Cat wore a frilly dress and droopy bonnet. Protection had always been part of her mother's objective when it came to Catrina. It had been the sole reason Cat had been forced to give up riding as a kid after she broke her leg. So what had all that safety gotten her?

She felt like a shell of a person, having lost her brother, then herself, and now Sis. And soon it would be Chris. Risk management had failed Cat a long time ago. She'd come on this trip to become more like her sister: wild and daring and free. So when the doctor at the hospital told her she was being released, Cat knew exactly what she needed to do. She wanted to bid goodbye to her formerly sheltered life and offer her siblings a proper goodbye. No one was here to guide her, or chide her, so Cat cracked open her trusty Triple A guide to establish one last adventure for their send-off.

Turning to the page that detailed Morelia, she searched for the tidbit about the midnight ceremony on the island of Janitzio that she and Sis had planned to visit tonight. "The festivities are dedicated to the goddess known as the *Lady of the Dead*," Cat read, "otherwise known as Catrina."

Cat felt like the Lady of Death as she sat on a wooden bench on one of the mariposas shortly before midnight. She wore two necklaces made of orange marigolds, which she planned to leave as an offering. She removed the leis inside the cemetery so she could use them to decorate the graves, and accidently knocked off the floppy hat that she had worn to disguise her identity. No one batted an eye at her as half a dozen people stomped on the hat, trying to squeeze their way in the dark through the skinny iron gates. Cat spent the rest of the night in full exposure, unafraid of what her past might define her as and ready to face the future anew.

When the last sliver of moon disappeared around 4:00 a.m., Cat began making phone calls in order of importance: Mom and Dad ... check, Chris ... *click*. She couldn't believe he hung up on her. After relaying the horrible story to her folks and listening to them wail over the phone, Cat needed Chris to just listen. He answered the predawn call with a fed-up sounding "What?" then huffed and hung up before she could get the frog in her throat out of the way to speak. It took her ten minutes to call him back.

This time he listened intently and offered an extensive apology. He didn't complain when she asked him for help; his narcissism waned in the face of Cat's astronomical problems. He was a real trooper when it came to Cat's requests: pilot hired ... check, money wired ... check, his anger expired ... check. The Lang sisters would fly home on a Gulf Stream V later today, courtesy of Chris's friends in high places. Cat asked him to handle Rey's arrangements as well. "Call the embassy," she said. "Do whatever it takes to get her back to the States."

After the tasks were completed, Cat realized she had yet to find a special shrine and make an offering. She planned to do it solo until Slick Rick called from Israel, where he was vacationing, and told Cat he would send his lawyer to accompany her. The man arrived on the same plane that would take the sisters to Texas. It would be Sissy's first flight ever. The only type of "flight" Sis liked was the kind that had her standing on the foot pegs of her bike while soaring. She was a land animal, dirt was her friend, and now she would spend the rest of time six feet under it. Sis had once told Cat: "I'd rather be a dirty girl than a princess incensed by a pea."

Now Sis's hard head was sitting in the morgue, and Cat wondered if her badass bod had been reattached to it yet. Cat hoped so, for her parents' sake. When Rick's lawyer arrived, he asked Cat what he could do: "Anything for a client of Rick's." He sounded like a dick.

"Just make sure Sis comes back in one box," Cat demanded. The douche bag nodded. He made a bunch of calls on his cell phone to confirm Sis's extrication with authorities.

"All set," he said. It was time to head to the airport.

"I need to make a stop along the way," Cat declared. In the middle of the sisters' soiree yesterday, Sis had pointed out the headstone of an eight-year-old girl who had been blessed with the name Cecilia. Someone had set a toy motorbike, car, and train on her grave.

"A girl after my own heart," Sis had exclaimed.

As Cat approached that cemetery again with her unwelcome handler, she asked him to give her privacy.

"I was told to keep a close eye on you," he explained.

"Fuck off," she said, channeling Sis.

As she walked solo through the graveyard, people meandered about, cleaning up the grounds after the final night of celebration.

A short walk through the colorful plots brought Cat to the spot she was looking for. Reaching deep into the pocket that held the key to her impounded Beemer, Cat retrieved the beans she'd recovered from Sissy's blood-stained jacket. Jiggling the box gently, she opened the top and dumped them onto her palm ... two of them vibrated, and one jumped.

"This one's for you, kid," Cat said. Then she kissed the beans and set them on top of the gravestone. Shivering in spite of the heat, Cat wrapped her jacket around her ribs and shook off the chill.

Moments later, the lawyer approached to tell her it was time to go. Inhaling one final breath of the floral scent of Mexico, she pulled her spine straight, set her feet firmly on the hallowed ground, and beckoned Sis's soul to accompany her back to El Paso.

ACKNOWLEDGMENTS

I'd like to thank my mom, who read and reviewed every story I ever wrote. I would not be the writer I am without her support, critiques, and encouragement. Thank you to my early readers of *The Last Cruz*, Steve Friree, Stephanie Friree, and Raye Carlton. Your expertise in the subject matter and enthusiasm for the story were invaluable assets on this journey. To the entire team at SDP Publishing: publisher, Lisa Akoury-Ross, editors, Kellyann Zuzulo and Stephanie Peters, proofreader, Karen Grennan, and graphic designer, Howard Johnson. *The Last Cruz* would be nothing without you—a dream team that helped me see my dreams come true. Last but not least, I want to thank any reader who spreads the word about *The Last Cruz*, especially those who write reviews, because word of mouth is the root of success for a budding author.

ABOUT THE AUTHOR

Caitlin Avery grew up outside of Boston, Massachusetts. After receiving a theater degree from the University of Colorado, she moved to Los Angeles, where she pursued an acting career for the next ten years.

Her love of writing was solidified when Caitlin chronicled her attempt to find love in LA. The result was her first book, *Lightning in My Wires*, and a chance encounter with a fellow Bostonian who would later become her husband.

After the birth of their son, the trio moved back to the East Coast in 2010. She published *Lightning in My Wires* that same year and got right to work on her second book. *The Last Cruz* is her first fictional novel.

Caitlin resides with her family in Newton, Massachusetts, where she works as an in-home personal trainer. The job that was meant to supplement her acting income has become a lucrative career, and her flexible schedule allows her plenty of time to write, hike, bike, and run. She is a three-time triathlete and recently competed in her first Spartan race. She is currently working on the sequel to *The Last Cruz*.

Want to know more about the author?

Go to caitlinavery.com

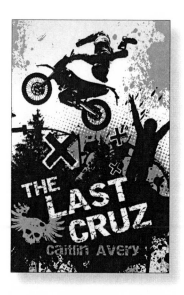

THE LAST CRUZ

CAITLIN AVERY

Publisher: SDP Publishing

Also available in ebook format

TO PURCHASE:

Amazon.com

BarnesAndNoble.com

SDPPublishing.com

Caitlinavery.com

SDP Publishing

www.SDPPublishing.com

Contact us at: info@SDPPublishing.com

CPSIA information can be obtained at www.ICGtesting.com
Printed in the USA
BVOW02s0348040616

450598BV00001B/1/P